A
Winnowing

By Robert Hugh Benson

Once-and-Future Books

For more fiction by Robert Hugh Benson,visit
www.benson-unabridged.com

A Winnowing was originally published in 1910

ISBN: 978-1-60210-005-3

Cover by R. L. Brohawn

Table of Contents

Foreword

With the possible exception of *Lord of the World* and *The Dawn of All* — and that only because of extreme familiarity with those two works — I cannot read any fiction by Robert Hugh Benson without finding some previously unsuspected treasure, another level, in the text. *A Winnowing*, from 1910, is a good example of this.

The novel struck me as particularly entertaining the first time I read it. There seemed to be something that outdid P. G. Wodehouse at his most sublimely ridiculous. Take, for example, a passage of which I quickly became enamored:

> I refuse to describe the flower show held at Sir Samuel Cohen's beyond saying that it was exactly like all other flower shows; and I forget whether it was in support of any charitable institution. I think it must have been; otherwise I do not think that even Lady Carberry would have made a speech. There were all the usual things — hot tents, moderately cold ices, awnings over the windows, grass trampled till it bled a dark green, a nerve-shattering noise of talking and brass-band playing, an enormous crowd that ebbed and flowed continually, motorcars, carriages, dust turnstiles, a good deal of crossness, small girls with black legs and white frocks, men in straw hats, women with Zulu headdresses: and there were some flowers, I think.

". . . and there were some flowers, I think." If a reader doesn't fall in love with Benson's writing on the strength of that line alone, then we must contradict Sir Walter Scott and declare that there *does* breathe a man with soul so dead. We can see why Evelyn Waugh was so fond of Benson's work.

But, of course, the glories of *A Winnowing* do not rest on that passage. Take the description of a character who drifts between being a major player and part of the scenery:

> I love contemplating people of this kind, because the subject is so endless and evasive. I have no certainty

of what Mr. Fakenham thinks about, but I am stimulated by him to form unverifiable conjectures forever. Thoughts undoubtedly pass through his mind beyond those to which he gives expression, but I have no idea as to what they are; words proceed out of his mouth — often, so long as the subject is on his own plane, shrewd and suggestive; and actions are done by him. He lives, and he will die; and as to what he will do then not even I dare to form conjectures of any kind. He is the strongest argument for the annihilation of the soul that I have ever met. . . .

I wish now to describe his appearance this morning — not that anything depends upon it. (He is not, later on, to be convicted by its means of some nameless crime.) I wish only to gaze upon him for a minute or two.

Such a character seems to be thrown into the story for comic relief. Despite his pretensions to gentility and his assessment of virtually the whole of the rest of mankind as cultural philistines, he is a boring nonentity, very nearly a boob. He isn't even amusing enough to challenge Bertie Wooster's preeminence as the quintessential member of the incredible Drones Club, serving to entertain the lower classes.

This is where Benson's superlative talent comes into play. At first reading we're tempted to think that the author throws these light, yet barbed comments in to lighten the mood. *A Winnowing* is, after all, seemingly drenched in an obsession with death. The novel opens with one of the protagonists at death's door. Every couple of chapters it seems as if somebody either dies, or is waiting for somebody to die. The French Carmelites who take up residence in the convent built for them by Jack and Mary Weston seem to be buried in death while still living behind their walls and grills. To add an even more macabre note, they bring with them from France the incorrupt body of their "saint," a sister who died some years previously, incongruously carted about in a cheap wooden packing crate.

Benson, however, wrote nothing without a definite purpose. Even *By What Authority?*, his first published novel, although it weighs in at nearly a quarter of a million words, doesn't waste a single one. Well-meaning editors who have abridged a number of Benson's works have not succeeded in improving the works, but in robbing them of much of their meaning.

Take *A Winnowing*, for example. As I hinted, at first reading it seemed to have a definite taste of being a pot-boiler. Despite the continual references to death, there is a flippancy, even breeziness in the writing that takes you off guard, especially if you've read any of Benson's earlier works, particularly the relentlessly grim *Lord of the World*. Reading *A Winnowing*, however, is so effortless that the reader is tempted to conclude that the author threw it together to meet a contractual obligation or make some extra money, and for a change didn't really give a damn about being "serious."

That judgment, however, would be a mistake. Benson did not write to make a living. He had independent means. He wrote because that was one of the ways he used to say the things he needed to say, not to churn out something to meet the monthly rent.

The problem becomes, What is Benson saying? *A Winnowing* is ranked among Benson's most obscure works. This is undeserved, even for Benson, whose novels as a body require a bit more effort to appreciate than a significant number of modern readers might be willing to put forth. Perhaps a better question would be, What was Benson *doing*?

Although these divisions are far from hard and fast, I see *A Winnowing* as marking the beginning of the third major phase or grouping of Benson's literary career. He had begun by setting out on a tremendous journey that he was unable to finish — creating an alternative to the (very) bad historical novels that afflicted the reading public of his day. The often-conscious (but usually not) assumptions in these productions color much of what many people to this day still believe is the absolute literal truth about the Catholic Church — and bears about as much resemblance to that institution as the shuffling, comic darky in bad films does to someone of African birth or descent.

The historical novels of this first period, *By What Authority?*, *The King's Achievement*, and *The Queen's Tragedy* are a splendid — and successful — attempt to present the "Catholic side" of the Reformation in England. Eschewing the bigoted and tedious "facts" cut out of whole cloth by other English historical novelists, Benson's concern for historical accuracy was so great that (had it not been for his native charm and the obvious importance of his self-imposed task), he was in serious danger of becoming a pest to a number of scholars as he checked and rechecked his work.

Oddsfish! properly belongs in this phase, for the first drafts were written (and endlessly rewritten) at this time before being set aside. *Come Rack! Come Rope!* however, would throw my neat categorization into a cocked hat were it not abundantly clear that the book is (as a number of authorities have pointed out) "in a class by itself." It defies an easy categorization — so we can safely let the novel rest on its own stunning merits.

Nevertheless, despite his obvious success as a historical novelist, it became apparent to Benson that he was not getting his point across. I could be wrong (and very likely am), but a growing conviction that historical fiction might not be the best medium for him could have been the reason why *The Queen's Tragedy* was such a difficult book to write, and why he was unable to complete *Oddsfish!* at this time — unconsciously he may have known that "it wouldn't do."

Benson seems to have caught on to the fact that, bad as the portrayals of the Catholic Church were in historical fiction, the view of the institution in early twentieth century contemporary opinion was worse — for it was current. This may account for the fact that the second phase of his career consisted of a "screaming" (Benson's own word) wake-up call in the form of his four "sensational" novels, *The Sentimentalists*, *Lord of the World*, *The Conventionalists*, and *The Necromancers*. Perhaps not coincidentally, these were also the years of his fortunately brief acquaintance with the weird "Baron Corvo" and "Marie Corelli" (both pseudonyms).

Yet these novels, too, failed in the sense that people still missed the point. The four "sensational" novels are possibly the most intelligent, clever, and biting satires of Edwardian England ever written. They are also Benson's most popular works — and for all the wrong reasons. *Lord of the World* in particular flays the assumptions and cherished beliefs of secular humanism (the real religion of upper class English Edwardian society) until there isn't a whole piece of skin left on the carcass.

Unfortunately, while he turned out what many regard as a classic of early twentieth century science fiction, many people even to this day take the novel — admittedly fantastic science and all — as a work of "prophecy." To counter that opinion, Benson took the time in 1911 to turn out *The Dawn of All* as a "counterblast" to *Lord of the World*, and to beat the horse from the other side. Naturally people took Benson's exaggerations in *The Dawn of All* as the blueprint of an ideal society, an interpretation that the author himself (tearing out his hair in frustration) explicitly rejected.

In 1910, however, Benson seems to have come to the realization that enlightens all good writers eventually. If you want to get your point across most effectively, write what you know. And what Benson knew better than any man alive was upper-class English society, both from the inside as a son of the most powerful Anglican clergyman in the British Empire — the Archbishop of Canterbury — and from the outside as a convert to the Catholic Church. This unique perspective supplied the raw material from which Benson forged half a dozen novels that, astonishingly, are little known today.

Thus began a run of satirical contemporary novels that delighted Evelyn Waugh and seems to have completely baffled generations of readers. Benson quickly found his "voice." He then turned out works that, read with a basic understanding of the author's goal — to discover the deepest meaning of life and discern one's vocation — are superficially easy to read and entertaining and yet at the same time contain such profound depths that they demand several re-readings.

The series began with *A Winnowing* and continued with
None Other Gods. Then in rapid succession came *The
Coward, An Average Man, Initiation*, and the posthumous
Loneliness? This achievement is even more astonishing
when we discover that it was during this time Benson also
completed or composed entirely a number of essays, two
historical novels, three dramas, and a science fiction epic
— in addition to a full schedule of lecturing, preaching,
and missionary work. At the time of his death in 1914,
Benson had already outlined yet another novel, set in
war-torn France during the German invasion.

So — what do we have with Benson's first foray into
"mainstream" fiction? Despite the seeming obsession with
death, it turns out that the subject of *A Winnowing* is not
death, but life — and the question, "What is life for?" Anyone familiar with the least of Benson's writings is aware
that, if anything, he was obsessed (if that is even the right
word) about his vocation, his calling in life. Why had God
made him and put him here on earth?

Good writers write about what they're familiar with.
Naturally, Benson being concerned with the question of
vocation, he wrote about the question of vocation in virtually every one of his novels. The subject is so vast, however, that we are not treated to a dismal parade of the
same plot, endlessly rewritten. No, the question of vocation is so important and broad in scope that, except in his
historical novels (written with another purpose in mind,
yet the issue is there, too), it, like life itself, provides endless permutations for study.

Reading Benson's different treatments of the question of
vocation reminds me of the story told of Picasso, in which
a friend criticized the artist for painting a picture of the
same vase over and over again. Picasso responded by
pointing out that he kept painting the same vase because
it appeared continually different to him, and he wanted to
paint the essence of the vase, not a fleeting impression of
the vase. Yes, Benson kept going over the question of vocation, but it is a different question for each member of
the human race, and each one has a different story to tell.

That brings us to the story in *A Winnowing*. At the most
superficial, yet still meaningful level, the novel is a study

in contrasts. Apart from the evident death-obsession, we find the utterly pointless lives of the local English gentry juxtaposed with those of the *nouveaux riches* Jack and Mary Weston and their newly discovered devotion to Catholicism. On a smaller scale, we see a continual rejection and misunderstanding on the part of the gentry of any life with purpose.

We see this later almost perfectly developed in *The Coward*, but in *A Winnowing* the picture is much starker. Life without death or even a purpose other than the trivial pursuits of upper class society as ends in themselves is, ultimately, devoid of meaning. Mary Weston, the central character of *A Winnowing*, seems to grasp this at some visceral level, yet is repelled by every shred of evidence or suggestion that pain and suffering — things she regards as obscene and something to be avoided at all cost (a theme visited again in much deeper terms in *Initiation*) — give meaning to life and are paths to something much greater than the mere world.

Mary's interview with a Carmelite appears to confirm her worst fears about being buried alive, of the sisters being dead in the midst of life. The fact that the sisters pay such veneration to the corpse of a sister — a nobody in life — who had died some years before and whose remains had been shipped to England in an ordinary wooden packing crate simply confirms this. The long memories of the sisters in regard to their "saint" offer a sharp contrast to the funeral of the local social queen, Lady Carberry, complete with silver-plated coffin and elaborate ceremonies . . . that are forgotten along with Lady Carberry a week after she's in the ground.

The description of Lady Carberry's funeral and its juxtaposition with the situation of the Carmelite "little saint" suggests that Benson may have had in mind the funeral of Sir Philip Sidney (1554-1586), which would have been familiar to him from his research for his historical novels. Sir Philip was considered the quintessential Elizabethan courtier, being (in Tudor terms) what every woman wanted, and what every man wanted to be.

After his death in the Netherlands Sir Philip was given a State funeral unequaled in England until that of Sir

Winston Churchill in 1965. Sir Francis Walsingham (the founder of the secret police and Sir Philip's father-in-law) staged and paid for the production, a description of which in sufficient detail to give the reader a good idea of the proceedings would be much too lengthy to relate here. Suffice it to say that "opulent" and "extravagant" are very weak words in some circumstances.

What would have struck Benson most of all was the near-total focus on the loss of Sir Philip and the orgiastic mourning instead of the solemn rejoicing that should accompany a Christian's "birthday into heaven" as the reward of a life (however short) well-spent. Yes, death is sad for those of us left behind, but should always be tempered with the knowledge that God is never unjust or wasteful. If we focus too much on our loss rather than on the deceased's gain, we risk falling into despair, a point that Benson was to make a significant subplot in *Initiation* a few years later — *Initiation* being a novel that, in a certain sense, may have been Benson's literary effort to prepare his readers for his own approaching death.

Benson saw one of the effects of the Reformation as turning people away from the spiritual and focusing on the material. Funerals such as that of Sir Philip Sidney and the fictional Lady Carberry exemplify this tendency by putting on an extravagant show that takes attention away from the reason and the purpose of death. Evelyn Waugh, who greatly admired Benson, made this same point even more graphically in his grotesquely funny novel *The Loved One: An Anglo-American Tragedy.* Waugh's story shredded the southern Californian manifestation of this tendency to "materialize" rather than spiritualize death — which specifically exempts Catholics and Jews (two groups that, in Waugh's opinion, viewed death properly) by noting that they "had their own cemeteries," and thus weren't good markets for elaborate funerals.

Benson would also have noted (probably with repugnance) the combination of genuine sorrow connected with Sir Philip's death and Walsingham's cynical exploitation of the staged production to take people's minds off the recent execution of Mary Queen of Scots and the planned

upcoming war with Spain. This, too, finds its echo in Lady
Carberry's funeral, in which Benson does not call into
question the mourners' sincerity, but at the same time
makes it clear that the real importance of the funeral for
them is as a social event and a promise of wealth that will
allow the heirs to do absolutely nothing of any real importance for the rest of their lives. This, again, is in sharp
contrast to the Carmelites, who spend their earthly lives
making certain that the next one fills its purpose.

Thus, is it not only the attitude toward death that sets
the Carmelites apart from the gentry. Benson describes
the life of Lady Carberry, James Fakenham, even the
Westons in terms that suggest they are merely taking up
space before dying and celebrating the happy event (for
the heirs) with elaborate funerals. He uses up virtually no
space at all on the lives of the Carmelites — their lives
are, in terms of this world, utterly repulsive, directed as
they are toward the next . . . thereby paradoxically making this one meaningful. The English upper class has everything except a purpose at the same time that the Carmelites have nothing — except a purpose.

All of the major characters in the story start out with
this utter purposelessness. The closest any one of them
comes to anything outside himself is Jack Weston with his
devotion to cricket. Playing for one's county or country is a
step in the direction of selflessness. It at least takes the
sportsman out of himself, doing something for the greater
good of the team instead of just himself. Ironically, when
Jack "gets religion," he burns his cricket bats, warning
the reader (and Mary, his wife) that something is wrong
from the first. A genuine conversion would not cause
someone to reject anything that draws him out of himself,
at least not without long and profound reflection and with
the concurrence of a sound spiritual advisor.

Unlike the opinion that some readers have of Benson's
endings, the titles of his contemporary novels are unam-
biguous. *A Winnowing* is no exception. The "winnowing" is
that of the wheat from the chaff, of those with a vocation
from those without one. James Fakenham as a stereotypi-
cal member of the upper class even succeeds in "rescuing"
Sarah from meaning. She returns the favor by persuading

him to resign from his government post after their marriage so that neither one is distracted by having a purpose in life.

The question that *A Winnowing* forces the reader to ask — and answer — is, Who, ultimately, is dead, and who is alive? Not just Catholics and Jews, but any sincere believer in any religion will be led inevitably to the answer that Benson forces the reader to confront in all its paradoxical glory.

— Michael D. Greaney, editor

A Winnowing

Prologue

(1)

He had passed down into the realm of pure sensation and association, losing for the time all that constituted his present objective life, inhabiting instead those inner chambers of memory where his past lay stored. Yet he did not regard them as the past, but the present. He did not criticize, weigh, or appraise his actions; rather he retraced, as it seemed, in his own proper person, his actual experiences.

For example, it seemed that he was a boy again, how old he did not consider; but somewhere at that age when the external world, rather than the internal, is the source of sensation. It was a summer morning; lawns were radiant in sunshine; there was a target somewhere and a bow and arrows; and the great house with green-shuttered windows dozed in the heat. There was a sense of ecstatic wellbeing within him, of tremendous and vital youth.

From within the house a piano, in some cool darkened room, poured out a torrent of melody; a gavotte danced in the air; and he knew that his mother, dead years ago, was playing. Presently she would come out . . . in fact, she was already come out, standing at the French windows in her big straw hat and white dress, looking out for him.

Then again it was the close of a summer afternoon; he was going out riding with his father — dead, too, years ago; and he stood, radiantly happy, listening to the champ and jingle of horses coming round from the stable. On the lawn, just out of sight, stood the tea table, silver, china, in the shade of the lime, with his mother and sister — the one who had died when he was ten years old — talking together there. From somewhere beyond the village came the crash of a band; there was some *fête* — a flower show, he thought — in progress. . . . His father came out and stood beside him, silent and smiling; but his face was altered, and it was plain he was a *revenant*, yet not terrible, only a little strange and mysterious: his head was lifted and his eyes looked out, seeing that which the boy could not see. It seemed as though he had returned from some long journey, and all was well again.

Or it was winter, as it was growing dark, and he was coming in through the park towards the garden. The great house, somber against the flaming west, shone from window after window, as if the sun were setting beneath the very roof. There was a smell of frost in the air, suggestive of frozen ponds, the glow of skating, the pulsating of tingling blood. Above all suggestive of a long evening within closed curtains, on thick carpets. The house was full of guests, aunts and cousins — friendly presences; there would be games tonight, acting, hide-and-seek — and again a piano crashed, chord after chord, inexpressibly solemn and uplifting, bearing within its sounds so great a wealth of association, memory, and at present excitement, that he nearly cried aloud with joy.

And once more it was summer, and he stood, naked and exultant, on a lawn, with the river racing beneath; the air was full of singing and the rustling of a myriad leaves from the beeches that sloped down to the very water's edge. In his ears, too, hissed the rush of air-laden water, plunging from the weir, and the bursting of ten thousand tiny bubbles; and in his nostrils the smell of water. He was thirsty, intolerably thirsty, yet reveling in the knowledge that satisfaction lay in reach. The breeze played over every part of his body, thrilling beneath his heart. In an instant he would have plunged. . . . He had already plunged, and was in a green world of twisting water, drinking with every pore of his body the exquisite refreshment. . . . And the gavotte pealing from the piano rang in the darkened room. . . .

Yet now and again the actual world for an intolerable instant thrust itself into his inner world; a face looked at him, like a face thrust through the silver, oily surface of water towards fish, cut off and detached from reality — the face of a woman — ah! That of his wife Mary, was it not? — pale, tortured, with dilated eyes of agony — and withdrew again. He sighed with satisfaction, closed his own eyes, and rolled again in his water-world among the

lush grasses and the shining brown pebbles, while the
river slid above him. . . .

Then again a face splashed in and stared at him with
moving lips — a ruddy face, clean-shaven, crowned with
gray hair; and he could see the fussy patch beneath the
nostrils where the razor had not done its work. The lips
were moving, and he could hear, incredibly loud, like detached barks of thunder, Latin words that roared at him
and ceased, echoless even in memory. They conveyed no
meaning; consciousness was not continuous enough to
carry on the sense from one to the other. . . . Why could
not the priests leave him alone even in his ecstasy of
drowning; they were pushing grace at him, bothering and
interrupting him in his joy of wellbeing. . . . He rolled over
with closed eyes, and the face vanished. . . .

The water roared louder above him. He was flying down
stream now with its thunder in his ears — a thunder
composed of many elements: the bellow over boulders, the
gush of a sluice, the dripping of a tank, the patter of rain
on leaves, the trickle of a runner. This water, he perceived, was itself Pure Joy. Not its symbol, nor its lan-
guage, but Itself. That was the secret of the world, he saw
now; the mystery at which all religions aim, which all fail
to find, the very quintessence of philosophy. How glorious
that he had found the secret at last — so appallingly simple, yet so convincing. It held all things — the peal of a
piano, the crash of a band, the joy of youth, the pleasure
of a house green-shuttered in summer, the inexpressible
comfort of parents, and familiarity and all sweetness. And
the secret had been in his hands so many times, and he
had failed to understand. How extraordinary that was! He
must make haste and explain quickly. Why! He had found
the key to happiness. . . .

"Mary: it's in the bathroom; it's everywhere; it's in the
water bottles. Don't you understand? It's right in front of
you. Oh! You must see. And you must remind me in case I
forget."

No. He had not been able to say that loud enough. It
had not gone up through the silver, oily surface. Well; he
was too tired to explain all over again. He must remember
when he woke.

There followed blankness. When he was conscious again
a completely new set of sensations met him.

(2)

The broad lawns of the upper gardens lay level in gold
and green under the hot afternoon sunshine, backed by
the shadowy woods, and broken here by a terrace fringed
with a blaze of flowers, nasturtiums, wallflowers, and
climbing roses, here by a mellow brick wall, here by broad
paths leading away towards the park beyond. And there,
a little below, on the curve of the hill, rose the jumbled
roofs, turreted here and there both in Tudor and Georgian
days, the gray window-pierced walls, and the fragmentary
restorations of old brick, of the house, Manningham Hall
itself. Beneath lay the valley, dreaming in sunlight.

It was the kind of house and place that can be seen in
England only in full perfection — a combination of art and
nature of such a fashion that each would seem to be the
other. The park below the house had a cultivated and ordered air; the gardens a look of pure nature. The very
brickwork of the buildings was toned down by time into
an appearance of primeval sandstone. All was finished
down to the smallest details. There was none of the careful artificiality of the French chateau; none of the deliberate wildness of an Italian country-house. It might have
stood for a symbol of the life of a man for whom conventions have become eternal laws and eternal laws conventions.

But the gardens this afternoon had a strange, deserted,
almost agitated air about them. In the center of the main
path, running upwards by steps and levels, stood a
wheelbarrow, still loaded with flower-pots, and a garden
instrument or two. Even a flung down waistcoat showed
the haste with which work had been interrupted. The
door into the enclosed kitchen garden on the north displayed within a manure-barrow on wheels, forsaken, it
would seem, upon the instant; and in a little fenced pad-
dock beneath the tall trees a pony, still in his leather
foot-mufflers and harness, released from his mowing-
machine, cropped the grass with a surprised kind of air,
raising his head now and again as if to look for his master
who had left him so abruptly a few minutes ago.

Yet if the gardens behind were deserted, the gravel plateau in front of the house was in a very different state. Two carriages and a motorcar were drawn up here; and a couple of servants, grave and silent, stood on the steps of the porch waiting in their liveries, now eyeing the cool hall within, now exchanging a look or a nod with the three drivers. The figures who so stood were no less eloquent of some crisis than the emptiness and silence behind.

So the minutes passed away. From the village below the park beneath came the usual little summer sounds — the trot of a horse's hoofs, the barking of a dog, and the whirr of some machine, as intermittent as the fiddling of a grasshopper.

Then a gate clashed, and presently, riding hard in the heat, up came a panting post-office boy on a bicycle. He sprang off without a word, handed a couple of telegrams to one of the men, who disappeared within, and himself sat down on the horse block. A few minutes passed away still in silence, until once more the man appeared, whispered a word or two, handed papers to the boy, and sent him again flying down the hill to the village. Gates clashed, in diminuendo, and all was still once more, except for the occasional stamping of a horse and a murmured growl from a coachman. The chauffeur had propped himself against a pillar of the porch, whence he was invisible from the windows, and was smoking a cigarette, held in the hollow of his hand.

Ten minutes later once more a gate clashed, and there came, riding up in haste, two figures, a woman followed by a groom.

She seemed a tall, attractive looking girl as she sprang off her horse, and stood whispering to one of the men, and gathering up her riding skirt before going up the steps; and there was a certain brisk, masterful energy about her, an air of confidence and proper assumption, that would have made a stranger think her someone of more or less importance.

"Yes, my lady," whispered the man. . . . "Yes, my lady. Sir James came an hour ago by motor. . . . No, my lady; we hear there is to be no operation."

The girl frowned a little, as if in thought, pursing her fresh lips, with a puzzled, anxious look in her clear face. She hesitated an instant; then she went energetically up the steps as the glass doors opened, and could be discerned within, talking with gestures to the grave butler in the hall. Then finally she disappeared into the interior of the house; and again the minutes began to pass.

The next person to approach the group was an ecclesiastic from the interior of the house, a middle aged priest with an air of extraordinary perturbation. He was a solidly built man, of no great impressiveness, ruddy-faced and genial, with dark hair streaked with gray showing beneath his biretta.

He carried three or four objects in his hands — a book, a strip of violet ribbon, and a little leather covered case. He appeared first hesitating in the hall; then he came abruptly out, nodded to one of the men who lifted his hat, and then once more paused.

"No, Pat," he said in an undertone. "He is unconscious. It is useless."

He shook his head gravely, came down the steps, turned to the right, and disappeared with an anxious, nervous kind of air into the doorway of a little turret, by the side of which rose up what was obviously the east window of some kind of chapel.

The sun was beginning to draw more obviously westwards, and the shadow of the house had completely covered the vehicles and the men before any other marked incident took place; and this was of a general rather than a particular nature — a stir everywhere, yet far more startling than the firing of a gun.

First, somewhere overhead, a window was thrown open, and a voice was heard talking in a rapid whisper to someone within; then very quick footsteps were heard, that rose and died again. The door in the turret opened abruptly; once more the priest appeared, and this time bareheaded; he ran straight up the steps and vanished into the house. The men at the porch exchanged glances, shifted their attitudes a little as if in expectancy; and the chauffeur hastily replaced a third cigarette which he had just drawn from his case. Then down from somewhere at the back of the house the figure of a man appeared running, drawing on a jacket as he ran; he waved his hand ominously to his fellows at the door, plunged over the sloping lawns; a gate clashed, and his footsteps died away into silence. The men looked at one another and nodded with a certain grimness. Then, as steps sounded on the flags of the hall inside, once more the mask-like look was resumed on their faces.

It was a little procession that was approaching; and the chauffeur, seeing his master through the glass doors, sprang to his car to make all ready.

First came a tall, lean, bowed man, with the face of an artist enclosed in short gray whiskers; he came through with a sort of noble courtesy, as if to deprecate his seniority to the short, stout doctor who followed. The butler, very grave and serious, came after, and stood awaiting any last messages that should be given.

But no word was spoken. The two doctors stood there, with that look on their faces so unmistakable and so eloquent silently awaiting the moving of the motor. Sir James Martin, the specialist, was neatly drawing on his gloves, and presently slipped his arms into the motoring coat that one of the men held up to him. The other doctor stood, meditative and serious, waiting till his companion was ready. A boy in a short striped jacket ran out presently at a gesture from the butler, and went down to open the gate for the motor to pass through.

Just, however, as Sir James stood aside for the other to mount before him, once more there was a step in the hall, and the tall girl who had entered an hour before came quickly out.

"One moment, Sir James," she said; and the two stepped out of the porch on a strip of turf that ran below the windows. But they were not far enough away for their voices to be altogether inaudible; and the man who stood nearest caught at least fragments of what they said, to be recounted later and embroidered and exaggerated beyond all reason, in view of the marvel that followed.

"I know," said the girl; "but she does not believe it. What can I do?"

A murmur answered her.

"Tell me again, exactly. I can tell her little by little. Quick, please. I must get back to her at once."

(The man only caught fragments of the answer.)

"Syncope . . . . Yes, that means failure of the heart's action. . . . Not the shadow of a doubt. Suggest to her. . . ."

"She won't hear of it."

". . . . Oh! It's natural enough. Poor soul. . . . You'll find tomorrow . . ."

"Yes, of course, I shall sleep here. . . ."

"Let the nurses do their work at once. She'll understand better then. . . . Certificate of death. . . . Certainly."

And so after a few moments the two came back; and the motor began to throb.

Then the marvel happened.

As the girl still stood on the steps with her grieved face and anxious eyes, and the butler behind her; as Sir James, after the door of the car had been closed and the chauffeur had mounted, was already lifting his hat, there came on a sudden a rush of footsteps; the glass door was flung back, and a French maid, her face mad with terror, stood on the steps raving —

"*. . . Il vive! . . . Il vive! . . .Oh! Mon Dieu! . . . Les mouvements . . . on a vu . . . Madame a vu . . . Il a parlé.*"

There was one moment of frozen motionlessness, then Sir James was out of the carriage and up the steps; and there poured back into the hall and vanished a torrent of men and women, running like hounds — more terrified, it seemed, by the possible tremor of life than by the certain descent of death.

"Why, yes; the whole difference. You must see that. I can't possibly go on with all this — this footling sort of life. I've got another chance, thank God — and by George —"

A discreet tap came at the door.

"Wait," he said, with that same unruffled air.

"I wanted just to tell you. It isn't fair not to. I want you to think it over. I think you'll see —"

"Jack, I will not hear another word. You can tell me tomorrow."

He glanced at her with a faint deprecating smile.

"Very well; I'll be good," he said. "But remember I've told you. Oh! And don't forget about Father Banting. I must see him this afternoon."

(3)

"Mrs. Weston wishes to see you, sir, in her own room, as soon as you have finished with the master."

The doctor nodded and went upstairs. And when he came down again he was more perturbed than ever.

He had never seen such a case before in his life; and he had Sir James Martin's authority for it that it was unique in modern experience. Here was a man pronounced dead by two physicians — dead so certainly that they had left the room. entirely ready to sign the certificate instantly, had it been presented to them; in fact they had actually mounted into the motor together to go to the village for this very purpose. All up to that point had been entirely according to precedent; they had feared syncope, and syncope had come and done its work. No symptom was lacking. . . . This was yesterday; and today he had had his third interview with the dead man, weak indeed, but entirely convalescent; and he had received during this third interview an explicit and apparently sane corroboration of his own and Sir James's diagnosis, given so fully in detail, so wholly without excitement or delirium, so well connected and so simple, and yet so extravagantly impossible, that thoughts refused to formulate themselves. It was not catalepsy, it was not any known form of paralysis. Certain details that need not be discussed here had put all that beyond a doubt. . . . Well, "suspended animation" was a convenient phrase; it meant nothing particular; but, well, it sounded all right, and at any rate it covered the truth.

He was therefore a little grave as he came into the morning room and the girl stood up to receive him. She looked rather white and constrained; but what wonder!

"What account now, Dr. Basing?"

He sat down in the chair indicated and clasped his hands.

"All perfectly satisfactory, Mrs. Weston. Temperature and pulse normal. A little weak of course, still; it will take a few days, but I see no reason, unless there is a quite un-expected relapse —"

He broke off.

"Ah!" said the girl. "And Sir James —?"

"He told me that there was no need for him to come again, unless, as I say, any new complications show them-selves. He wishes for news, of course. You see it is an un-usual case."

"Unusual. Yes. Have you ever known a case like it?"

He shook his head.

"Never quite like it. Sir James assures me of that. Oth-erwise —"

"I understand perfectly. You mean that you have never seen a case go so far and recover."

"Exactly, Mrs. Weston. Of course it was not death" (he smiled doubtfully), "it was not death; but it had all the symptoms — at least —"

"Ah! it was not death. You are quite sure?" she said, with sudden eagerness.

He smiled more confidently this time.

"Why, yes; in the very nature of the case, it could not be death."

She sat silent an instant.

"Did — did he — my husband, I mean — did he talk much this afternoon?"

"A little, Mrs. Weston. I would not allow him —"

"Was he quite clear and coherent?"

"Oh! Perfectly; remarkably so. But for all that —"

She interrupted him again.

"And no fever, I think you said? No delirium at all?"

He shook his head.

"He was perfectly reasonable," he said.

Mary stood up suddenly. Then she leaned back, half-sitting, against her writing table, and took up an ivory paperknife.

"Doctor Basing, I want to ask you a direct question. Please tell me the truth. Is his brain at all affected? I mean, even temporarily; as it is after typhoid, for in-stance? Is that possible?"

"Not the very faintest sign of that, Mrs. Weston. He seems completely normal in all respects."

"He didn't seem to talk wildly, even?"

"His brain is as sane as yours or mine."

"Ah!" (she paused.) "Did he — did he talk about relig-ion?"

He glanced up at her.

"Indeed no; not a word. He just answered my questions."

"And there is no fear of even temporary brain trouble?"

"There is not the smallest reason for it, at any rate. May I ask why you mention that?"

Mary hesitated.

"Oh! It's nothing particular. He doesn't seem quite him-self, that's all. I just wondered. Did he tell you he had ac-tually died, and saw himself in bed, and all that?"

"He said something of the sort. Of course, that was sim-ply a delusion — a kind of self-suggestion. That kind of thing is quite common, comparatively speaking."

Mary mused an instant.

"I see," she said. "But, you know, he thinks he came downstairs, and saw things that — that really did hap-pen."

The doctor smiled reassuringly.

"That would be all part of it," he said. "One mustn't pay any attention to that. That'll all go when he gets stronger."

She played silently with the paperknife an instant or two, twisting it nervously between her fingers. Then she laid it down and stood upright.

"Well, thank you very much," she said abruptly. "Good afternoon, Doctor. You have left all instructions with the nurses?"

"Everything, Mrs. Weston. I'll just look in again before dinner."

"And . . . and there's no harm in his seeing the priest? He wants to, very much."

"I think a quarter of an hour would do no harm. But he mustn't get excited."

"Oh! I don't think Father Banting will excite him," smiled the girl.

"Well — er — good afternoon, Mrs. Weston."

"Oh! By the way," said Mary, suddenly calling him back. "Have you any books you could lend me on — on this sort of thing?"

The little doctor blinked.

"I — I don't quite understand. As a rule, you know, we don't lend books on medicine. They are apt to do harm. Do you mean a book on diseases such as Mr. Weston's?"

"I meant rather on exceptional cases — like his."

"There is no such book, so far as I know. His case is quite exceptional, you know."

"But — but you are sure it was not death?"

"Quite sure, Mrs. Weston."

"Well . . . thanks very much," said the girl.

As he passed out through the hall he was wondering how far he had been successful in concealing his own perplexity. It was a comfort to him, at any rate, that Sir James had been there, and had been as bewildered as himself.

(4)

But the doctor's bewilderment was nothing to that of the priest, as, an hour later, he came out from the patient's room, and meditated to himself all the way down the park to his own lodgings in the village. On the spiritual plane the resurrection was as unique as on the physical.

Father Banting had had a rather hard time of it during his two years in the place. It was not that the squire and his wife were exactly irreligious. They performed their duties with tolerable care: they were at Mass on Sundays; they permitted the use of their chapel; and about four times in the year they asked their priest to dine with them. And that was about all. The atmosphere, therefore, was not ideal. Five-sixths of the people on the estate were Protestants; and the Catholics were not eminent for zeal. The result was a kind of respectable deadness, that had not in it even the stimulating sting of a grievance. Only, every single proposal made by the priest that was in the least unusual was met at the Hall by an attitude of mind that rendered enterprise impossible. Father Banting had recollections of certain public rites and processions suggested by himself, blocked, not by opposition, but by entire indifference. It was not that these great folk were at all wicked. On the contrary, Jack was an excellent young man, who played cricket really brilliantly, and looked after his tenants suitably; and Mary was an excellent young woman, who allowed her flower garden to supply the altar, who rode very well, was extremely kind and courteous always, and gave a certain moderate financial assistance to the mission. They were always quite polite to the priest; allowed him to use short cuts through the park; sent him a dozen pheasants each season and a tolerable supply of grapes; and never pretended for a single instant to be anything but Catholics. And that was all that could be said.

Well, matters seemed changed now: and Father Banting meditated them all the way down to his lodgings.

He reviewed the points.

First, the squire had made his confession. Well, that was a thing apart; not even to be thought over, except as regards the fact that he had made it. For two years past that ceremony had only been performed three times in the year — last year, indeed, only twice; and the month of July had not been one of them.

The second point was the check.

He had been instructed, when the religious part was over, to go to the writing table and bring thence a fountain pen, a checkbook, and a magazine to write upon; and there and then, before his amazed eyes, Mr. Weston had drawn out a check for one thousand pounds, made payable to the Rev. James Banting, to be applied at his sole discretion for the benefit of the mission. And that, Jack had remarked, was to be regarded as an act of restitution to begin with. (This had all been done, by the way, in a perfectly brisk and straightforward manner, unemotionally and naturally.)

The third point was the astounding series of questions put to him by this curious young man.

First, was it possible, under any circumstances, for a married man to enter a Religious Order: and, if so, under what conditions?

Secondly, would Father Banting kindly state, in as few words as possible, what were the usual signs of a Religious Vocation?

Thirdly, was it always a duty for a man living in an important and responsible position to keep up that position at all costs, so long as he was not unduly extravagant; and, if not, under what circumstances should he make a complete sweep of the whole of his life, having regard to the claims of his friends and relations upon him?

Fourthly, what would Father Banting think of coming to live at the Hall? The three rooms in the chapel wing, once occupied by the priest of the mission, should be put at his disposal entirely. Would Father Banting kindly think it over and let him know by and by his views on the point.

And these questions, too, had been put quietly and sanely, without any appearance of undue excitement, and the answers listened to with attention. No explanation whatever had been given as to the cause of the inquiries.

Finally, would Father Banting kindly bring him Holy Communion tomorrow morning; and would he cause it to be announced publicly at Mass next morning that John Weston desired to express his gratitude to Almighty God for signal mercies showed to him in his recovery from the grave danger of an unprepared death?

"You can put it as you like, Father," said Jack serenely, "but that's the substance. 'Unprepared' death, remember. I particularly want that; it's only decent."

Well, there was the situation. And the only conclusion to be drawn from it was that Jack had suddenly gone mad in a most unexpected but very edifying direction. The check, of course must not be presented; at any rate for a week or two; it must be locked up carefully. As for the announcement in church tomorrow, well — he supposed he must make it, as he had given his word; but he must tone it down somehow; it would not do for the squire to make this confession of unpreparedness. What an example!

It was a very curious position, thought the priest, as he climbed the staircase of his rather dingy lodging in the village street. Of course there was, too, that extraordinary recovery to be remembered; but extraordinary recoveries did not generally end in the patient's madness, especially in what seemed to the priest such a very sane kind of madness as this. He must think it all over and have a good talk with Mrs. Weston.

But it was a pleasant thought, on the whole, that he might not have to remain in those rather dreary rooms, so far from his church. He looked round them, smiling unknown to himself. The window commanded a view of the back premises of a tan yard. Certainly the chapel wing, with the fountain and the park, would be an improvement. But then, what about domestic arrangements? These might be difficult, if Mr. Weston were really mad; and if he were not —

The priest made a little movement with his head and sat down to say his office.

Part I

Chapter I

"Yes," said the girl gently. "The doctor says you may talk for half an hour; no more. Tell me, Jack."

The room looked out of its two wide windows straight upon the lawns and woods to the south of the house, where in the midday silence there was heard the contented cooing of the pigeons half a mile away. Beneath, in a little paved space, a fountain splashed gently in its basin.

The room itself calls for no particular remark. It was like a hundred thousand others, scattered in country houses wherever the well-to-do public sets itself down to be entirely comfortable. A dressing table between the windows shone with silver. There was a deep pile carpet on the floor; tall chintz curtains hung upon the window-poles; there was a high, white marble fireplace; there was plenty of opulent-looking mahogany furniture; a chintz covered couch stood at the end of the bed; and within the chintz curtains of the bed itself lay the young man who, it seemed, had had a very remarkable syncope from which he had recovered. And there sat by him his wife, a small, pretty, rather pale girl of about twenty-two years old. They had been married three years — ever since, in fact, Jack's Americanized uncle had suddenly died and left him wealthy.

About Jack Weston himself there is not a great deal to say. The most remarkable thing he had accomplished so far in his twenty-five years of life was his recovery from this syncope which Sir James Martin had actually mistaken for death. And the next most distinguished thing about him was the fact that for two years past he had played cricket for the Gentlemen against the Players; and, as every schoolboy knew, had three weeks before his illness made one hundred and seventy-two runs not out against the South Africans. Beyond these facts, and his inheritance of an immensely large fortune three years ago, there is nothing particular to say about him. He had been an only son; his parents had died while he had been at school at Stonyhurst. He had gone to Oxford, and he had married Mary. They were both Catholics, and had always been so; and there was a chapel in this house which they kindly allowed to be used by the village Catholics and by Father Banting. He was an ordinary, pleasant, straightforward, clean kind of man, without any subtlety at all.

Jack shifted a little on his pillows and took a firmer grasp of his wife's hand.

"He said I might, did he? Well, I'll try."

His blue eyes strayed out to the woods as he meditated his beginning; and his wife noticed with an inexplicable thrill the sane, healthy look of his tanned face and strong throat against the lace fringed white pillow. Certainly the sun-burning had worn off a little in his fortnight's illness, and the hand that held hers might have been stronger with advantage; yet there was no longer on his face that deathly grayness that had deepened so steadily only yesterday afternoon, and that had faded at last to that horrible tint that had thrown her all but screaming onto her knees. Certainly there was an odd look still on his face, but that would pass. Her hand closed with a yet tighter spasm upon his as she set herself to listen.

"Yes, half an hour, Jack," she said; "then you've got to be quiet before lunch."

His eyes rolled round to hers, and he smiled.

"Very well," he said. "Now listen carefully, please.

"I want to ask you first," he began, "to tell me once more what the doctors say. No, no; I don't mean about the future. I know that's all right; but about yesterday."

She swallowed in her throat. It was dreadful even to speak of yesterday.

"Oh! They say it was very remarkable. They . . . they thought —"

She could not go on.

"Yes," said the quiet voice. "They thought me dead? They left the room?"

She gripped his hand tighter, for answer.

"Thank you. I thought so. And Sir James was one of them, I think?"

"Yes."

He lay silent a moment.

"And they were perfectly right," he said suddenly. "I was dead. . . . No; don't interrupt. Just listen."

He shifted again a little on his pillows.

"Mary dear, I must tell you and get it over. You'll see why presently."

She sat back a little, still holding his hand; and her heart began that quick, low hammering that is one of the signs of a fierce nervous strain held in check by the will.

"It was about three o'clock that I felt I was going to die for certain. I heard the church clock in the village. I wasn't the least frightened; and hardly even interested. I suppose I was too weak. I know I ought to have sent for Father Banting then. Well, I didn't. I didn't care in the least. It seemed to me quite — quite external and useless. I just wanted to be let alone. Well, that went on. No, I can't describe it: it was like a steady slipping downhill, down into the dark. I remember just thinking that all religion was lies. It — it had nothing whatever to do with facts. This was the one fact — this dark. That was the end. Then things changed; and I began to dream — all sorts of things, one after another, connected with my father and mother, and going out riding, and bathing. There was some rot about water too; but I can't remember that." (Jack smiled.) "But it seemed awfully important then.

"Well; that doesn't matter. All that went again; and then after a time I came back again to nothing at all, except just knowing that I was I.

"I don't in the least know what time that was. But first I found that all my senses were gone except hearing. That lasted a long time. I couldn't move, or speak, or feel anything; but I could hear, long after everything else. I heard — I heard Father Banting come in sometime. You know the way he breathes through his nose? And I heard what he said — the absolution, the anointing, and the prayers. I heard lots of things. What time was that?"

"That was about half-past five," said Mary breathlessly.

"Very well. Well, sometime after that began a roaring noise; and that went on either louder and louder or softer and softer. I don't know which. There wasn't anything else at all, except that. It seemed to go on for days and days. And then, I suppose that stopped. At any rate that was the last thing, until —"

He stopped suddenly.

"Oh! Jack; don't go on."

"I must, my darling. I must tell you, while I remember. You'll see why directly. Besides, it's — it's not exactly frightening. Well, we'll put it like this. We'll say I dreamed something. This was the dream.

"I dreamed I was standing at the foot of my bed, looking at myself. I could see myself quite plainly. You were *there*, and Lady Sarah behind you." (He nodded to where she sat.) "Sir James was on this side, with his watch out; and he held my left hand. Old Basing was at the foot of my bed, close by where I stood. And the two nurses were by the door of the dressing room. I looked at myself; and I could see that I was practically dead. You were — were kissing my right hand, and after a kiss or two you looked suddenly frightened. Then I looked at myself again; and I could see that I was dead. Sir James shut up his watch and stood up. Then he drew the sheet over my face, and came round the bed, and said something to you as Lady Sarah caught hold of you —"

"Oh! Jack! Don't — don't go on."

"My darling; I must go on. Well, I'll leave that part out.

"When Sir James and old Basing went downstairs, I went with them. I was just frightfully interested. And as I stood there on the steps, I saw Lady Sarah come out and say something to Sir James. Then they went to the piece of grass by the horse block — you know — on the left. And then something happened."

He turned his eyes on her straight with an extraordinary look. For an instant she thought him mad. Then his look relaxed and he smiled.

"I've nearly done," he said; "but this is the point. I saw that it was time to go. I don't know where; but it was somewhere else; and then, all in a moment I saw that the whole thing was true — that — the Catholic religion was really true, not just in a pious sort of way you know, but solid, solid as a rock — judgment, hell, heaven, and the rest of it. And that I had to go and hand in my account. . . . . There were all sorts of people round me, looking at me. Real people, you know. . . . It — it was ghastly."

"Jack, I do ask you not to say another word. Why not wait a day or —"

"I can't — I may forget. I must tell you before I forget. Besides, I'm all right now, you know. Oh! I'm not going to die again just yet.

"Well, there are no words to use at all. All I can say is that the thing was as real as — as tables and chairs, only very much more so. It was all *real*, the whole thing from beginning to end; and — and I knew I'd made a most frightful mess of things. I — I was frightened to death.

"Well, I made the most awful struggle. I don't know what with, but it was with something. But it was entirely useless. No, I didn't see any one just then, or in fact, any-thing. It had all gone again. The last I had seen before those people, you know, was Lady Sarah and the man by the horse block — oh! And two carriages and a motor. Whose motor was that? It wasn't one of ours."

"Sir James came down from town in a motor."

"Where was I? Oh, yes. Well, I made this struggle. It was — just hell. I haven't an idea how long it went on. All I knew was that I couldn't and wouldn't go to that — place, or whatever it was, where I had to go. And then suddenly something happened — I don't know what. All I know is that it wasn't anything I did. There was some-thing that simply caught hold of me and swept me off. I thought it was the next stage. But the next thing I knew was that I was back in bed, and you were screaming. I couldn't see you; but I heard you and felt the bedclothes."

Mary made a huge effort to be serene.

"Dear boy, you've finished now, haven't you? . . . Really I think the half-hour —"

"Not quite. No; I will finish. It's just a question or two. Tell me. Was all that I said true? Wasn't it? . . . Of course it was."

"Well — er — certainly we were like that in the bed-room. But, you know, you saw us. My dear, do be —"

"And downstairs. The motor, and all that?"

"Why, you heard the motor arrive, of course; and re-membered it afterwards."

He nodded.

"Well, we'll let it go at that. And Lady Sarah and Sir James —"

"I — I think they did talk there for a minute or two."

"And they did tell you I was dead?"

"They — they thought so. But they were wrong, you see, Jack dear. It was just what they call 'suspended anima-tion'."

He made no answer to that; but she saw him smile con-tentedly to himself, and understood that kits conviction was unshaken. She stood up, still holding his hand, turn-ing her fingers gently in and out of his. Of course all this would pass in a day or two, she said to herself.

"Your beef tea —" she began.

He did not seem to hear; and she released her fingers quietly. He drew his hand in under the bedclothes, as if he did not notice.

"Of course you see the difference all this makes," he said quietly.

"Difference! Why —?"

Chapter II

(1)

I think Jack must have gone perfectly mad," said Mary, almost hysterically, to her friend Lady Sarah. "Tell me all over again, clearly and distinctly," said the girl.

The two were sitting together in the morning room on the evening of the third day. It had just gone six; and Lady Sarah had been contemplating a move homewards to her house a mile beyond the village. But after a long silence, broken only by obvious attempts to be conversational, Mary had suddenly burst out into such a torrent of incoherent information that a departure was impossible. (Jack, by the way, was doing excellently: that fact had emerged at an earlier point. He was even in his dressing gown upstairs before a small fire, as the evening was chilly.)

Mary sat down again abruptly on the low, wide window-seat, snatched a blind tassel, and staring desolately out over the box-lined beds in front to where the upper lawns rose to the fringe of the park, began her story.

"Well, the first kind of things I didn't mind. I mean things like asking Father Banting to come and live here. I think it's a bore, but — but there it is. Some Catholics do do it, and it's Jack's house after all. Besides, he'll be safely tucked away in the chapel-wing, anyhow. And I didn't much mind that — that ridiculous notice that was given out in church. (My dear! It was awful. You could have heard the tenants shiver. I thought I couldn't ever look Parkinson in the face again.) But I suppose he can do all that if he wants. But it's the other thing — the thing he asked me this morning — that's finished me."

"Tell me again," said Lady Sarah patiently. (She was thinking that husbands had their disadvantages after all.)

"Well, it was this. (Don't laugh, please.) Jack has been hunting up things in books. I never knew him do that before, by the way, except in Badminton, and so on. But he has. And he's discovered that the highest life in the world is to be a monk. And he wants to be one. And —"

"And what about —"

"Yes, just so. Well, it appears that I've got to be a nun. (No, really, don't laugh.) But that's his cheerful idea. It seems that he can't be one unless I'm the other. So he wants to sell this house, or give it away to some Order; and just go off — he to one monastery and I to another. And there we're to —"

"But I've never heard such —"

"I know. Nor have I. But he's quite serious, and — and not a bit melancholy or that. On the contrary, he's quite cheerful, and couldn't imagine why I bounced out of the room. And how in the world I'm to face him again!"

Mary broke off desperately, tossed the blind tassel away, and sat regarding her friend.

"Oh, Sarah! Don't look like that! It's I who ought to have the hysterics."

"But, my dear!"

"Yes, indeed. And the worst of it is that he's perfectly right in the head. At least the doctor says so; and — and —" (she fumbled in her pocket a moment) "here's Sir James's letter. It came yesterday." (She tossed it over to her friend.) "Just read that. You see what he says."

There was silence for a minute while Lady Sarah, her face a picture of consternation, turned the page. Then she laid down the paper. It is to be doubted whether she understood one word of what she read. (Hers was a mind which could contemplate only one fact at a time: she had no power of correlation.)

"And what are you going to say?" she asked.

"Say! What is there to say except No, No, No? I'd — I'd sooner die. If I wanted to be a nun, I wouldn't have married Jack — naturally. But that doesn't seem to have occurred to him."

"But what's put it into his head?"

"Why, all that I told you about. That nonsense about dying. Of course he didn't die. Why, he's alive. But he's got it into his head that the Catholic religion is — well — is true in a kind of way he hadn't guessed. He's — he's frightfully in earnest. It's awful."

"And he isn't depressed?"

"Not a scrap. He seems quite reasonable in anything else. Of course Jack and I have always been Catholics and all that; we've 'got the Faith,' as we say: I mean, we couldn't possibly be anything else; and we'd always go to our duties, and the Last Sacraments, and all that. But — but this sort of thing! Oh! I'm certain religion wasn't meant to upset people like this!" she ended passionately.

Lady Sarah meditated. She entirely agreed with the latter remark; and religion had certainly never upset her for even one passing instant. In fact her rector would have agreed with her that it would be a most improper thing for it to do. But you never quite knew where you were with Catholics, she reflected. She had known more than one case — However, that was neither here nor there. It was her duty to say something to poor Mary.

"I don't see what else you can do," she said rather feebly at last. "You must just tell Jack how the matter lies; and that you can't possibly be a nun. And that'll be the end of it. How fortunate —"

"Yes, indeed, there's some sense in theology after all. And at any rate he can't do it if I won't. And I won't. So he can't."

Mary got up. She felt rather better after formulating her conclusions. She came a step or two nearer and threw herself down on the sofa.

Certainly reflected Lady Sarah after all, there were some sensible Catholics. She looked at Mary, at that small, very determined face, her low eyebrows and her set lips. She looked perfectly charming, thought the girl: entirely fitted for her position, and entirely unfitted for any other. What a pity there were no children! That would have settled things.

"Well, there's not much to say. I expect it'll pass off in a week or two," she said. "And the other things —"

"Oh, the other things don't matter. I can stand them."

"Well, then —"

"Yes; I know. But it's such a relief just to have said out loud, 'I won't, I won't, I won't.' And when I say that I mean it. Oh, by the way, he's given a thousand pounds to

Father Banting. The poor man was dreadfully upset. He came and asked whether he should cash it."

"And did he?"

"Well, he's put it into the bank, with a note he made me sign about my approving of it provisionally. (That's just like a priest!) I'm afraid we have been rather brutes to him. Oh! I don't grudge that. Jack's frightfully rich, you know."

Lady Sarah sniffed slightly. It appeared to her a cruel waste of money. Such a lot might have been done with it. However, that wasn't her affair.

She stood up.

"My dear, I must be going. Come with me to the front door."

"Then you think I'm right?" asked Mary defiantly.

"Right! Why I should think so! What else did you expect me to say?"

"Yes, I suppose so. At any rate, I haven't got the faintest vocation. And Father Banting —"

"Oh, my dear, I don't understand about all that. You're absolutely, perfectly right. That's the end of it."

Mary got up.

"Oh, Sarah! What a comfort you are! I wish you were my confessor. Yes; I'll come to the front door."

As they passed together through the hall, Mary noticed a door left ajar, and remembering what room it was, went a step out of her way to shut it. She didn't want the smoking room to be disturbed until Jack came to disturb it again himself. So she peeped in (as one does), and recoiled with an exclamation.

"What's the matter?" asked the girl.

But Mary paid no attention. She vanished straight through the door; and as Lady Sarah hurried in after her she was confronted by Jack himself, in a dressing gown, cheerfully seated by a very large wood fire, and Mary staring at him.

"Yes, I know," the young man was saying with apologetic geniality; "it's strictly forbidden. But I had to come down — Good evening, Lady Sarah. You must forgive this."

"Jack," cried Mary suddenly, "what are you burning?"

"That? Oh, that's nothing. I found a little job waiting for me. That's all."

"But — but —"

Mary darted to the fire and dragged out from among the logs a large piece of smoldering wood. She held it in a kind of dumb consternation, by a curiously finished sort of handle.

"Don't. You'll be all over sparks," said Jack.

"But — but it's your bat. The — the South African —"

"I know. I thought it had better go in here, once and for all. I meant to do it sometime, anyhow."

Mary stared at him, white-faced, still holding the smoking wood.

"My dear girl; don't be so dramatic! Here; give it me."

Jack took it from her, and thrust it down again into the heart of the fire, with an odd sort of smile.

"But — but —" began Mary.

"Oh, don't let me have to explain. I should have thought you'd have known. I say, Lady Sarah, do sit down, won't you; if you don't mind —"

"But, Jack —" cried his wife again, as the girl sat down deliberately.

Then the young man's face changed a little. It is impossible to describe that change as the two saw it, but it had a curiously sobering effect upon them both. For the first time in her life to the elder girl it appeared that Mr. Jack Weston was not simply a jolly schoolboy. But as to exactly what he was at this moment she could not judge. His lips closed and his brows came down, and a new spirit looked out from his eyes for one instant.

"My dear," he said quietly to his wife, "I thought you understood. You didn't really think I was going to go on with — with all this sort of footle."

Mary looked at him for one moment longer. Then she suddenly burst into tears.

(2)

Mary got up next morning feeling just a little ashamed of herself. Yet she could not have said why. Every particle of reason that was in the situation at all lay on her side, and all the fanaticism on Jack's. "Fanaticism" — that was the word she wanted. It was kind, yet firm, like the pedagogues of childhood: it was charitable, yet just. Neither did it even hint at actual brain trouble; and it was loyal therefore to medical advice.

She looked in at Jack before going down to breakfast, exchanged a few pleasingly irrelevant remarks, and was just going out of the room, when he uttered one sentence that spoiled for her the next two hours.

"I say; I wish you'd just look in about eleven. I want to talk about something."

She spent those two hours deliberately screwing up her will, wandering vaguely with a newspaper and a pair of garden scissors up through the terraces that led to the upper lawns. And here she sat down on a white bench.

It was this part of the garden that was her particular joy; and it was looking simply heavenly this morning.

From where she sat there spread before her a great stretch of perfectly level velvet lawn, spread, so to speak, exactly on the top of the rounded hill behind the house, forming a large semicircle surrounded throughout its curve by a yew hedge. In this hedge were cut windows, commanding immensely long vistas of woodland, radiating out like the spokes of a wheel, showing the green gloom of trees and undergrowth for at least a quarter of a mile ahead. Immediately behind the hedge rose giant elms and beeches, shadowing, when the sun stood at noon, and through most of the afternoon, the whole lawn on which she looked. This was, so to speak, the sacred place of the gardens. It was the place where those who wished to be more or less alone retired: flaming beds, and fountains, and terraced walks, and so forth, were necessary for visitors, and these were profusely supplied down below. Down below, too, were croquet hoops, and bowls, and the rest, with their proper lawns. But here was peace. One could walk right up to the yew-windows, and, leaning there, be, so far as sight was concerned, in the heart of the woodland. Rabbits, even at midday, would sit up in the rides beyond and regard, with doubtful ears, the face looking at them — yet without panic.

It was, then, with this part in particular that Mary had fallen in love when Jack had first taken her over her new home. It seemed to her still a sort of solemn, yet friendly sanctuary, that made no demands on piety: she disliked, so far as it was proper to do so, with her whole heart the Georgian interior of the house chapel, with St. Peter and St. Paul, giant figures of plaster, regarding the worshiper from either side of the mahogany altar. This lawn was the place where she felt good.

It soothed her even this morning a little. She stared out at lawn and yews and elms, with a faint sense that they sympathized. Surely it was trying to be met by such an atmosphere as that which awaited her in the house! One thing only was certain: she must be perfectly resolute; she must give in, even genially, to minor discomforts, such as the perpetual presence of a priest, and impulsive gifts to him of heavy checks — even to the burning of cricket bats. But she must act as if she were entirely selfish in all matters directly connected with herself: she mustn't be swayed by Jack's moods. Of course all would come right in a few months at the latest; and a little resolution on her part would make that return more easy. Monk and nun, indeed! She smiled a little disconsolately.

This, then was her program. She must judge swiftly, by intuition, whether or not any new bombshell ignited by Jack would be likely to wreck her own comfort; if so, it must be firmly and kindly quenched. If it was only his own happiness in danger she must acquiesce instantly. . . . She wondered what it was that he wished to say to her at eleven o'clock. Surely it was not the cricket business. She had made her peace in that matter, more or less, after Sarah's departure. Yes, she had treated him like an invalid. An "invalid" — that was another useful word — almost as good as fanatic. Even his mind seemed to be like an invalid. He wasn't himself. He wasn't real.

She was interrupted by a sudden vision of Parkinson with a salver, appearing abruptly round the corner of the bushes that shielded her seat from the house.

"Please 'm, master says, would you kindly answer this? Master says he can't go himself."

She took up the note wondering.

It was directed to Jack; it was an invitation to either or both of them, written by a friend of Jack's, asking them to

dine and sleep a fortnight hence in a house the other side
of the county.

She hesitated.

"Is there any hurry?"

"Chauffeur's waiting, 'm."

She waited an instant longer, foreseeing, yet dreading
to foresee, the reason of Jack's refusal. It was the kind of
thing he usually jumped at. He was particularly sociable.

"I can't answer now," she said deliberately. "Tell the
man I'll write."

So this was the kind of thing she had to expect now —
for months to come, at any rate; until Jack's — Jack's fanaticism had worn out. Oh, it was intolerable!

Then she fell once more to considering the whole business: the illness; the apparent death; the recovery. And
yet she saw no light. The thing was a dream — just a very
vivid dream, of the kind that haunts one sometimes for a
few hours. Only in this case it had been more vivid than
usual; and was acting upon a state particularly ill-fitted
to resist its suggestion. That was the whole thing. It was
utterly and hopelessly impossible that what Jack had described had been really experienced. People did not die
and come back again. If they died they did not come back.
Therefore there was no means of knowing — knowing for
certain — that religion was — well, of course it was true;
all Catholics knew that: but true in the kind of way that
Jack thought it. Why, if religion was "true" like that, if it
was possible to verify by actual experience the realities of
faith, life would become impossible. No one could ever
think of anything else. The whole world would go about in
silence; everything would stop; nobody would marry anybody; nobody would dream of doing wrong ever; money
and motors and horses — well — all these would be value-
less; everybody would become a saint —

Then she broke off her meditations. But she could see a
little better what Jack meant. Poor Jack — an "invalid" —
a "fanatic "; just for a month or two. Then he'd become
reasonable again and buy another bat or two; and everybody would live happily forever after.

Well, well: that was eleven striking. She must be getting back. "Resolute "; that was the word; she must be

resolute and reasonable. She must just have common sense enough for two.

(3)

The doctor met her in the hall.

"Well?" she said.

"An extraordinary recovery, Mrs. Weston. I've given him leave to come down to lunch. It'll do him good. But please see that he eats well; he'll want all the strength he can get. I'll write to Sir James Martin. He's very deeply interested."

She said a word or two, and turned upstairs.

"Well, Jack," she said. "Here I am."

He was sitting in a deep chair by the fireplace, looking very nearly himself again. A little table stood beside him, deep in books, and three or four torn-open letters lay on the top. He nodded at her pleasantly, laying aside the book in his hands; and she sat down opposite on the couch that stood with its back to the window. The summer light fell full on his face.

"I saw the doctor just now," she said. "He gives an excellent account."

He said nothing for an instant. Then he turned to her full.

"Mary," he said, "I want to ask you a question. Will you promise to answer it truthfully?"

"Why, yes; if I know the answer," she smiled. (But she felt a little tremulous for all that.)

"Well then — do you think I'm mad?"

For a moment she was taken aback.

"Mad!" she said. "Why —"

"Yes; but do you?"

"Jack, of course I don't. I swear I don't. I think you're a little shaken by your illness, you know. People often are. I don't think you're quite reasonable always. But —"

"I see," he said. "Then that thing I asked you yesterday. Have you thought about it?" (Here was a fine opportunity to show resolution and naturalness.)

"Yes, my dear boy; of course I have. But only because you asked me. And I feel exactly the same, and I always shall."

"You're quite sure?"

"Absolutely. Why I haven't the faintest sign of a vocation. Jack dear, do you think I'd have married you if I had? You don't really wish —"

"That's final?"

Mary grew a little sore at his perfectly confident tone.

"Jack dear, I don't want to be beastly; but — but don't you think you had better consider my point of view just a little? I am your wife, you know. And —"

"But, my darling, what are you complaining of? I just made a suggestion. You don't like it? Very well. That's the end of it."

Mary sat silent. She had not expected such a swift capitulation. Plainly she was on the right road as regards treatment, however.

"Then I must just consider the next best thing to do," continued Jack tranquilly. "I perfectly recognize your rights as my wife. I've had a good talk to Father Banting about that. So we won't ever speak of that any more, unless you open the subject. That's all right, isn't it?"

"Er — yes," said Mary.

"Well, then; the next best thing. That's my point now. Do you like this place very much?"

"Why — I don't understand."

"Of course, if you're quite clear you want to go on living here, well, I suppose we must. But has it ever occurred to you that we should do better in a rather smaller house?"

Mary looked at him. This was worse than anything she had dreamed of. His persistence was horrible. Yet he looked practically himself.

"I don't understand," she said again faintly.

He smiled.

"It seems rather big for two people, doesn't it? Now I had thought perhaps we might get rid of this, and move — let's say — to one of the game keeper's cottages. Would you mind that very much?"

It seemed to Mary as if she were in some kind of appalling dream. Mentally she shook herself. Then she remembered the blessed words "invalid" and "fanatic," and took courage.

"Yes, dear," she said gently. "I should mind very much indeed. I couldn't dream of it."

"You mean that?" he said quickly.

"Certainly. Dear Jack, you must remember I've got the same ideas that both you and I had a week ago. If you haven't got them, I have. And, you know, they aren't wrong."

He considered this with his head a little on one side.

"No," he said, "that's fair enough. I'm not going to be selfish, you know; or, at least, I'm going to try not to be."

"But —"

"One instant. I want to say that I recognize entirely your rights as my wife; and, indeed, your wishes as well: so long as they don't actually interfere" . . . (He broke off.) "Then I understand you wish to live on here just as before — motors, horses, servants — everything — just the same?"

"Yes, please," she said quietly, though her heart almost shook her dress with its beating. Fortunately he was not looking at her. He sat, just as before, in his easy attitude, looking steadily at the fire.

Then a sudden spasm shook him.

"Mary!" he cried. "Mary darling!"

For an instant his face was changed, and an extraordinary appeal looked from his eyes.

"Don't — don't — Jack."

"My darling, I must — just one word. Oh! Don't you understand? The thing's real, real. God, heaven, hell, sin."

"Jack, I shall scream."

She was up, crouching back from him as if to ward off a blow. It was appalling that Jack should be like this.

His face relaxed first into a deep disappointment; then once more it cleared into that steady, slightly unfamiliar look that it had borne since his illness.

"I'm sorry," he said; "I know it's no good. I won't do it again. Look here; let's begin again where we left off. You really mean what you said?"

She nodded, and sat down again, trembling a little.

"Very good. Then that's clear. Then we'll both remember that. If I do anything, or propose anything that really interferes with your views, you'll let me know, won't you? You mustn't let me do anything, and then complain afterwards, will you?"

The reasonableness of this pierced her like a knife. Yet she knew she must not show it. She assented quietly.

"Then you must leave me, too, my individual freedom — my *individual* freedom," he repeated; "so long as it does not interfere with yours. That's all right, isn't it?"

She assented again. (What else could she do?) But it was hard to realize that this was Jack — Jack with his charming selfishness and occasional petulance. She began to see how much more pleasant it was to be ruled than to be deferred to. Yet anything was better than the hysteria of a minute ago.

"Very well."

He reached a letter from the little pile and handed it to her.

"Just read that," he said. "It seems to me to fall just pat."

She took it nervously.

It was in French. It was an appeal from a convent near Tours. It seemed that the nuns were to be driven out. They had no money and no friends. Mr. Weston's name appeared among the Catholic gentry of England. Was it possible that he could give them any assistance?

Mary sighed internally as she laid it down again. She foresaw, as in a flash, the interminable begging letters that would come now, so soon as Jack's new mood became known.

"I see," she said; "you want to keep them? That seems all right. You'll get references, I suppose?"

He smiled a little.

"Yes; I have been thinking it over. That letter came by the first post. I thought probably you wouldn't like my other suggestions, from what you said yesterday. So I've thought out a plan."

"Yes?"

"It seems to me that that lawn on the top of the hill would be just the place for them. There's a spring there, you know. And they're enclosed nuns, you know; so they wouldn't bother you much."

"I don't understand," said Mary faintly.

"Why, surely. Up there on the top seems to me just the place. It's an extraordinarily healthy situation; and I could build a really fine convent, and endow it."

"Jack! You don't mean that, really?"

"Yes, I think so. I've had a talk to Father Banting. He thinks it most suitable. You see, we should keep all the other gardens. And there's that road through the park by which the tradesmen could come, and so on. And then the people, too. I had thought of a really fine church, with a transept for the public. Don't you think it's rather a brilliant idea?"

She sat in silence, looking at him.

Chapter III

(1)

Old Lady Carberry always left London punctually on the thirtieth of June, and her daughter had to come with her. Some mysterious principle, no doubt, lay behind the selection of this day, in the great lady's mind; but whatever it was she kept it to herself. No disorganization of this plan was permitted on any pretext whatever. She had even been heard to say when the carriage that was to take her the thirty miles did not appear upon the instant that "they would never get to Hadham Park in time"; but it was still a mystery as to what engagement awaited her there. It would have made no difference to anyone in this world besides herself, her daughter, and her immediate dependents, if she had remained in London throughout the entire year; for she did nothing whatever of any importance to anybody either in Grosvenor Street or at Hadham. Her life consisted, so to speak, entirely of scaffolding, with no building inside. The morning was divided between getting up and preparing for lunch; her afternoon between "resting" from those labors and going for a short drive in a closed brougham with two horses and two men, in no particular direction; and her evening between "resting" again, dining, taking a little recreation at cards, and going to bed. Three or four other mysterious and solemn-faced old ladies spent a large part of the year with her in the same kind of pursuits, and nothing whatever happened ever to anybody. They were all rather religious in an Established sort of way.

It had been a real relief, therefore, to Sarah when the Westons had bought the place on the other side of the valley, and she had found that Mary was younger than herself, and of the same breezy sort of nature. They rode together now and then; they wrote letters to one another; and they learned the art of allusive conversation.

It had taken a few months before Sarah had quite got over, with respect to Mary, the odd sense of apprehensiveness with which she regarded Catholics. You never quite knew where you were with those curious people. Something rigid would suddenly emerge like a hidden rock from a smooth bay; and you spiked your boat before you knew there was any danger. This had happened once or twice to Sarah. There was an appalling memory still in her mind of a story she had once told to a middle-aged Catholic woman.

The memory made her hot all over. It was not at all a bad story, you understand; but it was just of the sort that nobody tells unless very certain of the company. The silence that had followed the story, and, when Sarah got indignant, the speech that followed the silence — well, it had all been exceedingly unpleasant. But Mary seemed different, somehow. And it was after a visit together to the hideous little chapel (that always smelt of soft soap), and a conversation afterwards in the morning room, that Sarah had lost her last trace of alarm.

"My dear," Mary had said very gravely, "I hate it all, exactly in the same sort of way that you do. It gives me the creeps. Yes, that small confessional that creaks and all the rest of it. I've got to do it, you see, because I'm a Catholic. But I try not to let religion interfere with my ordinary life at all. I think that's so important."

This was at least reassuring. It was precisely Sarah's own attitude to her own faith, and she found it satisfactory. After that the friendship had bloomed apace. And now an unsuspected mine had been exploded, and all was in confusion. She was sincerely sorry for Mary.

It was about a week later that the full significance of the situation burst upon her. She was riding through the village when she saw the first evidence of catastrophe. In front of a small enclosed court there was gathered a little group of round-eyed children, and in the midst stood a cart, drawn by an aged white horse, piled with the most incongruous looking objects she had ever set eyes on. As a foundation to the stack there rested several large pieces of painted furniture, "rained and varnished; from the midst of which protruded two bed-legs of iron like a pair of appealing arms; the castor of one was gone, she noticed. On the top of all this was a heap of rolled carpets, and on one side a mahogany bookcase, with all the books wrapped up in whitey-brown paper. But it was the crown of the heap that struck her most. A large plaster angel, painted pink, with one wing gone, lay on his face, as if in attitude to swim (she perceived that he was in an attitude of adoration reversed); and a pallid unpainted figure, terribly chipped, lay beside him on his back, grasping a small child in a position of benediction, lacking two fingers of his hand. Various other objects, like pieces of palm, a heap of pictures, a nondescript bundle, and bedroom china, were secured by string wherever room could be found. One picture in particular struck her thoughts dumb for an instant: it lay, fully displayed to the passer-by, and represented an immense, heart, blood-colored, surrounded by yellow flames, in a black, shining frame with a cracked glass.

Then, as she looked, the priest came out, in an alpaca jacket and a biretta cocked rakishly on one side, carrying a pair of indescribable yellow vases filled with dyed grass; and the moisture ran off his face.

Then she realized that the move was being made, and rode on hurriedly.

But the real shock came at the park gate.

The gate itself was open, and she saw standing within it two figures of men, beside a dogcart. One of these, whom she did not know, held a large parti-colored piece of paper in his hands, and the other was Jack Weston. He lifted his cap as he saw her.

"Going up to see Mary?" he asked cheerfully. "I think she's out."

"I wasn't thinking of it," said the girl, as she reined up for an instant. "So glad to see you out."

She was at that point of acquaintance when she called him Jack to his wife and nothing at all to himself. She had ventured about twice on "Mr. Jack."

"Oh, I'm all right, thanks. Look here; what do you think of this? (Stand still, will you?)"

Her horse began an ineffectual prancing as a map was suddenly displayed before her.

"Oh, may I introduce Mr. Farquharson. . . . Lady Sarah .
. . er . . . He's kind enough to undertake the building for
me."

"I don't understand," she said. "What's that for?"

"Oh, that's the Carmelite convent. Mary's told you,
hasn't she?"

"Convent! No!"

"Oh, I thought she'd be sure to have told you. We're going to build a convent on the top of the hill; just above the
house. French Order, you know — expelled from France;
at least just going to be."

"I don't understand," said the girl. "Mary hasn't told me
a word. When was it settled?"

"Oh, about a week ago. It'll be rather fine in its way; at
least I think so. This is only a rough sketch, you know."

She looked at the plan as well as she could, saw lines
and labels, and finally recognized the site.

"But — but where's it going to stand? It's not to be on
the upper lawn, is it?"

He nodded cheerfully.

"That's the idea," he said. "It's far the best site, Mr.
Farquharson says. There's a spring, and all that, you
know. And I'm rather thinking of an orphanage down on
this side, somewhere. But that's not settled yet."

She rode on after a word or two; and the horror deepened at every step. It really was to be; the whole place
was going to be changed. It was going to become a kind of
Catholic settlement, of an appalling kind — convents, or-
phanages; with Jack Weston in the middle as Universal
Provider — mad beyond a doubt, but with a madness that
could not be laid hold of; and Mary — poor Mary, distracted and miserable. It was simply wicked. But why in
the world had not Mary told her?

The reason was apparent when she reached home and
saw a pony carriage.

"Mrs. Weston's been waiting half an hour, my lady. I
said I thought your ladyship'd be home about half-past
four."

She was in Sarah's sitting room on the first floor, a
charming little square green and white place, looking out

on to a small lawn that seemed to belong to it; but it was a desolate face that looked at her.

"Oh, my dear," she wailed. "I simply couldn't tell you before I was certain. It's too awful. But the architect's come with his horrible plans, and it's really settled. I gave in; yes, I know I shouldn't have; but it's to be on the upper lawn — just the one place. It's too dreadful."

"You gave in?"

"Yes, I had thought it out so clearly, I thought; and Jack talked about his 'individual liberty' and mine; and I really couldn't see any excuse. And he gave in so instantly on the other things. He is so dreadfully reasonable — not a bit like Jack. And I had to. And the next thing I knew was Mr. Farquharson at lunch, and his plans propped up against the spiraea, and a fountain pen behind his ear. I'd no notion he really meant it."

"Why don't you tell him you can't," remarked Sarah, taking off her hat.

"I daren't. He'd think it so weak. Besides, it really wouldn't be fair. You know he did give in to me."

Sarah sniffed. Mary continued.

"And then, you know, it is really rather splendid — from Jack's point of view. Oh, I quite see that. I'm dreadfully reasonable too, in a kind of way; and — and if I felt as Jack does about religion, I suppose I'd do it too. But you see I don't."

"Why didn't you tell me before?" demanded the girl sharply.

"I couldn't. It was like telling a bad dream. It would have made it real, in a kind of way. Oh, but that's not the point. The point is, what on earth I'm going to do about it?"

"Cigarette?" said Sarah.

Mary took one without attending to it. She held it without lighting it, waving it about as she talked: and it was not until a match was thrust before her face that she put it to its proper use. Even then she continued her lament, pouring out horrible phantom schemes of Jack's, worse even than the visionary orphanage, describing the proposal to live in a gamekeeper's cottage and the rest of it.

"And he's given notice to his man," she ended. "He's been with him for years; but Jack says he simply can't be waited upon any more in that kind of way. Oh, and he goes to Mass every morning, and I've got to go too generally; and he makes his meditation every morning, just as if he was pious. Jack! Meditation! But he does; I've seen him from the gallery with a little paper book. It's too dreadful! And he tries to say the divine office. I came upon him and Father Banting at it in the garden one day. They were signing themselves like semaphores."

Sarah emitted a short chuckle.

"My dear, it won't last."

Mary shook her head dolefully.

"You don't know Jack," she said. "Cricket! That's the worst symptom. If you knew what cricket was to Jack! And he's given up the *Field*! He's — he's not like a real person at all. He's like a bad actor who's perfectly sincere and painstaking."

Sarah sniffed again.

"It strikes me it's the worst case of — do you mind my saying what I think, darling?"

"I want you to," wailed Mary.

"Well, it strikes me Jack's become the worst sort of prig."

"Oh, you don't understand. It isn't that. It's not the least that. He's not a prig. He doesn't think anything of himself at all. No, it's a sort of awful religious disease. Well, at any rate, it's a form that I don't like at all. Catholics do get it sometimes; and it's no good arguing. But it isn't priggishness."

"But what about you? Doesn't he think you very wicked and worldly?"

"Not in the least. That's the dreadful thing. He explained it all carefully a day or two ago."

"Tell me."

"Well, you see, it's like this. He thinks he's been sent a warning, at least that's what the poor dear says: that — that he was living an awfully careless life — and so he was in a sort of way; and that this has been given him as another chance. Otherwise he'd have gone to hell."

"Hell! You don't believe in that, do you?" asked Sarah, seriously shocked.

Mary stopped dead.

"Yes, I do," she said, "underneath somewhere. You don't understand, dearest. But it's all underneath. Now with Jack it's come to the top. Oh, it isn't only hell he's frightened of. He talks about ingratitude, and waste of his life and money, and all the rest."

"But you — what does he think about you?"

"Oh, he doesn't condemn me at all. He told me that he knew that it was quite possible to become a saint living as I do — think of that, Sarah! — but that he mustn't. Oh, he's raving mad."

"I saw Father Banting making his move this afternoon," observed the other after a short pause.

Mary gave a little resigned gesture with her cigarette.

"Oh, that's a mere trifle now. If that was all — yes; he'll be there tonight, and tomorrow morning, and so on."

Sarah sat silent.

The situation appeared to grow worse every instant. She was not in the least persuaded against Jack's priggishness: it struck her as an appalling example of the vice she hated most. It was odd that Mary didn't see it. However, there it was — the Catholic point of view once more; and she had run herself against it, full tilt. She must just back off, and sympathize. At any rate, there was some practical advice to be given.

"Look here," she said, "you simply must not give in about this convent. It would entirely ruin the whole place to have it there. If he must have it, why in the world not stick it down by the upper lodge?"

"There's no water there."

"Then they can go and fetch it; it would be an excellent mortification, as you call it. Or have it laid on. Besides, I'm sure nuns don't wash much — particularly French nuns."

Mary shook her head grievously.

"I gave in," she said. "I was mad; but I did."

"Then go and eat humble pie. Tell him you've changed your mind — that you simply can't have it there. You've simply no right at all to let that lovely garden be spoiled."

"He'd think me so changeable."

"Not more than he is himself."

"I don't think I can, Sarah."

"Stuff and nonsense. Of course you can. Stand up to him."

Mary shook her head slowly.

A gong resounded from beneath. Sarah jumped up.

"Oh, and I haven't changed my habit. Well, they'll have to put up with it. Come down to tea."

Mary rose.

"Do you think I must? I don't want to, you know."

"Of course you must. Don't be afraid. There's only Mother, and Miss Fakenham and her nephew. They're staying here."

(2)

Persons who have nothing whatever to do frequently succeed in investing that nothing with extraordinary pomp. Lady Carberry's afternoon drive, for example, was as carefully regulated in detail and etiquette as a state progress of Queen Victoria (whom, as a matter of fact, in personal appearance she rather resembled); and afternoon tea, dispensed in the shadow of her presence, stood, so to speak, for a banquet to foreign ambassadors. Things had to be done in this way, and not that; the tea-cake was never to be placed upon the slop basin; the toast was to be of a particular texture; and so forth.

In appearance, as has been said, her ladyship resembled the late Queen; in manner and mind a hanging judge. She was severe. Severity sat upon her like a crown. The only possible way of tolerating her therefore was to regard her from a humorous point of view; to elicit characteristic remarks and reckon them up afterwards — if possible in the company of a sympathizer; to take one's seat, so to speak, in the front row and look on at the play. Mary had soon learned this; and Lady Carberry therefore thought her charming and right-minded.

But this afternoon the girl was too much depressed to play her part; and a kind of despair fell on her as she watched and considered. (I have felt that despair myself sometimes on watching some stout and aged lady, let us say, setting out for a drive in a brougham; or a bald-headed nobleman reading his paper at the window of his club.) Nothing much happened for some time: words proceeded out of people's mouths; small things to eat were handed to and fro; the bell was rung; young Mr. Faken-ham, a slim and melancholy man of thirty years old, with hair quite beautifully brushed, did his duty; and the two old ladies discussed things like the view from the hill above Bachway and the iniquitous doings of the Liberal Government.

This was all enacted in the drawing room, a pleasant, low room, faintly suggestive of the early Victorian era, in spite of the Morris paper and the diamond-paned windows.

About half-past five the Rector appeared.

There is nothing particular to say about him, nor had he anything particular to say, yet his coming gradually switched off the talk to another line; and a sudden remark of his brought Mary forward, on that subject on which she would have most preferred to keep silence in such company.

"I saw Mr. Weston very busy over some plans at the lower lodge gate an hour ago," he said.

Lady Carberry stopped talking.

"Yes; that was an architect with him," said Mary.

"Indeed! You are contemplating some building —"

The Rector did not approve of the Westons overmuch. It had been something of a blow to him when this Papist couple had turned up; and it had taken nearly all the time that had elapsed since their coming to assure him that no harm would be done in his parish; He was a kindly enough man, getting on for sixty years old, with a very Established way of looking at things. Romanists were a superior kind of Dissenters to his loyal mind.

Mary hesitated for a moment. Then she reflected that it had to come out sometime.

"Yes," she said, "my husband is thinking of building a convent for some expelled French nuns."

The Rector stopped stirring his tea. (It is a significant detail that for the clergy Lady Carberry did not usually send out for a fresh supply. Sarah, by the way, did the pouring out.)

"But —" he began.

Mary felt suddenly defiant. She went on rather rapidly.

"Yes, you know. It's dreadful to think of those poor creatures; and, as Catholics, of course we sympathize with
them."

"But I should not have thought that Mr. Weston —" began the other.

Mary thought it better to elude this implication by a
swift interruption.

"Of course, it isn't exactly what we should have preferred, in itself. But things are really serious. My husband
got a most piteous letter a week ago; and — er — we decided almost at once."

"Do I understand you aright, Mrs. Weston?" began Lady
Carberry. "I am a little hard of hearing. It is that you are
really thinking of building a nunnery, here?"

"Well, on the top of the hill behind our house — yes, certainly — a convent; yes, a nunnery."

"In those beautiful gardens?"

"That seems the best we can offer," said Mary reck-
lessly. "It seems the obvious place."

(She saw Sarah out of the corner of her eye suddenly
bend to do something with the urn. She knew exactly
what she was thinking, but was too sore to care.)

Then Lady Carberry, having wheeled her battery into
position, opened fire. She was not exactly insolent, nor
exactly uncharitable; indeed, she professed a great
breadth of view; but she discussed the French question
with extraordinary frankness. It seemed to her, she said
(and would Mrs. Weston forgive her for saying so?) that
there must have been some reason why it was being found
impossible in one civilized country after another to toler-
ate the Religious Orders. She did not wish to say one word
against the Roman Catholic religion; indeed, she had
more than one friend of that faith; but it was politics —
was it not? — that made it so essential for no community
to be permitted which interfered in them. It was, of
course, most kind — most kind and charitable of Mr. and
Mrs. Weston to give shelter to those poor creatures, who
no doubt had erred in ignorance; but would it not have
been the truest kindness to have just given them help on

condition that they went to live in their homes again? And, again, what of convent life as a whole? Was it desirable in any case? Was it not unnatural and mistaken to shut oneself up within four walls (Mary had an intuitive flash of vision, and saw the brougham with closed windows, and Lady Carberry nodding inside) — within four walls, instead of doing useful work? And then, in any case, did Mrs. Weston think it wise to disturb a quiet little English village with foreigners, however unfortunate? Would it not he better . . . and so on.

Lady Carberry was extraordinarily difficult to stop when she got under way. She moved in conversation like a great brig; her wake affected all smaller craft within half a mile. Sarah made more than one attempt; but the silence that followed was so terribly abrupt on both occasions that she dared not do it again. So it flowed on to the end. Miss Fakenham, still in the hat with jet flowers in which she had shared in the progress this afternoon, nodded gentle approval, with closed lips. Mr. Fakenham, who had only arrived that evening from town, sat in an attitude of impartial deference, apart on the sofa; and the Rector ate and drank with an air of being fair to both sides.

The effect on Mary was, of course, exactly what might have been expected. She began by being bitterly amused at Lady Carberry's judicial attitude towards Carmelites. She did not in the least mind criticizing them herself, but for Lady Carberry of the brougham to do so was another matter. In fact, Mary had said most of the things herself, in expansive moments, including the "four walls" phrase; but it began to seem to her that the case was a singularly weak one when put by her hostess. By the end of the exordium she was cross; by the beginning of the peroration she was furious; and when the last words sank into silence she was speechless — though she preserved an admirable composure — and was almost persuaded that the top of the hill was precisely the right place, and that Jack's scheme was admirable in all respects.

She said one sentence as soon as her chance came.

"Yes, Lady Carberry; but you must remember that Jack and I are Catholics."

Sarah came out with her to the stable yard to fetch the pony carriage; and said nothing at all till they had turned the second corner.

"My dear, I'm so sorry. What can I say?"

Mary offered no suggestions. She was still trembling a little.

"What are you going to say to Jack?"

"I don't know," said Mary. "I — I think it's abominable of him; but —"

And she would make no more illuminating remarks.

(3)

The two dined together that night as usual in the small dining room that they used when there were no guests; and once more Mary was overwhelmed by despair. (Father Banting, it seemed, in the agonies of moving, preferred to sleep for one night more in his old rooms.) The thing that brought her misery to a point was her observation that Jack took no wine and refused two courses.

She remonstrated when the men had gone out.

"My dear, it's all right. I asked old Basing this afternoon."

"And — and do you mean always to starve yourself in future?" she asked, her voice trembling a little with dismay.

Jack laughed gently.

"Look here, Mary, do remember about individual liberty. And you must remember that I'm only just finding my feet. I haven't the least idea what I shall do later."

She was silent. Then she glanced up at him, as he sat there, serene in the candlelight. It was something for him to be alive at all, she reflected. Then she put her hands together on the table and her chin upon them.

"I want to have a long talk, Jack," she said. "Shall we have coffee out of doors?"

There was a small stone table fenced by seats in the little sheltered three-sided court where the fountain played; and here, when the windows had been shuttered behind them, and coffee had been set down under the summer stars, Mary began.

"Look here, Jack," she said, "I really do want to know how we stand. Are you going to spring any more surprises on me? That's the first thing. I want to know the sort of program you've got in your mind. I know perfectly that you mean to be fair to me. That goes without saying. Besides, you've said it. But I want you to explain exactly what you mean to do."

He looked at her without speaking.

"And I want to make a confession," she went on. "I'll tell you plainly that I thought you, not mad, but just upset by your illness; and I've been hoping it would all pass away again. Well, it doesn't seem to me as if it is going to. So I must rearrange my mind. Please help me. I don't want to be tiresome."

Jack crossed one leg over the other, and she could see him begin to finger his mustache.

"It's nice of you to have said that," he remarked quietly. "I was hoping you would. Oh, yes, I'm perfectly sane — for the very first time, it seems to me. Well, I'll tell you all I know myself."

He tilted his chair forward again on to its four legs.

"Well, this is the position," he said. "I've had a startler. It's no good going into all that again; but there it is. And it's just made the whole difference. It seems to me now that, knowing what I do know, it's everybody else that's a little mad — yes, my dear, even you. I see, in a sort of way, your point of view; after all, I had it myself till a week or two ago; but — but now it's exactly like a dream. Well, I want to fix that — my new point of view, I mean. I'm perfectly certain that nothing can change me again; but — well one never knows whether one mayn't get a little slack. I can see absolutely that it would be quite easy, in an ordinary way, to slip back again; and I want to take every precaution. I know now — at least, I saw it quite plainly in — in my illness, that the thing's solid. I can see now that religion, and so on, is the one thing that matters; but I can also see perfectly well that you don't. Very good. Then we must arrange matters on that footing. You've got your rights: I know that; and I'm not going to touch them. I wouldn't have touched that upper garden if you hadn't consented. By the way, you do feel that's all right, don't you?"

There was a moment's pause before she answered, long enough for her to see how much depended on it, not long enough for him to notice it.

"Of course I consent," she said quietly. "I said so."

"Yes, but — All right then. Well, I shall always consult you before doing anything that will affect you in the slightest. I mean I'm going to continue to dress for dinner, and so on; but, for the rest, you really must allow me to make experiments and go my own way. About social things — I don't know. They seem to me simple rot just now."

"We've got people coming soon," slid in Mary swiftly.

"Oh, of course here things must go on as usual. That's your affair; and I shall be polite, and all that; but about other things — I'm not so sure.

Mary, don't you see that it'll take a little time before I see things clearly, and what to do, and so on? You must really let me alone."

Mary put out her hand to the cigarettes. Jack wasn't smoking, she noticed.

"Do you see?" he said again. "It's not exactly easy for me, anyhow."

"Wait, please; I'm thinking."

They had always been on good terms, those two; almost like two boys together. They had made a special point of this, and it had worked admirably. Certainly it was good that such terms existed in such a crisis as this.

Overhead burned the myriad pin heads in their velvet setting. The great trees across the lawn stood silent and massive against them; and the fountain did no more than throw into relief the enormous stillness of the night.

Mary was thinking hard. That last sentence had struck her with a certain sense of hope. This afternoon she had been furiously hard against him, judging him sternly from the height of her own excellent sanity. But somehow the old lady's assault had thrown her, almost unconsciously, on to the other side. That strange Catholic pride, so incomprehensible to others, had come to her rescue; she must support Jack, in speech, at any rate, and in public, against all comers that were not of the fold. And the very action of doing this had contributed to make her ask for

this final explanation this evening, and to judge more le-
niently.

"*It's not exactly easy for me, anyhow.*"

A certain hope surely lay hidden in that sentence. It
was not a mere fanaticism that moved him then — not
such a drunkenness of spirit as that which enables the
fakir to find iron spikes his most pleasant bed: there was
still effort; and effort involved the possibility of cessation
of effort. Further it was even rather admirable.

Jack's voice broke in on her silence, as if designed to
emphasize her new thought.

"For instance, you don't suppose I like giving up that
upper lawn. I know it's the best of the garden. But that's
exactly why they must have it. You see that, don't you?"

She nodded meditatively.

"Yes, I see that," she said mechanically. "Wait a second,
Jack. I want to put into exactly the right words what I
want to say."

Again the silence came down. Then Mary broke it, with
an abrupt movement of her head.

"Jack," she said, "I think I'd better say it plainly. It's
this. I can't think that all this is more than a mood with
you. I'm not saying anything against it. It's much better
than a good many moods. So I'm not going to fight any
more. But you don't seem to me to be quite yourself,
somehow. . . . Of course it may be a complete change, and
I may be quite wrong; but —"

"My dear —"

"Yes, I know; of course you're bound to think that."

"My dear, I tell you the whole world's absolutely
changed. Tell me; I'm not excited, am I?"

"Well, no, but —"

"Oh Mary —"

Mary turned her head to look at him. She had said just
now that he was not excited; yet even already she was
beginning to doubt that. There was, again, a very odd look
in his face, so well as she could see it in the dim light, an
almost mask like look, with some hot passion burning
through the eyes. Certainly it was Jack all right; yet there
was entirely gone from his features that placid, utterly
natural, almost animal expression that simple well-bred

people wear. Again she hesitated. Which of the two was
the real Jack? Was it conceivable that his soul had only
now awakened for the first time? Or was this some gust of
feeling, working on a slightly unbalanced brain, that
would pass again? She strove to reassure herself that it
was the second.

"No," she said. "Please don't try to persuade me. I'm being quite reasonable. Just talk to me simply about your
plans."

He dropped his eyes.

Then, while he continued to talk, she continued to
think, answering him only when necessary, pursuing
meantime that new point that she had only just perceived. It was really a relief, she saw now, to know that he
found it just a little difficult. It made him somehow more
human. Perhaps even he might already be regretting the
burning of the cricket bat. Of course it was intensely annoying — though she kept that annoyance loyally suppressed — that this new course of life should interfere
with things like the upper garden, and that Father
Banting should be in the house, and all the rest of it. Yet
there began to come into her mind a certain faint sense of
admiration that had been wholly lacking. She knew that
she would probably be annoyed very often again; but it
was a consolation to know too that it cost Jack something
as well as herself. It would be easier to cooperate on that
understanding, or, at least, not actively to hinder.

Yes, it was rather admirable — this furious even fanati-
cal response, to — to an illusion such as he was suffering
from. There appeared in it a certain nobility.

. . . "Yes," she said suddenly, in answer to a suggestion.
"Get the plans and a candle, and let's look at them. I understand better now. Give me a kiss, Jack. I'll try not to
be tiresome."

Chapter IV

(1)

Mr. James Fakenham was walking on the gravel path behind the house with a cigarette after breakfast.

He was a very harmless and entirely respectable young man of thirty-two years, with a thin, mask like face; black hair so beautifully ordered that it resembled a discreet wig; narrow black eyes, rather melancholy; very delicate, hairless hands, with blue veins showing on the back; and was dressed this morning in that costume which he considered absolutely appropriate to a small country house where there was nothing to do except riding and trout-fishing.

His history was as correct as himself. He had had the dignity of orphanhood for thirty years; he had been sent to Harrow and Oxford by his aunt, in whose house he spent his holidays; he had entered the Home Office at the earliest possible age, and had remained there ever since, discharging his duties with the exact proportion of zeal, punctuality, and indifference that was compatible with and appropriate to his proper position. His aunt, whose heir he was to be, allowed him four hundred pounds a year and the hospitality of her house in Queen's Gate. He kept a small, trim horse in the mews round the corner, and might be observed riding in the Row, carefully and slowly, with his toes out, in the proper manner at the proper times. He had a small group of persons whom he called his friends, with whom he dined, danced, smoked, motored, and went to the theater. He moved gently about in town among extremely correct people, and went dutifully with his aunt for at least a part of his vacations. He had no vices worth mentioning; he did the duties of his state of life; he was very far indeed from being stupid; and if it was impossible for anyone to be enthusiastic about him, it was equally impossible to be enthusiastic against

him. One is not enthusiastic about a quiet, inhuman machine.

I love contemplating people of this kind, because the
subject is so endless and evasive. I have no certainty of
what Mr. Fakenham thinks about, but I am stimulated by
him to form unverifiable conjectures forever. Thoughts
undoubtedly pass through his mind beyond those to which
he gives expression, but I have no idea as to what they
are; words proceed out of his mouth — often, so long as
the subject is on his own plane, shrewd and suggestive;
and actions are done by him. He lives, and he will die; and
as to what he will do then not even I dare to form conjectures of any kind. He is the strongest argument for the
annihilation of the soul that I have ever met.

He is religious? Well, he goes to church nearly always in
the country, and even sometimes in town, and I imagine
that his philosophy consists in regarding himself as a philosopher.

He is artistic? Intellectual? Well, he collects a few en-
gravings and first editions of artists and poets whom no
one has ever heard of except a group of persons in London
and Paris of which he is one. He published a small volume
of slightly improper essays ten years ago, and is extremely pained if anyone mentions the fact, for that was
in the days of his youthful enthusiasm and indiscretion,
before he had learned that self-repression was the epit-
ome of all the virtues. (It was in those days that for about
two years he had been accustomed to dress in the fashion
of George IV, with, I think, straps to his trousers and a
high satin stock. It had caused quite a sensation for a
time.) He is really rather shrewd about people and human
nature generally, though his outlook is not as catholic as
it might be.

I wish now to describe his appearance this morning —
not that anything depends upon it. (He is not, later on, to
be convicted by its means of some nameless crime.) I wish
only to gaze upon him for a minute or two.

He went up and down the path between the laurels neither slowly nor fast — the former would be self-conscious,
the latter enthusiastic; he carried in his left hand a small
silver matchbox with "Jim" engraved upon it in a femi-

nine handwriting. I have no idea who gave it him; perhaps he bought it. His right hand held a small round
Turkish cigarette. He wore upon his body a gray flannel
suit, with a single carnation in his buttonhole, and upon
his head a neat Panama hat with a dark green ribbon; he
had a high collar of the new fashion round his neck, em-
braced by a beautiful little very dark red silk tie that con-
trasted admirably with the soft blue-green flannel shirt
beneath. On one finger he wore a gold ring with a coat
lightly engraved. He had pumps upon his feet, and green
clocked socks. A couple of documents in long envelopes, of
no importance whatever, protruded from his jacket-pocket
on the left side.

So, then, he walked. Below him was the shrubbery that
shrouded the house; above him, beyond the laurels, stood
the summerhouse and the woods behind. Birds sang, and
insects hummed, and the sun shone in an unclouded sky.
And this lord of creation walked up and down, formulating thoughts, no doubt, though no living man could con-
jecture with any certainty as to their contents — in a gray
flannel suit and Panama hat. He had breakfasted half an
hour before, and would go indoors presently to the smoking room to see if the papers had come.

Probably he was a little annoyed, therefore, when Lady
Sarah appeared, radiant, flushed, healthy, and hatless,
but carrying a dog-whip, and accompanied by a trio of fox
terriers. He was first aware of their approach by the sudden apparition of a young rabbit, panic-stricken, but running like a streak, which burst from the lower shrubbery,
as a chorus of shrill barks broke out below, and vanished
again upwards in the direction of the summerhouse. Then
the quartet appeared, *en echelon*, the girl last, cracking
her whip and issuing orders. But the thing was useless;
the pack had disappeared in full cry among the woods;
and the two began to saunter together to await their return.

They knew one another quite well, in a flat sort of key;
for there was no emotion available with Mr. Jim Fakenham. Their elders were old friends, and this was perhaps
the fourth or fifth time that Jim had come here for a week
or so in the summer. Further, they met fairly often in

London, and were each of them perfectly acquainted with the tastes of the other. Jim was a little critical sometimes of the lack of repose in Lady Sarah, and she, in moments of expansion, rather impatient of the extreme self-repression and colorlessness of Jim. But they were good friends; they had quite finished at least two years ago those remarks of mutual disapprobation that were bound to be said and had survived them. They accepted one another now as final. Sarah, even, had begun to repeat some of Jim's sayings as her own.

"Sorry there are no men here," she said presently. "What'll you do with yourself today?"

"Oh, I'm all right," he said vaguely. "I've got one or two papers to finish; and — and there's the trout stream."

"By the way, the Westons' stream's in better order than ours. You can always go there, if you want, you know."

"Perhaps I will," he said. "After tea."

This was Jim's one physical accomplishment. It was impossible to call it a passion; for he had no such thing; but, so far as things interested him at all, trout fishing interested him most. His enthusiasm had never yet risen — since one fatal holiday in Norway which he had spent with zealots who refused to dine at eight — to making anything resembling a business of that sport; but he certainly quite liked to take out his beautifully polished split-cane rod, his fly book and net, half an hour after tea, and go down to some slow-flowing stream where monsters dwelt, subaqueous and alone, beneath the tangled roots of chestnut and lime. (He would always, however, be back at half-past seven.) He was just a little ashamed of his liking for it; for in his dim philosophy indifference was the greatest of virtues: and no doubt he would give it up, like everything else, in a few years' time. Meanwhile, if the weather was really pleasant, it was worth while just to go down alone for an hour or two, and see what could be done. It gave him an appetite for dinner; the sport was not noisy, and he could enjoy it without perturbation, in a really nice-looking suit.

"You might go to tea with the Westons," said Lady Sarah presently. "It'd give you an extra half-hour. Mother takes rather a long time, you know; and there's the walk afterwards."

Jim nodded gently. I imagine that he was considering whether it was worth it. He had nothing particular to say to the Westons, and was inclined to regard their religion as something corresponding to a slight air of ill-breeding. It had a fatal capacity for the production of enthusiasm.

"Yes, I might," he said. Then he glanced at Sarah.

"Yes, I know," she said. "It's very early to be so untidy. But those dogs, you know."

"I was thinking how charming," said Jim.

This was a little unusual from Jim, and the girl wondered why he had said it. She was quite sure he did not mean it. She decided to pay no further attention to it.

"I must see after those dogs," she said. "By the way, I wish you would go to the Westons. You heard all that last night? I can't make out Mary."

"Yes, I heard it," he said. "I suppose it's all right?"

"How do you mean?"

"Oh, the sort of thing Catholics do. It seems to me very odd. But, of course, I'm very narrow-minded. And up in those gardens, too."

"I can't make it out. Mary seemed to hate it as much as I do; but she's given in; at least, I think so. It isn't like her. I told you about Mr. Weston, didn't I?"

"His recovery?" asked Jim, carefully lighting a new cigarette from the stump of the old one.

"Yes. Well, that's at the bottom of it, of course. It seems to have sent him perfectly mad."

"Sort of revival, in both senses," remarked Jim.

"Exactly. Well, I wish you'd look in and see what you think. I think you're rather good at that kind of thing, you know."

"I daresay I will," said Jim, secretly pleased.

Sarah understood his attitude perfectly; in fact, it was largely her own. It seemed to him slightly indecent that religion, or indeed any instinct of the kind, should so display itself in outward action. It was not meant for that. And as for this form of display, no reprobation could be strong enough. They were both a little shocked, as if acquaintances of theirs should suddenly manifest bad taste. It was kinder not to say too much about it.

Then a dog arrived suddenly, miry-nosed and panting, and regarded them with his head on one side, from the vantage of a high bank; justice had to be administered and further search made. Jim went discreetly indoors to look at the papers.

(2)

The Manningham stream, Jim thought (and said late at dinner), as he approached it along the inside of the park palings (he had not been to tea at the hours, after all), looked extraordinarily like a certain sort of Academy picture this evening.

It moved leisurely along at the foot of the slope on which the house was built, looping itself generously here and there, full-brimming, translucent; with here a wa-ter-meadow, dark with clumps of rushes, here an opulent may-hedge, while overhead towered the chestnuts, limes, and beeches that formed the front rank of the woods that trooped to the water's edge. The stream itself was a joy to the eye of the observer as well as to that of the dry-fly-fisher. It was full to the very brim just now, after the rains of early July, yet clear as glass; the chestnut blossom had for the most part floated away long ago, and lay now only in thin rims of faded pink above the lines of posts that here and there broke the even flow of the water into tiny cataracts. The rich evening sunlight poured across the western slopes, turning the green to gold, and the gold to an indescribable radiance; and as a foil, just beyond the stream, lay the heavy scented gloom of the deep woods. The air was full of evening sounds, the liquid talking of birds, the steady organ-hum of insects, the far-away suggestive jangle of cowbells.

Jim was aware of all this with a certain pleasure. It was a little common and simple and English, of course — he preferred Italy — but it had its charm; and he hummed softly to himself as he set up his rod, passed the line through the rings, and at last, cigarette in his lips, sat down on a stump to select his fly.

It was a "coch-y-bonddhu" that he chose at last, after a careful stare at the surface of the water — a fat little fly, consisting of iridescent feathers standing all ways at once, with disheveled wings of a light brown — altogether an important-looking little beast, that would fall with a small succulent plop, would float detached on the liquid mirror, and — above all to be considered under the circumstances — would dry quickly.

It was attached; the reel was looked to; the fly book put away; and business began.

It would be about an hour later that Jim, now half a mile upstream and immediately below the northern side of the house, became aware of footsteps that approached and halted. But it was impossible to attend just then. Not two minutes before, as the "Welshman's button" (female), who had succeeded the "coch-y-bonddhu," floated, an apparently agonizing moribund, just beyond a small clump of rushes, beneath an overhanging beech, there had appeared for one instant a solemn fish-face of incalculable size, seen magnified beneath the surface, and gone again, with a single ripple to mark it, inspecting the fly and vanishing with a hesitating air. All now depended upon a perfect cast. Jim, crouching unseen, kneeling in spite of his beautiful gray flannel trousers on a damp tussock, was waving the fly softly to and from, waiting for that psychological moment when first impressions should have faded from the fish mind and a second temptation should prove irresistible.

That moment came. There was a long, careful movement of the rod backwards (the fly whirled exquisitely in the sunlight), an indescribable pushing swish forwards, and simultaneously the sudden plunge of a rat opposite, and the consequent destruction of that mirror of peace. The rod checked, the fly flew up and wrapped itself affectionately about the beech leaves that sloped from the further bank.

"Damn!" said Jim softly.

Then Jack came forward.

There was a short exchange of greetings and technical explanations. It appeared that Jim had caught one two-pounder in the pool below the keeper's cottage (this was exhibited); that his rod was by Farlow, with double-brazed suction joints and a greenheart top; that the stream would be the better for just one thunder-shower; that Lady Carberry was extremely well and was to open the flower show next Thursday; that Mr. Fakenham himself was to stay at least another week, then he was going to Norfolk; that he hoped Weston was really all right again; that he thought he must be getting homewards, and would Weston have a cast or two first?

Jack did not say much beyond what was necessary for courtesy's sake. These two had never got on very enthusiastically together, though they had smoked together perhaps half a dozen times, and the trout stream had been put at Jim's disposal in a general kind of way whenever he was with the Carberrys. Jack had secretly considered Jim rather an effeminate fool, and Jim had hinted gently to Sarah that Jack was rather bourgeois and Philistine. The two points of view were quite characteristic and quite untrue. Yet as they talked now each ratified emphatically his previous judgment.

"I suppose you won't stop to dinner," said Jack, with a regretful air that was completely hypocritical.

"Thanks very much; but Lady Carberry mightn't like it, you know," said Jim, with a sorrow he did not feel.

That courtesy was exchanged; and the two walked in silence.

Then suddenly Jack broke it, quite uncharacteristically, thought Jim.

"You've heard about our change of plans?" he said.

"I — er — heard something," said Jim vaguely. "Mrs. Weston was talking —"

"Yes," said Jack, with an air of finality, and walked again in silence.

He seemed a little jumpy, thought Jim; it was just like these slightly bourgeois people to lack repose. If Jim himself was ever compelled by circumstances to embrace the profession of an acrobat, he would say nothing whatever about it: he would simply appear one evening in exceedingly well-fitting fleshings of a slightly unusual tint, and would silence criticism by his assumption that all was as it should be. He sincerely hoped now that there were going to be no confidences. But Jack broke out again presently, with an effort.

"Look here," he said. "I want just to say this. I daresay it'll seem quite mad; but — but you've heard about my illness. Well, it's that that's made the difference. And — and I just want to know what Lady Carberry and that lot think about it. Not that it'll make any difference," he added; "but I want to know."

"My dear Weston, I don't think it's anybody's affair but your own — and Mrs. Weston's."

"Well, then — what do they say?"

Jim reflected an instant. He recalled very vividly a conversation at dinner last night — or rather a monologue, which it would be hardly discreet to report.

"Oh, she doesn't like it, of course — since you've asked me," he said. "But I don't see that it's her affair."

"And you?"

Jim smiled with his melancholy eyes.

"Oh, my theory is, Live and let live. You see, I'm not a Catholic, and don't understand."

Jack nodded.

"Thanks," he said. "Well, you'll come and dine one night?"

"I shall be charmed," said Jim. "Ah, here's Mrs. Weston."

They had come in sight of the lodge gate by now, and a pony-carriage wheeled in as they looked.

"Mary," cried Jack. "No, don't bother."

The girl climbed out, for all that, as the groom ran to the pony's head. Then she came towards them across the thirty yards of grass. She looked very well indeed, thought Jim, with his artistic perceptions, though again regrettably like an Academy figure against her background — small, trim, and brisk, rather flushed and bright-eyed, with sun and breeze and the west behind her. But she was just a little bourgeois in character too, he considered: she was too enthusiastic and decided to be quite perfect. She was not at all of the solemn number of the elect. He took off his cap and smiled as she came up and linked herself to her husband's arm.

"How do you do again, Mr. Fakenham?" she said, and made an inquiry after the sport.

The three walked together slowly, and halted to say goodbye. But there was plainly something the matter with Jack, for he again recurred.

"I've been telling him," he said almost defiantly, "that I don't care in the least what people say, and he quite agrees."

"Why, of course," said Mary, with an astonished air of whose genuineness Jim was not quite certain. "Of course we do as we please with our own things."

"It's nobody's business but ours, I think," repeated Jack.

Jim looked at him gently. He was quite a tolerable judge of moods, according to his own standards.

"You see it's like this, Fakenham," went on the other. "I've had a shock. I needn't go into it, but there it is. And I'm going to make a change. My wife didn't much like it at first, but we had a good talk last night, and she sees now as I do, at least in some of the things, anyhow. I know it's ridiculous talking like this to you, but I want you to let them know — oh, in your own words, of course — that we really mean business. So we do hope they'll mind theirs."

Jim looked for a fleeting instant at Mary. He felt as if the whole thing was slightly indecent, and wondered how she took it. But she was looking at her husband with an expression he could not understand, a kind of set look, one of a kind of admiration too, that was inexplicable.

"Oh, I'm sure —" began Jim, almost uncomfortably.

"Yes, that's exactly it, Mr. Fakenham," said the girl. "Jack and I entirely agree in this business. We want that to be quite clear."

Again she glanced at her husband, and again Jim was a little puzzled. What he read in her face was not at all in accordance with what he had learned of her through her friend Sarah. However, he told himself, it was not his business.

The rod had to be readjusted now, and it took a moment or two while the others waited. Then the usual things were said, and Jim went off. The two stood looking after him.

Mary took her husband's arm again and pressed it.

"Oh, Jack!" she said quite inconsequently, "I'm glad we talked last night."

"Yes," said Jack.

Jim Fakenham seemed doomed to fill the role of confidant just now, and it was one for which he felt himself possessed of no ability, except for very subtle temperaments.

He came down this evening an hour later, in a costume of dinner jacket, braided trousers, and a shirt with just the hint of a frill, and feeling that a flower was demanded, stepped out of the drawing room window immediately to obtain one.

There he ran into Lady Sarah, also dressed for dinner, but with an air of unusual perturbation. She held a note in her hand.

He made a remark or two, selected a white rose and pinned it daintily into his buttonhole, while she looked on abstractedly.

"Look here," she said suddenly. "It's frightfully indiscreet of me; but do just read this — oh! And don't breathe a word, of course."

He took it, glanced at the name at the end, then turning back read it through. He made no comment at all as he gave it back.

"Well?" she said.

"I've no remarks to make," observed Jim, with his hands in his pockets, looking at the sunset.

"But I don't understand it a bit," said the girl peevishly. "It's not like Mary. Do you think she's trying to be loyal, or what?"

Jim creased his lips tightly. (It was a substitute for a shrug of the shoulders.)

"I hardly know her, you see."

"Mary shan't play-act with me," said the girl vehemently. "I'll soon have it out of her, if that's all."

"No, I really don't think she's doing that," said Jim. "I met them both just now. He seemed more uncomfortable than she did — if I may venture to say so. . . . Oh no, I don't mean he was giving in at all. On the contrary, he seemed extremely pugnacious. But he asked me right out what Lady Carberry thought of it all; and she didn't."

"But she knew."

"Perhaps that was it," said Jim.

Sarah stood silent for a moment, creasing and uncreasing the note.

"I don't understand all this about her talking to Mr. Jack last night, and the difference it has made. What difference can it make? He's perfectly mad. Don't you think so?"

"Yes, I do."

"But Mary's not. Far from it. Oh, do tell me what you think."

Jim moved on a step along the garden path without speaking. The ground fell steeply away behind them, and far across the valley to the eastwards Manningham Hall pricked its chimneys among the woods. The sun was gone down, but the sky was still glorious with color.

"They're Catholics," he said at last. "And with Catholics you can never know. There's a touch of fanaticism always, and it flares up." (He felt extremely shrewd and large as he uttered this sentence.) "Personally I should guess that Mrs. Weston was — well, piqued by what — er — Lady Carberry said yesterday. She probably went home rather angry. Then they talked, as she says; and she just chose, partly out of pique, and partly, I daresay, because she's very fond of her husband, to wish what he wishes."

"And you think that's all? Why she talks as if she was repentant about something — all that about 'understanding,' and so on. And then there's that other mysterious sentence on the last page, about there being something she can't ever mention to a soul."

Jim smiled.

"You think that means nothing?" asked the girl.

"No — I mean yes."

"You're sure?"

"I think it's just part of the pose," said Jim magnificently.

Sarah sighed.

"Well, I'm sure I hope so," she said. "If Mary's going to become religious too, I shan't ever trust anyone again. Why are you smiling, Mr. Fakenham?"

"Only — only it's all so odd. Do — er — women always watch one another like that, and get interested and excited?"

Sarah smiled.

"Mary's a dear," she said. "No, of course they don't, yes; I think they do more than men."

Dinner was as august an affair in this house as it was possible to imagine, and was conducted with a solemnity of demeanor entirely unimaginable. Other persons might make alterations, and begin with this and end with that, and dine in the garden, and have iced soup and frozen coffee on hot days, and permit cigarettes to appear on the very cloth itself; but here were no modernities. The date of eighteen hundred and seventy, I believe, was the year in which Lady Carberry first shone upon the social world; and the details of custom in that year — I forget at this moment what they are — were for her immovable and sacrosanct. Poor Jim was conscious of committing a hundred solecisms; even his dinner jacket had once been eyed through a pair of long glasses; but he was determined not to yield, and he compensated by his extreme deference to the old lady in conversation for those little ways of which she did not approve. It is a cheering and a pleasing fact that young men of this kind have a strange attractiveness to severe old ladies of Lady Carberry's kind; and she permitted herself to talk before him with a confidence she did not give to everyone. She even allowed him to smoke his cigarette in full view of the very drawing room windows themselves.

It was as cheese appeared that she diverted the talk in the dangerous direction.

"I have been thinking a great deal," she said, "about that poor Mrs. Weston. I think it's terrible her being put upon like that."

That struck the key. It was evident that Lady Carberry's attitude was to be one of commiseration. She had two methods in dealing with antagonists: one consisted in severe and public reprobation or in yet more severe silence; the other in a vehement compassion which there was no resisting. It was under this scourge that Mary was to be brought; she was to be represented as a victim of her husband's folly. It did not matter in the least that the whole thing was not at all the old lady's business; as she herself said in a phrase that was irresistible — she made it her business; and that was an end of it.

Sarah glanced up and down again.

"Of course we can do nothing," continued her mother severely; "we shall have to wait and see the whole village turned upside down and all the Rector's work undone. We must just submit; I know that. But I am sorry for that poor woman."

Sarah flushed a little.

"Mother, I don't think you need be," she said.

"I've had a note from Mary. She seems quite reconciled."

The old lady shook her head with a bitter smile. Jim noticed, in that kind of paralytic state which the old lady's more emphatic conversation tended to produce in him in spite of himself, the miniature of the deceased Lord Carberry — a nobleman in a red coat, with whiskers and a long upper lip — rise and fall upon the lace-shrouded throat of his widow. (I cannot find that this nobleman ever did anything beyond writing four pamphlets on Indian Administration that are very severe against the Liberal policy of his day. He seems to have been a man of almost startling obscurity; and I suspect him of having been henpecked by his wife.)

"She may say so," said the great lady; "of course she must be loyal to her husband. I admire her for that. But she's far too sensible to agree with him. I shall make an opportunity to have a good talk with her."

Miss Fakenham murmured an admirative assent.

It is an appalling, and yet a fascinating spectacle — this tyranny of the old. Here was the whole situation staked out, regardless of others' claims; or, to change the metaphor, here were all these persons, attached like marionettes to their wives, set to play those parts thought suitable by this one old lady. I despair of describing her forcefulness. Jim was aware of it, no doubt, in a detached kind of way; after all, he was only her guest. He could hardly remember a single conversation under his hostess's auspices in which he had sincerely said what he thought (that is the one drawback to forcefulness). Sarah was aware of it — no longer with anything that could be called resentment: that had flared, perhaps ten times in as many years, and seemed dead within her. A dull, half-humorous resignation had taken its place. Miss Fakenham was aware of it, and reveled in its power. The men behind the chairs were aware of it; in fact, it was worth their respective places to forget it. The very furniture of the room — the hopelessly inconvenient sideboard, purchased in the year 1873; the gouty-legged mahogany chairs; the stuffy carpet; the terrible splendor of the pictures — all were aware of it, or at least retained their positions only by its power. The presence brooded over all, and made all its own. Yet it resided in but one old lady, stout and ill-formed, of no great position, of second-rate faculties, always rather unwell, with the portrait of her deceased husband round her neck, a bracelet of his hair on her wrist, a rich black dress trimmed with lace, a small country house, a town house, and two thousand a year.

Why are such things permitted?

(4)

It is a characteristic of Catholic clergy, politicians, and diplomats that they usually say less than they think — in distinction from the rest of the world, who usually say more than they think. The priest, that is, usually makes up his mind before he utters it; the layman employs utterance as a method of thought. (Of course there are exceptions to both rules.)

Father Banting, for instance, had not in the least made up his mind as to the new situation that had unfolded round him, and accordingly said nothing whatever about it to anybody, except as regarded the barest external facts. He did not know whether the development would advance or recede; whether Jack would become more or less of a *dévot*; whether Mary would resent the change less or more as time went on. But he thought about it a great deal.

Now it is a fact, if the world would only believe it, that a priest is usually an extremely common sense and cautious man. He knows perfectly well, from books, if not from experience, that there are few catastrophes so great and irremediable as those that follow an excess of zeal. He has read of, if he has not seen, shipwreck after shipwreck caused by the mere crowding on of too much sail with the best will in the world; the disease that he has to combat at least as often as any other is the state of mind called Scrupulousness — the result, in most cases, of some unbalanced excess of virtue.

Father Banting, then, was not as content as might be thought with Jack's sudden burst into devotion. He was pleased, naturally, with its very solid fruits so far; but he had not in the least made up his mind as to the future. As to the origin of it all — the apparent resuscitation from death — well, he put that into a small pigeonhole in his mind labeled "doubtful," that already contained a certain number of well-wrappered packets. He did not know: that was all. He marked time; and meanwhile was in correspondence with his bishop as to the bestowal of his thousand pounds.

The rooms he occupied were an enormous improvement on his old lodgings. They were three in number, in the chapel wing; his bedroom, a small rather stuffy apartment, chiefly occupied by a large bed and a chipped-winged cherub in pink plaster; his sitting room, where his pipes lay about and his books; and a small prim apartment, where he could eat when the squire was away. But they were comfortable and convenient, and it was a pleasure not to have to trudge up through the park every morning before breakfast. He interviewed people when necessary in the sacristy down below.

It was here that Sarah was requested to wait one morning, a week or two later, when she asked for him.

She had never been in a sacristy before, and looked about her with a superior sort of curiosity. It seemed to her as if she were very much behind the scenes indeed. Two chairs called "Gladstonbury" stood before a disreputable-looking pine table on which rested a large flat book, an ink bottle, a clogged pen, a grimy book of devotion, and two or three crumpled pieces of linen. There was a kind of tallish cupboard on one side, with drawers covered with American cloth; and at the back small glass vessels, a dish, a bottle of wine, and a mysterious sort of calendar lay huddled together. Other objects met her eye as she looked round — a sheeted flat thing hanging on a pole; a couple of staves bound with brass; a censer. An open wardrobe between the windows was half-open and disclosed a vision of linen within. It was all rather dingy and unswept. There was not much glamour here, at any rate.

She sat down; and almost immediately Father Banting creaked in, in new boots with elastic sides and sham laces.

It was rather difficult for Sarah to approach her business, for it was nothing else than to pump the clergyman of all the information she could gain. She was persuaded, of course, that he knew a great deal about the whole matter, even if he were not somehow at the back of it all. She did not actually suspect him of having engineered the entire affair from the beginning, but she was quite positive that he had pulled the strings very adroitly ever since. There was that thousand pounds, for example, of which Mary had told her.

"I came to talk to you about Mrs. Weston," she said presently, with an air of great frankness. "Of course she doesn't know I've come, and you won't say anything, will you?"

Father Banting smiled gently. He had not a notion what to say.

"Why, of course not, if you wish me not to," he said. "Won't you move your chair, Lady Sarah? I'm afraid you're in a draft there."

He got up and satisfied himself that the door into the chapel was closed. Sarah repressed her impatience admirably.

"It's all a terrible upset," she said, when he had settled down again. "Of course from your point of view, Father Banting, it's all as good as can be. I quite understand that. But I wondered whether there wasn't anything I could do to smooth down matters. Mary — Mrs. Weston — seems to be quite changing."

The priest took off his spectacles, drew out a magenta silk handkerchief from the breast pocket of a very old cassock, and began to polish the glasses carefully. But still he said nothing. Sarah thought him very stupid indeed, and certainly he did not look very clever. He had what is called an amiable expression. He was going gray fast, and his forehead above his eyes — more weak-looking than ever now that his glasses were off — was a gentle moist pink. He wore a celluloid collar, rather yellow at its rim, Sarah observed.

Something in his air of timidity irritated her. She felt it was dreadful that this stupid old man — not even a strong, crafty personality such as a priest ought to be — should so control people like Jack and his wife. It was just because he was a priest, she supposed. Well, at any rate, she had no superstitious awe of him. So she became a little more rude than she had intended.

"It's a very serious thing, you know, to the neighborhood — all these changes. I don't think your — your Church will gain by it at all in the long run. People are beginning to talk."

He replaced his handkerchief in his pocket. A corner of it still showed, vivid against the dusky shiny cloth. Then he put his spectacles on again and cleared his throat.

"What do you want me to do, Lady Sarah? I don't quite understand. What are people saying?" (Ah! That had gone home, then! She congratulated herself on the stroke.)

"Well, I don't want to offend you," she said, smiling, watching his rather stout old hands folded on the table, "but you know what people do say about priestcraft, and so on. Of course I don't believe it, but —"

"Then why do you tell me of it?" came gently back.

She started a little. It almost sounded like a reproof. But that, of course, was out of the question.

"I thought it my duty," she said, with patient tolerance. "I knew you wouldn't wish to do anything that brought disrepute —"

"Do I understand you to mean that you think I am urging Mr. Weston on?"

She was genuinely surprised.

"Why, of course," she said. "And I don't blame you in the least. It's perfectly right and natural from your point of view. I quite see that."

He cleared his throat again, rather suddenly, and she heard him uncross his feet beneath the table.

"And you have come to say —"

(She seemed to have been so successful up to this point that she determined on a far bolder stroke than she had imagined possible. She had had no idea that he would give in so easily. He seemed to have no personality at all.)

"Well, I've come to see whether it isn't possible, even now, to dissuade Mr. Weston from this scheme. You know Mrs. Weston can't bear it, though she's given in at last. Don't you think that a few tactful words, dropped at the right time, might make him pause even now? I'm sure you know the way — in the confessional, perhaps — or —"

Again he took off his spectacles, again drew out his handkerchief and fell to polishing.

Sarah felt her spirits rise incalculably. She had prepared herself, with some timorousness, for a really formidable interview; for there lurked in her, in spite of her protestations to herself, an indefinable kind of fear of this old man. She had very seldom spoken to him before — perhaps half a dozen times altogether; but she had a sort of innate distrust and awe of a priest, as of one who possessed arts and powers beyond the reach of the average worldling. (Of course she would have denied this vigorously, if she had been challenged.) And now that he was really bearded, he was nothing at all — just a nervous, short-sighted old man among his shabby instruments of worship. She waited for his capitulation. It surely must come soon.

He put his spectacles on the table before him and wiped his nose carefully.

"Lady Sarah," he said, "I'm sorry to have to say this; but I'm afraid I am obliged. I don't think you quite understand what you are doing."

She looked at him in the blankest astonishment.

"I understand you," he went on carefully, "to have threatened me with the displeasure of your friends if I continue a course of action with regard to two of my own people — a course of action which you credit me with without any evidence at all. I shall not discuss whether or no that course of action is mine or not; but in any case I

am bound to tell you that I cannot for one instant allow —
er — your ladyship to interfere, even with the best intentions, or to suggest to me what I am or am not to say in
the confessional."

"But, Father Banting —"

"I am very sorry that your ladyship should have thought
it possible —"

"Father Banting —"

He rose steadily, picking up his spectacles; but his old
hands shook uncontrollably.

"I trust that your ladyship will not bear malice against
me for having spoken so. I — I thought it better to explain
the situation as clearly as possible."

Sarah too stood up — white with anger and disappointment. And the worst of it was that she knew perfectly well that it was her own fault.

"I shall not trouble you again with the matter. Good
morning, Father Banting. I am sorry that you should have
so misunderstood me."

Chapter V

(1)

I refuse to describe the flower show held at Sir Samuel Cohen's beyond saying that it was exactly like all other flower shows; and I forget whether it was in support of any charitable institution. I think it must have been; otherwise I do not think that even Lady Carberry would have made a speech. There were all the usual things — hot tents, moderately cold ices, awnings over the windows, grass trampled till it bled a dark green, a nerve-shattering noise of talking and brass-band playing, an enormous crowd that ebbed and flowed continually, motorcars, carriages, dust turnstiles, a good deal of crossness, small girls with black legs and white frocks, men in straw hats, women with Zulu headdresses: and there were some flowers, I think. Sir Samuel walked about indefatigably, in a frock-coat and white waistcoat, and his wife sat in the drawing room and said the same things over and over again during three hours and a half. There seems to be a vacuum in life which this kind of business fills; and it filled it on this occasion; at least everybody said it would have been a great success if only the champagne and strawberries had been a little better iced.

The point of it, however, so far as I am concerned, lay in a conversation that took place in the morning room — a small place with the blinds drawn down, whither Lady Carberry retired with Miss Fakenham after her opening speech in the biggest tent.

Mary had come, as befitted her position, though without Jack, and was wandering with Sarah, whom she had suddenly met to and fro, up and down an unfrequented path behind the shrubbery. Sarah could not altogether make out her friend; and she had hardly begun to put a few leading questions when Miss Fakenham's sunshade appeared round the corner. The summons was issued, and Mary, after one enigmatical glance at the girl beside her, disappeared in captivity.

Sarah remained conscience-stricken, and sat down to consider the situation. She had been on the very point of disclosing her mother's intention to deal with the matter in person, when the summons had come: she wondered what in the world would happen.

To her entered presently Jim Fakenham, cool and unperturbed, round the corner of the protecting shrubbery. He did not know a great many people here. He had strayed into the dining room to look at a reputed Gainsborough, and out again after a glance; he had stood absorbed in a small green book, leaning against the library shelves; and he had soon afterwards congratulated his host on possessing a book of which the owner was not aware, though he pretended to be; and had said nothing at all about the Gainsborough. He felt it would have been very painful if he had. Then he had wondered where Sarah was, and had wandered gently away to look for her. I think he very likely wanted her to observe him as the Philosopher at a Flower Show.

He said nothing at all. He sat down beside her, placed one knee over the other, drew out his cigarette case and the little matchbox engraved "Jim," and went through the series of actions necessary for smoking with a precise air.

"Mother's started on Mary," burst out Sarah suddenly.

"So I perceived," said Jim looking at her.

Sarah looked charming in her afternoon party costume — far more charming to an esthetic eye than in her rather short skirts and blouse and jacket that she wore usually, more charming even than in her riding-habit. She had that simple and fundamental kind of good looks and healthiness of the rather fair sort, that fitted most costumes; but her large, shady hat today, trimmed with red roses; her white dress, which I do not propose to describe, beyond saying that it presented a general appearance of grace and white lace and cambric and silver; her silver-buckled brown shoes, and the rest — all this made her more feminine and youthful and even delicate. Jim looked and approved. . . . Besides, she had expectations of two thousand pounds a year and two houses — and that would make three. All these things were combining consciously in his mind, this year for the first time.

Jim too, to her eyes, looked all that he should. I really cannot bother with his dress too; but it suited him. His clean-shaven, clever face, thin and black-eyed and cool, his precise, rather fastidious mouth, his pleasant detached air — in fact that air which he wished to carry — his assumption of homely friendliness and intimacy in sitting down beside her like this, away from the crowds who buzzed like bees forty yards away behind the screening shrubbery — all this made her feel friendly and confidential.

"And I don't know what to do. Shall I go and interrupt? I don't think I dare."

"Shall I do it for you?" suggested Jim. "I might go in and forget to throw away my cigarette. That would cause a diversion."

Sarah smiled with one side of her mouth, and looked serious again.

"Really," she said, "I'm rather anxious. Mary will be driven quite desperate. She had just time to tell me that Mr. Weston wouldn't come, when your aunt fetched her away. And now Mother's at her."

"I can't make out why you bother so much," said Jim.

"Oh, you can't help it with Mary. I've got frightfully fond of her. She's the sort you can't help liking."

"But what are you afraid of?"

"I don't know. Catholics are so hopeless. And their priests! . . ." She broke off eloquently.

Jim nodded gravely.

"And — er — Weston too?" he asked.

"Oh, you know him as well as I do. He's exactly what he looks. He'd be quite sensible — in fact he was — until this absurd thing happened. It doesn't suit him at all. You can see it in his face."

Jim considered this. By "sensible" he knew quite well what Sarah meant — she meant what he himself called Philistine — cricket-playing, sunburned, conventional — that is by conventions that were not Jim's — quite transparent and rather dull. It seemed a queer thing — almost ironical — that this elusive thing called religion, above all that most elusive aspect of it that is called Catholicism, should have been overlaid on such a foundation. It was like looking at a green meadow through a magenta glass. The two things didn't mix: they looked just ugly and rather repellent.

He presently put this more or less into words with a wistful air of not being understood. The air was justified.

"Magenta glass! I don't understand. Please don't be clever, Mr. Fakenham."

Jim sighed inaudibly; but he determined to be tolerant.

"I mean that it doesn't suit Mr. Weston," he said. "He isn't really religious, you know; it's only a phase."

"Yes, I think that's true. But he's a Catholic, you know."

"Only by education."

Sarah reflected. Her face looked delightful in meditative repose.

"Yes, I think I agree. That's rather clever, Mr. Fakenham. How did you notice that?"

"Oh! It's pretty obvious," said Jim. "He's rather dull, you know, really. Now it seems to me that the only point of religion is to make people interesting."

Sarah glanced at him sideways.

"But —" she began.

Jim said nothing. He felt more a philosopher than ever.

"And do you think it won't last with him?" she asked.

"I shouldn't think so. You've got to take away the magenta glass sometime, you know. Besides, you can see it in his face, as you said."

Sarah got up suddenly.

"Well, let's move about a bit. We can't sit here all the afternoon. It isn't polite."

The crowd wore rather a fatigued air as they emerged into it again. There was not the previous activity visible: the hot tents were almost empty; groups were tending to sit upon and lean against everything that could support the human frame; and there were distinctly fewer people. Suddenly Sarah made a small sound.

"Look," she said, "there's Mr. Weston. I wonder what he's doing here, after all."

Jack was indeed coming towards them, alone; but he was eyed a little as he came, and people dropped their voices. It was obvious that he was beginning to be talked about. For one thing, at least, Sarah was thankful: he was, at least, respectably dressed. She had not been quite comfortable on the point: visions of sackcloth or camel's hair had moved before her, or the absence of a shirt collar, or even of shoes and socks. Another thought also struck her, and she moved quickly towards him.

"Are you looking for Mary?" she said. "She's with Lady Carberry in the morning room, I think."

Jack saluted her.

"Thanks very much," he said. "Yes, I was beginning to wonder —"

"So you came after all," said Sarah as they went together, with Jim looking philosophical in the rear.

"I — I thought I would," said Jack, rather feebly.

She glanced at him again. Yes; he looked uneasy somehow — it was in his face — but it was so slight an air that she hesitated to draw any conclusions.

"Here's the window," she said, and rustled in before him.

(2)

It was quite a dramatic scene, on a very small scale, that opened before them. Miss Fakenham was absent; no doubt she had discreetly withdrawn. But the two figures were placed admirably. Lady Carberry's likeness to Queen Victoria was quite extraordinary; her dignity was supreme. She sat in a tall chair with her handled eyeglasses on her knee, and a look of furious commiseration on her face. Opposite her, on a sofa, sat Mary, also bolt upright, rather white in the face, but so exceedingly composed that it was obvious that she had determined to remain so against all odds. Her voice when she said a word of astonishment to Jack was cool and high-pitched.

"Ah!" said the old lady; "so here is Mr. Weston, after all."

Jack shook hands carefully and drew himself up.

Sarah began, hypocritically, to hope that she had not interrupted, but that Mr. Weston —

"Not at all," said her mother. "I am most pleased that Mr. Weston came so opportunely. Do sit down, Mr. Weston."

Jack sat down, and a small conversation followed that Sarah followed with all her powers at full stretch. Jim

Fakenham looked in for a moment; then withdrew to a chair set outside the windows, from which he could hear every word and pretend not to be doing so.

Lady Carberry began by a little arch scolding, in which her voice now and then cracked with passion. She knew and they knew, and she knew that they knew, that it was not in the very faintest degree any business of hers if they had chosen to bring the Pope of Rome or the Grand Lama of Tibet to their upper gardens; so she was unable to loose such vials of wrath as she might have done under other circumstances; so she assumed a motherly attitude towards these two young things, with the veins on her forehead swollen with indignation. To Jack was assigned the part of the enthusiastic boy who did not know what he was doing; to Mary that of the blindly adoring, though timid wife who followed his lead. Lady Carberry's own experience of above sixty years was spread before them: her deceased husband's name appeared more than once; they were entreated to consider the situation more tranquilly, to let at least a year elapse, to make a quantity more of inquiries, to have a good talk to the Rector, to beware of the influence of the insidious Father Banting, who must, of course, have planned the whole thing from beginning to end.

"My dear young man," she said at last. "You really must let me call you that; I am more than old enough to be your mother. You really ought not to let a little thing like this — oh yes! I heard all the story of your illness from Sarah over there — you ought not to let this little thing make all the difference in your life — and the life of your wife."

Sarah glanced at Jack, in time to see him pass his tongue softly over his lips, and then back again to Mary. For it was not mere impatience or resignation that she saw there. There was a look she could not understand. She did not have to wait long.

After one more paragraph from the old lady, Mary rose suddenly, whiter than ever, but, it seemed, completely herself.

"Lady Carberry," she said, "I am sure you mean nothing but what is kind. You have talked to me now for nearly half an hour, and I've hardly said one word. I must say to

you now what I haven't even said to Jack yet — I suppose
I've been too shy — but it's this: and Jack can hear it too.
I wasn't convinced at first" — she broke off — "I mean I
wouldn't let myself be convinced at first, though I knew it
perfectly well, and I know it now beyond the shadow of a
doubt, that Jack really did die (I don't care the least what
the doctors say; what else can they say from their point of
view?) — that Jack really did die and was brought back
again in answer — well, I needn't go into that" (her voice
faltered) — "but that he came back in order to have another chance . . . and — and that I might too. You're not a
Catholic, Lady Carberry, and you can't possibly understand."

"My dear girl —"

Then the pent-up nerves flashed a little.

"Please mind your — Please don't trouble to say any
more. We're perfectly determined, both of us now. It's not
the least good —"

"But, Mary —" began Jack in such a tone that Sarah
glanced at him again sudden and quick-eyed. But Mary
seemed to notice nothing. Sarah, herself excited now, saw
how she trembled as she turned to her husband.

"Yes, Jack; you've been right and I've been wrong. I'm
sorry. I agree with every word you've said. Come, let's go
home."

Lady Carberry arose in majesty.

"I am very sorry for you, Mrs. Weston," she said emphatically. "But I quite understand. Of course you must
be loyal —"

Mary flashed again a little.

"It's quite useless to say any more," she said. "I don't
think I can possibly persuade you, if you insist on thinking that that's my reason. I think Jack'll tell you that
that's not the reason."

She turned to him swiftly; but before he could answer
(certainly he seemed a little troubled, thought Sarah) she
wheeled again.

"No, I must say it," she said, "right out. It's this. It's
partly you, Lady Carberry, who have helped me to see
more clearly. (I'm not being in the least sarcastic or bitter.) But first when you began to speak against the Car-

melites you made me rather angry; and — and I suppose
when one's angry something melts. Well, my — my sham
opposition melted. You made me go right over to the other
side. Then I talked to Jack the same evening — a long
talk; and I found I'd believed all along that his recovery
was very extraordinary, and that we must do something.
And now you've finished me."

She stopped abruptly; and Sarah saw the defiance fade
from her face. Then she seemed to make an effort at recovery.

"Tell them, Jack," she said. "Isn't that true?"

He had been looking at her doubtfully. But he responded with a jerk; his fair-skinned face flushed a little,
and his eyelids came slightly down.

"It's perfectly true," he said. "We had agreed to differ.
Now we don't — I mean, we agree. We — we see perfectly
together. We're going to carry it through — that — and —
and perhaps other things too."

Lady Carberry's mouth mumbled a little in excitement.

"Well," she said, "it's your affair, of course; but —"

Mary made a little impulsive movement forwards. "Oh,
I'm sorry," she said. "Really, we don't mean to be rude.
But, you know, we are Catholics — real Catholics, both of
us — and — and you can't understand."

The great lady drew herself up a little. She saw her advantage, and took it shrewdly.

"Well, I've no more to say, Mrs. Weston. You must do as
you please. But you mustn't expect the rest of us —"

Mary again twitched suddenly. Then she came forward
and held out her hand.

"Goodbye," she said. "We must be going. Oh, don't be
angry, please."

There was but one instant in which a confidential sentence could be exchanged between Sarah and Jim. And
that instant Sarah took. It was as the elaborate
leave-takings and congratulations were passing with
Lady Cohen.

"Well, that's clear enough, anyhow," she murmured a
little bitterly.

"Oh, do you think so?" said Jim.

(3)

It was not until after dinner that Sarah was able to pursue the subject.

Dinner was rather terrible. Lady Carberry discoursed upon the garden party, upon the duties of landowners, upon Sir Samuel's virtues — of which she did not usually make much account; but all present fully understood her motive — upon the enormous responsibilities that rested upon persons like herself, to foster the welfare of people who lived in the country; and Miss Fakenham played a sincere, and her nephew an insincere, chorus.

Sarah contented herself with listening and pondering the situation.

Lady Carberry retired early that night, worn out, she said (presumably with the admirable discharge of her responsibilities that day), and Miss Fakenham disappeared into the morning room. Miss Fakenham was one of those persons plainly intended by Providence always to fulfill the function of tactful admirer. Her silences, her movements, her glances, far more than her words, conveyed flattery and agreement with an eloquence that must be taken on trust. She revived like a flower in sunlight beneath Lady Carberry's presence; and, like a flower, wilted in her absence. She was a good soul, but she must be figured while living in her friend's house as a mere appreciative shadow of that friend without any perceptible personality of her own. At home she was sufficiently real; here it was almost impossible ever to remember that she was in the room. She vanished into the social atmosphere, like an animal with protective coloring. I have caught myself in the very act of soliloquy in her presence when Lady Carberry has been absent for a moment — at least that is a vivid way of putting it. But I have found her pleasant and kindly, an excellent housekeeper, even almost a little formidable, seated at her own table in her own house in Queen's Gate after a course of Lady Carberry has had time to fade in its effects. In fact, she was a kind of shadow of Lady Carberry in the latter's absence as she was her reflection in her presence. I cannot imagine why she had never married; I suppose there was not anything of her to marry. She was about fifty-eight, and dressed in black; and that's enough of her just now.

Sarah and Jim then found themselves alone on a garden seat outside the drawing room windows. Lady Carberry's bedroom was overhead, so they talked but cautiously. The valley lay dark and silent beneath them, seen but incoherently through the foreground of gravel and shrub and grass viewed in the light of the drawing room windows projected from behind.

"I want you to explain," said Sarah suddenly. "Why did you say it wasn't clear this afternoon?"

(The fact that she made no preface made it obvious even to herself how much this queer little situation was on her mind.)

"Why did you say it was?" asked Jim. "At least I suppose you mean the Weston affair."

"Well, Mary's changed; that's all. Surely that's obvious. You can't say she didn't mean what she said? Somehow she's come round to the other point of view. I was afraid she might, when she was so weak about the lawns."

"Ah," said Jim.

"Well, isn't that so? Oh, do say what you think."

It was but proper for a philosopher to show a little reluctance; and Jim showed it.

"Really, you know, I was hardly attending."

"I don't care; please say what you think. I'm wild about Mary, you know. I can't think why; but it is so. Go on."

"Well," said Jim meditatively. "I think she meant more than she said; and — and Mr. Weston —"

"Yes?"

"Weston, less."

"How do you mean?"

"I think — well — that she's as keen as he is, now."

This was rather a tame conclusion; but Sarah was not very sharp.

"Oh, is that all? That's what I said, isn't it?"

Jim ground the heel of his shoe gently into the gravel in a quarter-circle.

"I think there's something more behind, in Mrs. Weston, at least."

"Why?"

"Well, she interrupted herself once or twice, in rather an odd way. And didn't it strike you she was a little feverish in her manner?"

"She was angry."

"Perhaps that was it," said Jim.

This was all so very philosophical and allusive and suggestive that Sarah entirely failed to take it in. She thought only that Mr. Fakenham was a little obscure. She pondered it by herself a moment or two.

"Well, I think it's extraordinary — such a sudden change."

Jim smiled to himself in the shadow.

"Oh, do you think people change much?" he said.

"How do you mean?"

"Well, I should have thought it was only that they showed themselves more — that they're really what they finally are, all along."

"I don't agree at all," said the girl decisively. "And there's Mr. Weston to prove you wrong."

"But he's just a case in point," murmured Jim, who was enjoying himself.

"Why, he's utterly different! Don't you remember —?"

"I mean," said Jim, deliberately interrupting, "that I don't believe he has changed. He's just put it on, like — like a hat."

Sarah made a small sardonic sound resembling a laugh.

"He's crammed it on pretty tight, then," she said. "He'll never get it off again."

"Oh, I daresay the head'll come with it," murmured Jim.

Sarah made an impatient movement.

"You're so dreadfully clever," she said. "I wish you wouldn't."

Jim's soul expanded in him like a flower. He was quite aware of his extreme capabilities; but it was pleasant for someone else to recognize them. He felt more attraction towards this girl than ever. It was this common confidence that did it. He glanced at her with approval. She was still looking perplexed and bothered.

"Did I tell you about Father Banting?" she said suddenly.

"What about him?"

"Oh, my interview with him."

"No; tell me."

Sarah's face suddenly looked pinched.

"I think I won't," she said, "after all. He was abominably rude to me."

Jim pursed up his mouth.

"Why do you look like that?" she asked abruptly.

"Nothing."

"Tell me. I will know."

Jim glanced at her.

"Well, I imagined you put your finger into the pie, and got it scalded."

Sarah's face positively froze.

"Suppose we leave the Weston's for a bit," said Jim generously.

I cannot bring myself to write down the conversation that followed, because it has nothing whatever to do with the story, and depends only for its interest upon those two persons. Certainly they enjoyed it, since they talked for the next ten minutes almost exclusively about themselves.

Jim described with something very nearly approaching pathos the hardships and routine of his life in town. He spoke, allusively again, of papers upstairs on which, it seemed, the foreign policy of England entirely depended. He had drunk a certain amount of wine — I hasten to say not at all too much — but sherry, five glasses of claret, and three of port produce a certain expansiveness even in the most self-contained of philosophers. He did not actually say right out that nobody really understood him, but Sarah gathered as much.

Then she too began. Her life also was spread beneath the stars in the light from the drawing room window. She acknowledged that she liked an outdoor life exceedingly, but that there were certain moments — and so on. It was quite well done. A little more crudely than Jim's, yet never passing a certain point. It was rather a hot night. She was very slightly feverish. She too had drunk two full glasses of claret. (Yes, I acknowledge that is rather a coarse thing to say.) And they were actually beginning upon religion. Jim had just conveyed an intimation that

no system of belief hitherto known to the world really satisfied him, when a shadow and a rather heavy footstep
behind interrupted them.

"A note, my lady."

Sarah took it, read it in the light from behind, made a
small exclamation, and paused. It took a perceptible time
to read.

"No answer," she said.

Then she handed it to Jim.

"Read it."

The paper was headed Manningham Hall, no date. The
handwriting was an excellent one — firm, self-contained,
without flourishes.

"My dearest, —

"I want you to understand at once. It is this. I take
back all I said to you the other day. I was perfectly
sincere in everything I said this afternoon. I really
have changed entirely after my talk with Jack. I fully
and entirely agree now that the convent ought to be
built, and that the lawn is the best place. This recovery of Jack's is really an extraordinary thing. Oh, it's
no good going into that, but I am sure now that I
knew all along, and that we must really do something big. Please don't think me tiresome, but you
don't know what religion means to us, really. Of
course we shan't alter our life very much in ordinary
things, but we're going to be different. Jack's simply
a dear — so simple about it all. He half-withdrew
this evening, thinking that perhaps I really did mind
after all, but of course I wouldn't let him. So we're
beginning at once. The architect's got everything
ready, and the nuns ought to be here in about four
months. Don't be angry.

"Yours, M."

Jim handed it back. "Well, well," he said.

End of Part I

Part II

Chapter VI

(1)

Manningham village fell into a state of curious suppressed excitement on the afternoon of the nuns' arrival, just before Christmas.

It was that cheerless kind of day that occasionally falls in mid-December, neither honest wintry frost nor tempestuous storm, but a heavy, weeping sky, an earth in which all seems contracted and starved; the bare trees shivered and stood patient in the wind, the pavements were damp but not dripping; there was a general sense of discomfort and unhappiness.

The entrance to the park lay on the station side of the village, fifty yards before the houses began, but a tolerable little crowd had collected to see the carriages drive up. A dozen children were, as usual, in front; a couple of tradesmen's boys loitered carefully towards the point of interest a minute or two before the rumored time of the arrival; a little way away gathered a group of aproned women, and, behind them, in twos and threes, a dozen men.

Mary had found it difficult to arrive at exactly the point of view that lay behind the quiet, mannerly suspicion of the villagers; she had made one or two attempts, but the worst she could gather was that it was believed that these nuns were probably rather wicked in a suppressed kind of way, that they had designs — of what nature it did not appear — upon the British Constitution, and that their life was one of entire idleness and luxury. There seemed too to be a faint suspicion abroad as to the fate of English girls who should venture too closely in the direction of the new convent — a danger of some sort of bewitchment, also undefined.

She had done what she could to reassure the village by a few purposely short and easily repeatable sentences, planted here and there with emphasis.

"They are some French ladies, with an English lady or two among them, who are coming here to settle down."

"They are very good people, who just want to pray, and be left alone. . . . No, you won't see them about at all; but they will be pleased to see you sometimes."

But it seemed pretty useless. It was unintelligible to the English rustic mind that anyone, who had not designs of some sort behind, should wish to live in a large, rather uncomfortable-looking house, merely in order to pray, and never to go out visiting.

A kind of despair had fallen upon Mary at the railway station just now, as the train had drawn up, and out of two reserved second-class compartments, there had emerged a dreary-looking company of French ladies, in indescribably sordid-looking, rather respectable dresses, with black bonnets. Most of them were spectacled; and all were nervous. They reminded her faintly of a procession of hens, rather agitated, entering a new farmyard. She nodded and smiled reassuringly, saying a few French sentences, till an old lady, stoutish, with large round spectacles, pale, pendulous cheeks, muffled round her face with a black comforter, had been ushered through the crowd, and been announced in English by an unknown voice as the Reverend Mother Prioress.

It was something of a disappointment. Mary had expected rather more of a stage effect — a certain dignity at any rate, an augustness, a few tall, dignified figures, chastened by sorrow; instead here was this reminder of a fowl house.

She uttered a sentence or two of welcome, gave assurances that the luggage should be seen to and after another explanation or two, had led the way to the close carriages drawn up outside, where Jack awaited them with his bicycle.

Jack had come forward, also nervous and a little awkward, had promised his assistance for the identifying and safe conveyance of the luggage; then, when all the others had been bestowed behind, Mary with the Prioress, a tall woman, obviously English, and a very young-looking, round-faced French girl — presently introduced as the single novice of the house — entered the front carriage, and the procession set itself in motion.

The horror of dreariness and agitation fell more and more heavily on Mary as they drove up the country road, passed the groups at the park entrance, and turned up through the lodge gate. There was hardly anything to say, but she said it. Things seemed so extraordinarily different in actuality. It appeared to her like a bad dream come true. She had not realized even while the workmen came and went, and the walls rose on the hill above the house — the graystone court, surmounted by the gable of the bleak chapel — how all this would dominate and color all the life that she knew. Here was the house and place that she had learned to love, associated in her mind with that normal English life in which even Father Banting had been a faint discomfort — now and henceforward to be overlooked and affected at every instant by the knowledge of these Frenchwomen in the heart of it all, not two hundred yards away. The dead building had scarcely given her a hint of the impression that the living people would bring to bear. And now they were here; and actual responsibilities had begun. . . . She dismissed the horror with a violent effort and began to talk again, now in French to the Prioress, learning a little of the journey's adventures; now to the tall Englishwoman who sat opposite.

The face of this one seemed more homely, though not in the least beautiful. She was tall and rather largely made, thin-faced with big cheekbones and large brown eyes. She had been in the convent, Mary learned, about four years. There was a certain friendliness about her that Mary found pleasant, though she sat back silent in an instant when the Prioress made a movement to speak.

Mary made one or two attempts to point out various things as they went — the trout-stream, the group of old oaks, finally, where the road branched halfway up the park, the Hall itself a hundred yards away. But the Prioress seemed not to be attending.

"The baggage, Madam — that will be all safe, will it not, with Monsieur your husband?"

Mary reassured her.

"There are all our treasures there," she said; "our chapel furniture, our vestments: all that the Government would permit us to remove. And there is our greatest treasure of all."

Mary asked genially what that was — thinking it to be an old crucifix, perhaps, or a monstrance.

"It is the body of our little saint," said the Prioress beaming through her round glasses, "our little sister Catherine."

Mary jumped, thinking she could not have heard aright.

"I beg your pardon," she said, "you don't mean —"

"But yes: in a packing case. She was a saint, there is no question. We had leave to bring it with us. She has worked many miracles, we think, already. You shall see her tomorrow, Madam."

Mary sat aghast.

It seemed to her the gilded pinnacle of her house of fears — the very incorporation and symbol of her forebodings. It expressed in a form which there was no mistaking the enormous gulf between her own methods of thought and those of these women whom she was bound now to befriend. To carry a dead body about! She had faced, more or less, in imagination, all those details of routine which were so entirely absent from her own instincts the bell-ringing, the endless trifles, the silence of the new great house above her own; she had thought it possible that she could still live her own life in spite of them — for her attempt during these last four months to modify it had been a remarkable failure; but somehow the mention of this horrible dead body, transported from Tours in a packing case, counted as the chief of the treasures — this seemed to focus in a burning point all her terrors and unwillingness. . . What in the world would Sarah think? . . .

She sat silent.

"Yes, you shall see her tomorrow, Madam," said the old lady again. . . . "Ah! We are arrived?"

"Yes, Reverend Mother," said Mary mechanically. "We descend here."

The building could not be called beautiful, yet it was not ugly. It stood here, like a contemplative in a ballroom, severe, cold, self-contained, graceful, yet with a grace that did not in the least accord with its surroundings. Obviously it was an afterthought.

The little lodge at which they stood, built, like all the rest, of graystone, was placed exactly at the crown of the hill, where the slopes began to descend to the Hall. There was a short covered way, as Mary knew, paved with flagstones, immediately beyond the lodge, leading into the glazed cloister, court-shaped, above which ran the cells on this side and to the west. The chapel stood at the further end of the cloister on the left, the refectory to the right, and the kitchen offices beyond. In the center of the cloister garth, where a few shrubs still lingered disconsolately, a pump and a well had their position. The whole place had been built after a good deal of correspondence, and included a walled garden approached through the tiny ante-chapel. The court and the garden formed the whole "enclosure," technically so called, beyond which, later on, no nun might pass. Visitors would be admitted through the lodge into a couple of small parlors, where a double grating would separate them from those on the other side.

The rest of the ground was comparatively unchanged, though it looked a little dreary now with the marks of recent mortar heaps and certain chips of wood that blew about in the December wind. The semicircular hedge was still in place, though part of the walled garden approached it very nearly in one place. Mary had arrived at the perfectly just conclusion, more than two months ago, that the peculiar charm and value of the place had been completely destroyed, and had already made her plans for another garden elsewhere, entirely out of sight of the convent.

Well, here they stood; and at the first pull on the bell the lodge gate opened, and one of the gamekeeper's wives, who had been educated at a convent and had volunteered to make things more or less ready, stood there smiling and curtsying. Smoke went up in the background from the kitchen chimney.

But the place was indescribably dreary to Mary's eyes as she went through with the Prioress, and the flock followed whispering together. There was a horrible newness about it all, yet it was far from bright. All was gray about them; and their footsteps, marked by the creaking of new boots, echoed dismally upon the stones. The daylight was darkening every minute, for it was drawing on to sunset, and there was no welcoming warmth of carpet and firelight to suggest a refuge from the gray world.

They went together through the place, first to the chapel, where the white bare altar seen beyond the screen glimmered like a sheet, and the painted deal stalls ranged themselves on either side. Across the foot of the chancel the screen, not yet closed, barred the way, beyond which the nuns later would not be able to pass; and on the left again, lightly barred, rose the opening to the transept that, projecting outside the walled garden, was accessible to the public, and would serve in future instead of the chapel of the Hall for the small Catholic congregation of the district. From a door at the side of this opening there emerged the figure of Father Banting, who had been busy in the sacristy, and now after a word or two of greeting in execrable French (the poor man had a French grammar lying open in his room down at the house) stood smiling behind the iron bars like an amiable lion, until he excused himself again and disappeared to finish his work.

But worse even than the cold welcome of the chapel was the appearance of the cells and the corridor that united them on the upper floor. It seemed natural somehow that the chapel should be austere and forbidding, but the new, clean deal boards of the passage, the frosted-glass panes of the windows, both in the passage and the cells, the appalling emptiness of these rooms where the nuns would pass most of the hours of their solitude — this was too much for Mary altogether. She had seen them before, of course, again and again; but the thought that on this night women would sleep here — and that in the luggage to be brought up were no such things as pictures, or carpets, or wallpaper — this appalled her.

Each cell contained four principal objects, and no more. A bed stood against two sides — at least, what was called a bed. It consisted of a rectangular, shallow box of wood, covered now with a brown blanket; and beneath lay one of those thin straw mattresses which Mary had obtained with some difficulty from London. At the foot of the bed stood a *prie dieu*, with an enormous black painted cross hanging above it on the white wall. In the center stood a deal table and chair; in the further corner a wash-hand stand. And that was all. There was no fireplace — a black iron radiator stood near the door. There was the pale deal under foot; all the rest of the room was dead white. In the twilight filtered through the frosted glass the desolation was overwhelming.

The refectory was not much better. The eternal deal was again underfoot; deal tables ran along the sides of two walls with a small cross table uniting them. The one tolerable feature was the brown painted paneling that rose to the height of about four feet up the walls, and suggested — faintly indeed, yet suggested — a kind of echo of a thought of comfort. A radiator also stood here, near to the door.

Mary was almost dumb with dismay as she came out again with the Prioress and the Englishwoman, now known to her as Sister Teresa, and stood to make her farewells for the present at the entrance to the lodge-passage. The Prioress had entirely refused any further help in the work of settling in, beyond that supplied by the gamekeeper's wife.

"We are accustomed to work," she said. "All shall be finished tonight; and Holy Mass is to be at seven tomorrow, is it not?"

"I believe so," said Mary.

"Then nothing remains but to thank you, Madam," said the Prioress, peering at her through her round spectacles; "and our Lord can do that better than I. Then if you will come tomorrow, Madam, sometime after ten, you shall see our little Sister Catherine."

And as Mary came out at the lodge gate, there, among the valises and bundles, over whose disembarkment from the van Jack was presiding, she thought she discerned a tall packing case, grim and ominous against the pale sky.

(2)

Half an hour after dinner the two were sitting in the smoking room talking together. There was an enormous amount of detail to be discussed, and Mary at least had found it a certain safety valve for her feelings.

They had been a curious four months since the building had once got under way, and in them again the quantity of practical things to be done and decided had been a kind of refuge from the facing of principles. Jack, as Mary had related in her note to Sarah, had once at least offered to give up the whole idea, saying that he understood better now the demand that it made upon her; but Mary would not hear of it. Since then, with a kind of furious ardor, the two had thrown themselves into work — Jack into long consultations with the architect and hours spent among the workmen; Mary into interminable correspondence, first with the nuns, then with tradesmen, and almost weekly excursions up to London. It was amazing how much had to be done. The crockery was obtained from Spain, and the cooking-vessels from France. The garden also had to be overseen, and proper selections made for its stocking.

But the end was in sight.

For an hour before dinner they had discussed details connected with the new chapel, and one or two arrangements concerning the gardeners; through dinner they had continued the same kind of thing; and now, half an hour later, by common unexpressed consent they had dropped the rest, and both sat suddenly silent before the fire.

It was a delightful little room in which they sat — the room in which, five months ago, Jack had accomplished the holocaust of his bats. In August she had found him again preparing to remove certain books on sport from the room; but on her pointing out their suitability at least for guests, he had left them as they were. (This was on the day after the flower show, and he had seemed a little depressed that day, she had thought.) For the rest, the room was ordinary enough. A semicircle of vast leather chairs, five in number, were ranged round the fire: a deep window seat ran from its edge; there were horns, books, glass cases of stuffed birds, a deep Turkey carpet, and heavy, comfortable curtains over the windows. No one would have suspected that it was the sitting room of a fanatic; and Jack had begun once more to make it his sitting room, and had acquiesced in its appearance.

In fact, in a good many ways he had shown his reasonableness after the first excitement had expired. He still said his office (Mary had peeped at him more than once from an upper window, going up and down the broad walk beneath); he meditated, frowning rather, for a smart half-hour each morning; he went to the Sacraments once a week, and to Mass every day. But in other matters he had gone on very much as before. He had pointed out to her that his position certainly did go for something; saying that Father Banting agreed with him; and that, on reflection, he considered he had been rather hasty in determining to give up all social duties. He now took a glass of wine again at dinner, though he had not yet resumed smoking; and he still refused to have a manservant of his own. The butler now looked after his clothes.

On the whole Mary was content with him. He was now what would be called an excellent and devout Catholic; there was very little trace of the fanatic about him.

And Mary?

Well, the account that Sarah would have given of her — in fact did give of her, fairly frequently — was that she was perfectly charming, though a little given to brooding sometimes. She no longer said the kind of things she used to say — except during one week in October, when she had raged about as usual, denouncing the convent, Jack, religion, herself, and everyone concerned. But she had repented of this so abjectly, explaining with such misery in her eyes that she had been maddened by neuralgia, that this scarcely counted. Obviously there was something going on in Mary that Sarah did not understand. It hardly seemed probable, as Jim had pointed out before he had left for Scotland in the summer, that a conversation with Jack and two with Lady Carberry should have worked a complete conversion of outlook. But as to what the other element was Sarah had no idea. She had fished, with ill-success. Veils had descended upon Mary's eyes, and her face had fallen a little. Sarah dismissed the whole affair

— at least she said she dismissed it, though she continually pulled it back to look at it again — by attributing it to that Catholic temperament so inexplicable to other people.

Here then the two sat — Jack and Mary — suddenly silent before the smoking room fire.

For some while Mary was not conscious of it. Their last words had been as to having breakfast at half-past eight in future instead of half-past nine. This appeared as a necessity, since Mass was to be in future an hour earlier than usual. And from that point Mary had run on, thought by thought, dwelling on little vignettes of memory — on the Prioress' spectacled face, the deal boards on the cells and corridors, and the rest. She began to picture to herself the life there, so far as she knew it — the silent row of figures passing in the dead night hours to prayer, the hooded faces in the refectory, the interminable silences, the even more interminable "recreations," at which all must talk, in whatever mood. She passed on again to consider the packing case and its contents . . . the grimness of the thought of the body of this French peasant girl, as she probably had been, being hauled about on railways and a steamer, guarded by jealous, anxious eyes, stored now in some little white room, probably the refectory — these nuns had no imagination — till its translation into the white iron-barred church.

So she sat thinking, staring into the wood fire, unconscious of all save her own thoughts.

She was disturbed by a small sound, faintly familiar, and looked up.

Jack also, it seemed, was meditating. He lay there in the deep chair, also staring at the fire, frowning a little as he stared, and further holding in his hand to his mouth a small wooden object, through which he was sucking in a contemplative manner, with a hollow and whistling sound.

Mary perceived it was an empty pipe.

"There!" she said. "You're a backslider!"

Jack smiled lazily and said nothing. They were both rather tired with the labors of the day.

How nice and clean he looked, thought Mary.

Never, even in the first days of his enthusiasm, had he omitted to dress for dinner. He lay there now with his long legs extended. One shoe had fallen off from a large foot, and his toes twisted luxuriously up and down before the blaze. His chin was sunk on his white shirt-front, and his eyes blinked at the fire. He looked extraordinarily comfortable and pleasing to the eye.

Then Mary thought again of the nuns, and sat up instinctively.

"You lazy pig," she said; "and think of those poor creatures up there in the cold."

Jack smiled again and made a small contented noise. Plainly he was sleepy.

"Oh, Jack, what a dear you are to have done all that! They are so happy. What a brilliant idea it was! And they're really there."

"Yes, they're really there," murmured Jack. "It's finished; and Mass tomorrow at seven. Don't forget."

"It seems awfully luxurious to them, you know," went on Mary. "It's only out of concession to us.

"No. Is that so?"

"It's about four in France, you know, or five or six. I forget, but it's certainly long before seven."

"Oh!" said Jack.

Then he added, "Oh, by the way, I'm going out for a ride tomorrow."

"That's excellent," said Mary.

Again there fell a long silence. Mary went on thinking. There were a thousand things to think of. She rehearsed again the past, the present, and the future.

She began to feel rather sleepy at last. The fire swam up more than once before her eyes, and dropped down again with a jerk into its place as she winked the sleep away. Finally she sat bolt upright and looked at Jack with that kind of reproachfulness with which an awakened dozer always regards the rest of the company.

But she need not have done so. Jack himself was sleeping like a child. The pipe had fallen from his fingers and reposed against his cheek.

(3)

The weather was no better next morning, nor even satisfactorily worse. The same gray clouds fled across the sky, the same wind shrilled uncomfortably with spatters of rain, as Mary, after interviewing the housekeeper, set out in furs to pay her visit.

She had been to Mass in the early morning, a minute late or two, with Jack five minutes later again; but that did not count, so to speak. One sped only over the ground in the dark, carrying a lantern, and back again. The Mass itself had been oddly dreary in that bare sanctuary, seen through iron bars, with the single figure of the priest moving about, the tiny server from the village motionless on his heels, the naked glimmer of candle-flames seen against the white stone surfaces. It was too queer to arouse any emotions but that of curiosity, and a faint contemplative wonder as to the process of events that had made it a fact. One thing only thrilled her to the least degree — the knowledge that out of sight, behind the screen she had seen yesterday, kneeled in deal stalls seventeen Frenchwomen and an Englishwoman who thirty-six hours ago had crossed the Channel from home to exile.

They had talked a little at breakfast; Jack had displayed slight symptoms of a morning crossness, and had presently sunk into a study of the *Westminster Gazette* of the evening before. He said he was going to ride at twelve.

The door of the lodge was opened to her by Mrs. Truman, the gamekeeper's wife — a thin, active, energetic woman with Irish eyes.

"Mother says, will you step into the parlor, please, Ma'am."

It was a bleak little room this, on the right-hand side, carpeted like the other — and these the only two in the building — with new coconut matting. A small rosewood table stood here, and an early Victorian sofa in green ribbed silk that had once done duty in Mary's mother's schoolroom. These things had been placed here by Mary herself; but there hung now on the wall opposite the door an astonishing picture, framed in black shiny wood: with gilt pins at its corners, representing, in oleograph, a woman in a Carmelite habit, clasping in her hand the feathered end of an arrow apparently piercing her heart, while her eyes — and no wonder, thought Mary — were turned upwards with a painful expression. In order that there might be no mistake, the words "Sainte Thérèse" were printed at the foot in gold letters. Mary gazed at this object in horror, wondering what was the emotion for which it stood, or which was proposed to be elicited.

Then she looked at the side opposite the window, and examined the gratings which she had watched in process of erection. The entire wall consisted of grating — on this side of iron bars set trellis-fashion; and from each point of crossing protruded forward a short iron spike. Then, after a space of the thickness of the wall, came a second grating of horizontal wood, and behind that blackness. The blackness was new to Mary.

She sat down after a moment or two, wondering as to the reason of her having been shown in here and the cause of the delay; but almost simultaneously there came a little sound from the convent side, and one square of the blackness vanished. In its place appeared the head and shoulders of a human being, swathed in black, with a glint of brown beneath. No face was visible.

"Good day, Madam," came a voice in French.

Mary made her greetings, understanding that it was the Prioress who spoke, and drew her chair a little nearer.

"You will pardon me for not having received you in the cloister," went on the voice. "I thought it better that we should begin at once as we shall continue. The enclosure is not yet commenced; but we had best act as if it were. You will pardon me, Madam?"

"Why, of course," said Mary, a little disconcerted all the same.

"And Monsieur, your husband, our benefactor — he is well?"

"Oh, Jack's always well," said Mary — "except last summer —" Her voice faltered.

"Ah, but so many prayers will be offered for him here," went on the tranquil old voice, "for his goodness to us. Our Lord will surely reward him a hundredfold."

"I hope you are all comfortable," said Mary, conscious that the word was scarcely the right one in this place. But it was taken up enthusiastically.

"Comfortable! Why, yes; it is luxury; it is too good for poor nuns."

"Isn't it dreadfully damp?"

"Ah no; the walls perspire a little; but it is nothing. We shall work the better, to keep ourselves warm."

"Surely it is bitterly cold," said Mary, suddenly aware of the fact. "The furnace; is that all right?"

"It will serve us very well," said the voice.

"Is it lighted?" demanded Mary, putting out her gloved hand to the radiator beside her.

"We have not kindled it yet," said the voice. "We have had so little time. But we shall do it presently. And you have come to see our little sister. Well, she is in the chapel now, all ready; we shall place her in her tomb this afternoon. You will come to the little ceremony?"

Mary had a sudden revulsion.

"I think not, Reverend Mother. I — I half-expect visitors this afternoon; and you see —"

"I comprehend perfectly, Madam. Then you shall pay your devotions to her this morning; she is all ready by the screen. But wait, Madam; let me tell you of her first."

Mary sat and listened as in a dream, while the story was told. It will be told again publicly, some day, no doubt, in a certain court in Rome; but nothing would persuade me to tell it now. It concerned, as Mary had half-guessed, the life of a French peasant-girl, and nine-tenths of it would be entirely devoid of interest to most English people — a life lived behind bars like those through which Mary stared, of small obediences, of sayings, of minute actions, of rhapsodies; and the tenth part of it would be regarded as medieval nonsense; of rose leaves, of sick persons healed, of a broken bone restored, and of what the Prioress called "Spiritual Favors." It seemed amazingly unconvincing to Mary — full of holes through which a coach could be driven, of omissions, of exaggerations; yet the old voice went on, serene and confident, with a little ring of complacency infinitely pathetic.

"And she was one of my daughters," ended the old motherly voice. "I received her at seventeen years of age, and she went to our Lord when but twenty-two."

Mary asked what seemed to her an intelligent question or two, rustled as if interested; and in her heart despaired.

"And you will come and see her now, Madam; and ask her prayers for yourself and your dear husband and for us all. Will you pass round the garden, Madam, and enter through the sacristy?"

"One moment, Mother. May I see Sister Teresa?"

"Afterwards, Madam," said the voice firmly.

It seemed stranger than ever to pass on such an errand over that familiar lawn outside, now gray with December growth, through a gap cut in the hedge, to the new little doorway of the sacristy Father Banting was there again, and a tray, from which he had breakfasted a couple of hours earlier, still rested on the table in the middle. He greeted her with that nervous little manner he had always shown, and himself took her through into the sanctuary. The two genuflected side by side, and then approached the grating. Mary's heart beat, quick and hot, as she observed that that part of the screen had been removed through which the nuns received Holy Communion, and that there lay beyond, guarded by the Prioress, a long box, supported on trestles, covered with a white cloth.

She knelt down, hardly knowing what she did. The next instant, as, without a word, the veiled figure swept aside the cloth, she knelt, suddenly gone white, staring at what was disclosed.

Certainly it was a human figure that lay there; that could be seen by the shape and the attitude; but it took two or three seconds before she understood that she looked indeed upon the face of a girl. The head was shrouded in a hood, and a veil passed below the chin; and in the midst, a gray-brown thing lay, with. sharp jutting nose, a slightly prominent chin, sunken eyes, and a sunken mouth like a cut. The texture seemed that of polished wood; and two hands, of the same aspect, crossed on the breast, and emerging from wide sleeves, held a rosary and a crucifix in the fingers. One thing only relieved the horror — the incapability of the imagination to grasp that this had once been a human being.

There was a dead silence as she looked. Father Banting behind, either standing or kneeling — she did not know which — was as still as death itself. The Prioress was motionless.

Time meant very little as the moments went by: there was nothing to measure them by. And at last, as she still stared — with every instinct of repugnance and terror mounting at every second, the standing figure stooped, kissed that wooden, shiny forehead once, as a mother might kiss a sleeping child. Then the cloth swept softly into place again, was smoothed down and adjusted; and Mary drew a long breath and stood up.

"You have prayed well for us all, have you not?" whispered the old voice.

(4)

The parlor seemed scarcely the same place when Mary found herself back in it a minute or two later. It had become indifferent; it no longer mattered, in face of the horror that had fallen and enveloped her. . . . She did all mechanically — passed again through the daylight, in again through the lodge door, and so to the parlor and sat down. Time and space seemed, so to speak, flat and superficial; to be but scenery for the reality of that gray, fallen face with sunken eyes and mouth. There lay a kind of dazing blankness on her, in which she was scarcely conscious of herself.

So she sat down mechanically and waited; no longer interested in the thought of the Englishwoman she was about to see. She wondered only whether the Prioress had noticed the shocking impression that had been made upon her.

Then again the curtain disappeared; and this time she was allowed to see plainly the nun who spoke to her. The swathed face seemed very different from that of the bonneted, black-dressed woman whom she had seen first as Sister Teresa. The lines of it were infinitely more graceful. In spite of herself, Mary glanced at her with interest; yet again and again there recurred the vision of terror she had seen in the chapel.

For a while Mary said little or nothing except the most ordinary remarks; but she watched the big eyes with the dark beneath them, the thin nose and the sensitive lips. This was an Englishwoman, she reminded herself, of one blood with herself. Then suddenly the lethargy passed and she became interested.

"You are a convert, you say?"

"I was a convert when I was about eighteen. My father was a Wesleyan minister."

"Ah! And did he — what did he do? You don't mind my asking these questions?"

"I never saw him again," said the nun simply.

There was a pause.

"Tell me something about the life," said Mary suddenly. "Don't you get fearfully tired?"

"Oh yes; but it's different somehow. There's not time to get tired in the ordinary way. (The nun smiled.) At least there's no time to think about it, which comes to the same thing. We always sit upright, you know."

"Upright! Do you mean you never lean back?"

"No, it's our custom. Oh, you soon get accustomed to it. It's just habit."

"But — but what do you do? I mean what outward work?"

"Well, my work was always the garden. I expect it will be so here. I'm quite a tolerable gardener."

"But in your habit!" exclaimed Mary, glancing at what she could see of the heavy brown folds.

"Oh, we've a way of tucking that aside. It's a great pleasure to have the garden to do."

Suddenly Mary realized that the nun was kneeling, not sitting, on the other side of the grating. There was a little stool behind her; and for the rest, just the deal floor, the walls and the ceiling.

Then, once more, the whole thing rushed on her (as blood rushes back to compressed veins) — the amazing hardness of the life, and its absolute mad folly as judged by any merely physical philosophy of the world. If the body were the real person, and the soul, at the best, but a department of it, what wildly conceivable justification could there be for such a life as this? Yet the nun looked serenely happy. And — and that gray face in the chapel was the end of it all.

Mary gripped the bars.

"Tell me, Sister," she said. "How can you bear — Are you really and truly happy?"

The nun looked at her straight for one instant. Then she dropped her eyes and opened her lips to speak.

"No, let me finish," said Mary, oddly excited — she scarcely knew why. "Let me say it right out. . . . You won't be offended? . . . I've just been to see — to see Sister Catherine. Reverend Mother made me. Well, that just sums it all up — that dead body. It seems to me horrible — horrible; it's utterly impossible that God can really want that. And you all seem to me just like that — all dead and yellow, without any of the advantages of being dead." . . .

She stopped breathlessly, excited and shocked by herself. Yet it was exactly what she meant. The bars shook a little in her hands.

"Are you really happy?" she repeated abruptly.

The nun looked at her again.

"It's very hard to put into words," she said slowly in that thin, very slightly tremulous voice. "Words mean such different things to different people. Let me answer it like this. For no conceivable reason on earth would I leave the convent. I would sooner die ten times over. Suppose I woke up and found the whole thing a dream, and that I was living in the world, I think my heart would break."

Mary interrupted abruptly. She felt that her side was winning.

"Ah, but you aren't really happy. You've only killed your capacity for happiness — spoiled it — starved it to death. Now isn't that true?"

The nun's steady eyes lifted and dropped.

"There's a good deal of truth in that, Mrs. Weston. I don't deny that. But —"

"It's exactly as I thought," said Mary, conscious simultaneously of triumph and disappointment. I've always felt that must be so, and now you tell me it is so."

"Ah, but I hadn't finished," said the nun gently. "It is perfectly true that one sort of happiness goes entirely; I mean that things that give pleasure to people in the world after a time aren't even any temptation to us. And it's perfectly true that that comes from their being 'starved to death,' as you say. But another sort of happiness comes that's entirely different. You can't even call it happiness. It's something else."

Mary made a sound as if to interrupt.

"Let me finish, please. I can't put it into words. No one can. All I can say is that the life inside is just a different thing altogether from life outside. There's sorrow too; but that's different again. It isn't at all the same thing. It's like a new set of faculties for pain and pleasure, and another world altogether. It's all different."

Mary dropped her own eyes as she met again those of the other beyond the bars.

"Do you know the last sermon I heard my father preach?" went on the nun. "I've forgotten the sermon; but the text was, 'Ye are dead; and your life is hid with Christ in God.' Well, I understood that for the first time. It was the last straw. I don't remember a word he said. I was just thinking all the while of the text, and I've been thinking of it ever since. You were quite right when you said what you did about Sister Catherine. That's exactly it."

Mary listened with a new kind of sensation enfolding her more swiftly every instant. She understood absolutely what the other meant. She saw its horror and its inexorableness, and she saw also, what terrified her still more, a glimpse of the enormous possibilities of an entirely new kind of joy that lay hidden under the horror. It was as if a great hand were on her, grasping in an irresistible soft pressure every surface of her mind and soul, and she loathed and resented the touch. She dropped the bars abruptly and sat up, rigid and resisting. Her own voice sounded strange at first in her ears.

"I think I see, Sister." (She drew a long breath as the pressure relaxed.) "It's extremely beautiful; but it seems to me quite unreal — unreal to me, I mean." (Ah! that was better. Sanity was coming back like a tide. She noticed again the texture of the painted iron she had grasped just now.) "But thank you so much for trying to tell me. I hope I haven't been too inquisitive. It's always so interesting to hear other people's points of view, even if one can't take them oneself. After all, we can be good Catholics, even if we don't understand the religious life, can't we?"

"Why yes," said the nun, smiling. "It's all a question of vocation."

"Of vocation — yes; just so," murmured Mary, drawing a long breath of relief. "I do think that's so splendid in the Church. Why, I heard a very holy priest say once that it might be a vocation for a Catholic to be the best-dressed woman in every room she went into."

The nun smiled once more.

"I must be going," said Mary. "Thank you so much."

(5)

A great scraping of hoofs greeted her as she turned the corner of the house, and Jack's voice sharply raised. Then, as she stepped on to the gravel sweep, she saw a delightfully distracting scene.

There revolved in the middle of the gravel two living beings, a horse and a very young groom. They faintly resembled a chain-shot, and the link between them was the bridle, which the horse had slipped over his head, and now held, so to speak, at nose-length with his head in the air.

"Get to his head, you fool," bellowed Jack, who was standing, in riding gaiters, capless, and with a large smear of mud and gravel all down his back, just below the mounting-block.

The horse had that appearance of patient complacency that horses do have when they have won the first round of a conflict. He seemed to move on tiptoe and on springs, delicately prancing; he appeared to be divided between pleasure and apprehensiveness.

"Is that the new horse?" asked Mary. "I say; take care, Jack!"

Jack that instant had done a thing he certainly ought not to have done. He launched himself straight at the horse, snatching at the reins and saddle, and the horse very properly responded by an indescribable movement that left Jack empty handed, and that pulled the groom as nearly as possible off his feet. It was obvious how Jack's back had become gravelly.

"That's no good," said Mary impulsively. "Here, let me try."

She went straight across the gravel, past her speechless husband, and took the end of the reins from the groom's hand. The horse eyed her carefully.

"Poor dear, then; did they bully you?"

"He's a beast," said Jack.

"Not at all," said Mary. "Are you, my dear?"

She was gently shortening her grip on the reins, up and up and up. The horse rolled his eyes once towards the gaitered figure with the riding-crop, and then decided to attend to this new personage instead. Very slowly the gloved hands advanced and advanced. There was a delightfully soothing sensation of his ears being pulled, and he thought it better to lower his head a little; then something went gently over it, and the next instant he was slouching forward, as tame as a cat, to the mounting-block.

"Up and down first, my dear. Now are your nerves quite quiet again? Did the nasty man jump at him and frighten him out of his wits?"

"I didn't," burst in Jack. "The beast swerved violently just as I was getting on. I'll teach him."

"No you won't. You must be quite quiet too, or you shan't get on. Now then — no; not from the block. Probably he isn't accustomed to one."

But it was no good. The horse wasn't going to be cajoled like this for one instant. Again he swerved violently, and dragged Jack, hopping frantically with one foot in the stirrup.

"There then. Will you behave?" said Mary sharply. "Give me a handkerchief."

The groom, anxious not to be left out in the cold, produced a large red bandanna so suddenly as nearly to bring about another catastrophe.

"Jim, that's not the way to quiet a horse," observed Mary. "Thank you."

The handkerchief seemed really harmless after all, thought the horse, after he had inspected it by means of long snuffles and blowings out of his nostrils. He would permit this lady to do what she liked with it. Then, of course, so soon as it was firmly across his eyes and tucked into the cheek-straps there was no more to be said or done.

"Thanks," said Jack, as he settled himself in the saddle. "Cap, Jim."

"Where are you going?" asked Mary, standing back, a little flushed, still holding the handkerchief.

"I don't know. I must see what this beast's made of."

"He's a dear if you take him right. . . . What's that?"

The horse pricked his ears too as a confused sound broke from the direction of the lodge below — a strange yelping cry, the clatter of hoofs, and voices shouting.

"It's the hounds," cried Jack. "Good Lord! What a chance!"

Over and through the palings below, beyond the stream, came a torrent of white and gray specks, breaking, mingling, breaking again like quicksilver. From a group of trees appeared a flash of scarlet, then another; while round through the lodge gate, bending sharply to the left, came a stream of riders; the hollow drumming of hoofs on turf grew louder and louder; and the shrill cheers from the village street turned thin as the bellowers tore up the road outside the park to get another view further on.

"Oh, Jack, do —"

But her voice failed, as she understood.

This, then, was one more of the things that Jack had given up. He had never hunted much; but it would have been inconceivable in the old days that he should have refrained at a moment like this. There below passed the hunt; the hounds had already vanished up the park, their cry fainter every instant; the last stragglers were following; it was not yet too late to pick them up at the bridge. . . . She looked again at Jack.

It was not until that moment that she realized how entirely his old self had come back to him during their little struggle with the horse. He had been during those minutes so obviously himself, indignant, impatient, and very human. But even now that odd constrained expression had descended on him again: his lips looked thin and tight; in his eyes only the pair of moods still fought one with the other. Then he dropped his eyes suddenly and settled himself again in the saddle.

"I shall go round by the Carberrys'," he said deliberately. "Thanks very much for helping Mary. I'll be back to lunch."

(6)

Mary felt extraordinarily better that afternoon. She informed herself that the horrid discomfort that had descended on her during her visit to "Sister Catherine" was quite removed by her victory over Sister Teresa. It was a real relief, she said to herself, to know from a nun's own mouth that the apparent victory achieved by religions over what were called worldly temptations was nothing else but their starvation. Of course she had known so all along really, but it was pleasant to be corroborated.

She had one more corroboration, too, at tea; and she thought it really providential when she considered it afterwards. Certainly there were some unpleasant accompaniments to the evidence, but those could be dealt with separately.

It is an unhappy drawback to the possession of an old house that courteous and inquisitive archeologists are apt to be brought by neighbors to inspect it — brought with many apologies, but none the less brought. So it fell out this afternoon.

Professor Peters did not happen to be an archeologist, by the way; he occupied the chair of psychology at a new American university, but to the layman all these things amount to the same. He was a professor, and that was enough. He was bound to be interested in old oak, a winding stone staircase with pentacles inscribed on each step to keep devils away, and a chest covered with human skin, presumably Danish.

It was half-past three that he arrived, towed up to the house by an earnest young squire from the next village, whose name is of no importance; and ran straight into Jack, who that instant was emerging through the garden door. There was no escape; Jack was obviously unoccupied, and after sending a message to Mary that there would be two people at tea, he resigned himself and went off with them.

The Professor was so overwhelmingly learned in psychology that he had forgotten everything else except his manners. (Professors are usually like this, except that most of them have forgotten their manners too.) He was so certain that psychology was the very center of knowledge that he imagined it the circumference also, and sought to bring all phenomena within its radius. He made some very valuable remarks about pentacles and the modern revival of magic, alleging that the value of symbols lay in the fact that they enabled the naturally diffuse mind to concentrate itself upon the point symbolized. There were no devils, of course, and nothing in a pentacle as such; yet the Pentacle-idea could be made to counteract the Devil-idea with very happy results. He used a German phrase or two at this point, and Jack assented politely. It was all very convincing indeed.

He seemed a pleasant old man, thought Mary, as she gave him his tea half an hour later. He was neither deaf, nor lame, nor blind, as professors usually are; nor did he wear his hair particularly long. He was a thin-faced, clean-shaven man, respectably dressed, with very bright and piercing gray eyes, and a long upper lip. She talked to him, therefore, on a settee, while Jack and the earnest young squire entertained one another on the other side of the table.

When two persons are, permanently or temporarily, possessed each of one idea respectively, and talk together, it is not surprising if the two ideas are brought forcibly into contact. Mary was thinking just then of the convent; the Professor was thinking then, as always, of psychology. Within ten minutes, therefore, they were discussing the psychology of the Religious Life.

"Of course, to us psychologists," said the Professor presently, "there is nothing at all remarkable in the phenomenon of persons wishing to shut themselves up in order to concentrate on one idea. Neither does it matter at all whether or no the idea is a delusive one —"

"I am a Catholic," said Mary rather quickly.

The Professor made a little sound that might stand equally for assent or compassion.

"The eremitical life is, however, common to all religions," he said gently. "The Buddhist monk, no less than the Christian, is a person possessed of one idea to the exclusion of others. He finds, therefore, to be quite tolerable conditions of life impossible for others."

Mary shifted her position a little and took another piece of toast.

"I don't quite see why," she said.

The Professor smiled.

"It is a familiar phenomenon in psychological studies," he said. "A mind under the stress of any sufficiently strong emotion will be impervious to all others. If he is in love, for instance, his appetite will go. An artist will forget his meals and his duties. It is a perfectly commonplace —"

"I see," said Mary abruptly. "And in their place a new set of sensations will appear."

"Exactly. The possessing idea will produce them. And, as I said before, it is of no importance whether or no the idea corresponds to fact or not."

"I don't see that."

"Well, Mrs. Weston; a young man in love will —"

Mary nodded. This was a little more than she had bargained for. She retraced a step or two.

"The whole state, then," she said, "is an *exalté* one."

"Just so. We should call it 'morbid' — not in any opprobrious sense, you understand: merely pathological. But we are only in the very beginning of the science. The word self-suggestion, for example. What a world of possibilities lies there."

"And you believe it accounts for all these things?"

"Undoubtedly. So far as we see at present, there is no boundary in sight. There is scarcely any abnormal phenomenon established — I may say, I think, not one — which cannot be brought under the range of this force."

A little mental vignette of Sister Teresa's face, as she had seen it through the grille, passed before Mary's eyes. She regarded it an instant. Was it really possible?

"Isn't it possible to push that too far?" she said.

The Professor made an indescribable little deprecatory movement resembling the ghost of a shrug.

"It is possible, of course," he said.

"I mean," said Mary, with a glimmer of humor in her eyes, "that it may even be true that psychologists themselves bring their main idea to bear too much on phenomena. We are all open to that danger."

The Professor wrinkled his face up in honest mirth. He was perfectly good-humored.

"A palpable hit," he said. "You silence me."

Mary sat pensive over the fire when they went out at last. She was thinking very hard indeed. But underneath she was conscious of a considerable relief. It was at least pleasant to her pride to remember that the very trying life of the convent was not so trying after all, that if one could but be possessed sufficiently by one idea, all things became possible. "All things are possible to him that believeth."

Then what about other things — her religion, for instance; Jack's remarkable developments? Why the key fitted appallingly well.

But that's quite different, she assured herself, entirely different. Why at that rate —

Then Jack came in.

Chapter VII

(1)

Somehow the thing had to be faced: Sarah had to be shown over the convent, or rather admitted to the parlor, and allowed to express her views by comment or silence. Mary dreaded it unspeakably; yet she could hardly have said why. She supposed it was because of the need of defending the indefensible; at least, she said it was that. Soon after the beginning of the New Year, therefore, she sent a short note across to the following effect: —

"My dearest, —

"We may as well get it over. You've got to see it all sometime, and grasp the fact that it's now part of me, so to speak. I know you'll be kind, and not say too much. Come to lunch on Tuesday — Jack's away that day — and we'll go to the convent afterwards: they're in working order now.

"Yours,

"M."

Sarah was agreeably impressed by the letter. It seemed to grant her own superior position. In fact her faint resentment gave way to a certain pity. She determined to be very kind indeed.

Mary seemed rather feverish at lunch, she thought: she talked rather quickly, gave her statistics and a few external facts, and never even approached the attitude of her mind manifest in her letter. But when the servants had gone, and coffee had been set in the morning room, she threw her arm round Sarah's waist as they went across the hall.

"Oh, dear me. Be very nice to me, Sally dear. I need it."

This was delightful. Sarah felt more of a strong-minded friend than ever, and rejoiced in the sensation. She thought she understood everything now — that there was this strain of weakness in her friend — deplorable, though natural in a Catholic born and bred — and that it was her own part to comfort and console.

She implied this delicately in the conversation that followed.

"I don't see why you need mind so much," she said. "I often think our own clergymen rather fools. . . . One isn't responsible for all that."

Mary said nothing; she just lifted and dropped her eyes.

"You see," went on Sarah, remembering fragments of Jim Fakenham's philosophical conversation, "you see there are all sorts of temperaments; we mustn't be narrow-minded. I daresay those old Frenchwomen are happier there than they would be anywhere else. I am sure it seems to me all very harmless, in spite of what Mother says."

"Is she very —" began Mary.

"Oh, she can't bear it. You knew that. I don't think she'll come here much. But she was very clear that she still regarded you as neighbors."

The ghost of a smile came and went across Mary's face. Sarah reflected it more broadly.

"Yes; I know," she said. "But Mother's like that. Oh, Mary, need everyone be so dreadfully responsible?"

"I've got to be," said Mary gloomily. "I'm a sort of nursing mother now, you know."

She turned a little and sat staring out of the window.

"Have a cigarette," said Sarah.

"I don't fancy it, as the lady said," answered Mary dismally. "Oh, Sarah, be nice. . . . Here" — she jumped up — "let's go and get it over. Then we can talk about other things. Yes — this very instant."

There was a touch of frost in the air today, and things were not, therefore, so utterly depressing as a fortnight before, when the nuns had arrived. Mary put on her furs, and they always suited her. Sarah thought she had never seen anyone so entirely suitable to this world — her face touched now with excitement, her eyes bright, her quick, alert movements over the frozen ground. She hardly said anything on the way up, and even Sarah refrained from depressing comments upon the way in which the peculiar charm of the place had been entirely ruined by that stiff

little lodge, that seemed to dominate the hill like a convict
warder. As they rose higher the roofs rose with them, till
they stood at last before the gate, and comment was impossible.

It was one of those mysterious dependents that always
seem to haunt convents who opened the door — a small
brisk young Frenchwoman in a nondescript black dress
and a frilled cap. She broke into smiles and voluble
half-finished sentences at the sight of Mary, showed them
promptly through into the parlor, and a single stroke of a
bell was presently heard to sound somewhere in the cloister within.

Sarah could not resist a little silent triumph in this
room. She observed the grating, fingered one of the spikes
with a suede-gloved hand, glanced at the table, gave a
long and careful inspection to the picture of Saint Teresa,
and said nothing whatever of any sort.

A deep sigh broke from Mary.

"Don't," she said feebly.

"My dearest, I didn't say one word. I'm behaving beautifully."

"Yes, I know," sighed Mary, who had sat down on the
sofa. "That's just it."

But Sarah's heart beat a little quicker for all her supe-
riority, as she caught a faint sound from beyond the
shrouded grating.

Her views on nuns — except on those who, as she would
have said, "did something useful" — were, for a wonder,
very much what she had stated them to be. It appeared
that there were people who were, unhappily, endowed
with a morbid sort of temperament that could find satisfaction in nothing except some sort of self-inflicted misery.
Now here these people were in the world, and had to be
provided for; so convents of this sort had naturally come
into existence. There was no shadow of doubt in her mind
but that her own point was the saner, and that Almighty
God, at the best, only tolerated with a kind of pity those of
less healthy minds. She did not for an instant, like her
mother, think that nuns were actually wicked. At the
worst they were but dangerous, like people suffering from
an infectious disease. Yet since the type was uncommon,

there was something rather interesting in it, and she prepared to visit the convent in the kind of mood in which she would have gone to see a hospital, or a lunatic asylum warranted to contain only amiable invalids.

Naturally, therefore, her interest quickened almost into excitement as she heard the footstep stir beyond the grating, and she settled down in her chair determined to observe her hardest, while — and this was seriously a kindly thought — to humor so far as she consistently could the harmless old thing that would immediately make her appearance.

The square of blackness slid away. There was the murmur of a voice, and the head and shoulders of some human being appeared on the other side.

(2)

For an instant Sarah was taken aback. Her expectations had been either of an old person in a cap and spectacles with weak blue eyes, or of a dramatic figure in an attitude: she had oscillated between these two conceptions. The reality startled her. It was a trifle ghastly, yet not at all menacing or theatrical.

She was reassured by Mary's voice at her side — speaking in French.

"Good afternoon, Reverend Mother. This is Lady Sarah I've told you about — a Protestant. I've brought her in to see you."

"Good day, Madam — good day, Madam. I'm very happy to see you, Madam. So you've come to see the poor nuns and to promise them your prayers."

"Er — *oui*," murmured Sarah. (She was not very good at French, and had explained so to Mary.)

"My friend cannot talk French very well, she says," went on Mary, "but she can understand perfectly. She has never been inside a convent before."

"Ah, you think us all very wicked, then?" went on the quiet old voice almost apologetically.

Sarah hastened to defend her broad-mindedness.

"No, no; not at all. I'm not like that. It isn't that. I know how good you are. Mary, my friend here, has often talked to me of you."

"Ah, then, that we are very foolish then, is it not so? And you are quite right, Madam. We are all of us very foolish — very foolish and simple. You must pray for us the more."

Was that irony, thought Sarah, or a pretense of humility? She had no idea; the voice sounded sufficiently simple.

"We owe all our beautiful home here to Madam," went on the voice, "to Madam and Monsieur her generous husband. God will surely reward them. . . . And you would like to hear of the life we live, would you not? All our visitors ask us of that."

Then, extraordinarily simply, the voice went on to give a little sketch of the day, such as Sarah had already heard from Mary, laying stress upon the quietness and regularity of the life, speaking with something that might or might not have been humor, of the excellence of the meals, largely provided for the present from the Hall, telling her of the little manual works that they carried out — one in embroidery, another in writing out music for churches, another in the garden.

"But you must understand, Madam, that our principal work is prayer. Not only must we work for what we need but pray also; and for all sinners who will not let men work for them."

Sarah listened, but with half her mind. She had determined, of course, that a great effort would be made to convert her; and had resolved to be thoroughly magnanimous in return. She would humor the old thing; she would not utter all those convincing sentiments that she had rehearsed in private — such as the "four walls" business, or the obviousness of the fact that since God had made the world it was meant to be enjoyed; and that it was far braver to meet in open field those obstacles to perfection that were called temptations rather than to try to run away from them — not even the final argument about "selfishness." After all, why should she upset and anger the poor old creature? It could do no good. No, she would be patient.

It was a little disconcerting therefore, even disappointing, that nothing at all was said about religion, as Sarah understood it — not one word about the superior light enjoyed by Catholics. The voice went on serenely, telling of the external details of the day, assuming that they would be heard with interest, though with a deprecatory remark or two thrown in as to the dullness of all this to one who had so varied a life as Madam, and nothing else.

"And you are very happy?" asked Sarah at last.

"Yes, Madam, very happy," said the voice tranquilly.

"And the young girls who come to you? They are happy too — always?"

"If they are not happy we find it out very soon, Madam; and then, of course, they leave us. I was obliged to send away a novice shortly before leaving France — the poor child!"

"She was a peasant?"

"No, Madam, she was of noble family, and it nearly broke her heart."

"Why did you send her away?"

"She became a little melancholy, Madam."

This was all quite outside Sarah's range. She thought it safest to be content with a sympathetic murmur. That committed you to nothing.

"And you would wish to see our Sister Catherine, of whom Madam Weston has without doubt told you?"

"I should like —" began Sarah politely. But Mary's voice broke in, swift and tremulous.

"Not today, Reverend Mother, thank you. I don't think that's quite —"

"I understand perfectly, Madam," came the gentle old voice. "Then some other day, perhaps. Madam Weston will explain to you. And you will come to see us again, Madam — the poor nuns, and bring Madam, your good mother?"

Sarah made a confused sort of answer; the voice bid them good day, once or twice; there was some sound again beyond the grating; then, once more, blackness and silence.

The two made their way round to the chapel almost without a word, and came into the public transept by the side door.

Things were a trifle better here now. There was at least a carpet before the altar, cheap, but not outrageously ugly; a statue of not quite the worst possible taste stood in the transept itself, just on this side of the screen, and the altar itself showed on its gradine the gleam of gilded wood and flowers. But there was nothing particular to be said about it.

Sarah sat and considered it all, as Mary knelt, not precisely in a mood of hostility, certainly not in a mood of appreciation. She told herself that she must just take in impressions, and be very kind to Mary when they came out. Mary's anxiety just now in the parlor had been almost pathetic.

So when again they left the chapel and began to go homewards down the hill, for a while Sarah said nothing. It was hard to find exactly the frame of words to use. Mary drove her to it first.

"Well?" she asked, without looking up.

Sarah made an effort.

"I liked that old nun," she said generously. "I thought her very nice not to argue."

"Argue? Why should she?"

"Oh, I thought she'd want to convert me."

"And that she'd begin to argue?"

"I thought so."

"Oh," said Mary.

"Well, but doesn't she?"

"Doesn't she what?"

"Want to make me a Catholic."

"Of course she does, and anybody else too. But, of course, she doesn't argue."

"But what'll she do then?"

"Oh, she'll pray," said Mary wearily.

Sarah pressed her arm sympathetically. She thought she understood so perfectly the mood of the other. But there was no responsive pressure.

"Who's Sister Catherine?" asked Sarah presently.

The arm stirred a little in her own.

"Sister Catherine's dead. She died ages ago." Sarah was amazed.

"But I thought she said —"

"Oh, you may as well know at once," burst out Mary suddenly and vehemently. "Sister Catherine's a dead body that hasn't decayed. And they carry it about, and kiss it. They brought it over here from France in a packing case, and it's somewhere in that chapel now. I don't know where."

"But, my dear," interrupted the shocked Sarah. "Yes, I know. It's perfectly horrid. They think she's a saint. And I daresay she was too; but I think it's all horrid — at least — Oh, I don't know. Let me alone!"

This sounded like hysteria. Sarah faced about suddenly on the path, still holding Mary's arm, and looking straight and stern into the flushed face and tearful eyes. But there seemed no hysteria there — nothing but a face tortured by some sudden revulsion, or some hidden conflict suddenly revealed. Mary tore herself free like a petulant child.

"No, I'm all right. Leave me alone."

Sarah stood, grave and reproachful.

"My dear, you oughtn't to treat me like that. I've done my very best. I haven't said one word —"

"I know you haven't. But that doesn't make it any better for me! Let's talk about something else. Come on."

(3)

Sarah had entirely failed to form any satisfactory conclusion by the time that she had reached home. Mary had accompanied her to the lodge gate, saying she mustn't come any further, as Jack might be home soon from his magistrates' meeting; and Sarah had gone the rest of the way in solitude.

It was all very puzzling.

After that outburst on the path, just after they had reached the first terrace, no more had been said. They had talked of almost entirely other things; the nearest they had approached again to the subject of the convent was the matter of its being visible from Lady Carberry's windows. This, it seemed, was another unfortunate detail.

What, then, was the matter with Mary? She determined to write to Jim Fakenham, who would be sure to have an illuminating word to say.

Then she reviewed her own impressions.

That nun had been very unexpected — chiefly in her mildness and her curious little air of dignity that even beyond those two abominable gratings had made itself perceived. There it was — there was no question of it — it was the air of one who ruled and was obeyed. Yet what of those little humble sentences that had been interspersed? Sarah decided that these had probably been uttered for the sake of effect. That then was settled.

And as regards the whole thing.

There Sarah failed to correlate her impressions. It was all so unusual. In the parlor there was ugliness naked, and not only unashamed, but complacent. There had not been a hint of apology for the miserable little room with its dismal picture. It was not even dignified. She supposed that the nuns thought that that was the kind of room in which worldly people lived. No wonder then that they despised the world!

To that had to be added the bleak chapel, and — a note that reflected it — the horror of those prison bars. These, Sarah was quite certain, were merely stage effects. Finally, there had somehow to be reconciled with the tame feebleness of the parlor the desolation of the chapel and the unspeakable horror of "Sister Catherine." . . . And there were quiet old Frenchwomen who somehow combined these impressions into a coherent whole! Well, it was more than Sarah could do. She could but contemplate them severally.

Finally, again, there was the problem of Mary. . . Oh, these Catholics!

She took considerable pains about her letter to Jim — with whom by now a kind of skirmishing correspondence had been established. Secretly she felt a little proud of enjoying the intimacy with a man of Jim's evident powers. He was so very philosophical, so aloof, so well finished; and he took the trouble to say such shrewd things to her — things that he never said, apparently, to her own aunt or her mother. It was pleasant to think that she understood him. So she wrote her letter with considerable pains.

Dinner, alone with her mother that evening, was a little difficult. Somehow her mother had to be informed of the visit to the convent (she would be sure to find out anyhow), and yet neither alarmed nor ruffled.

Sarah did it rather well.

"I was lunching with Mary Weston, you know, today, Mother."

"So I understood from you, my dear."

Sarah then discoursed for a while upon Mary — Oh! she had learned, she thought, how to manage her mother by now — touched upon Jack, and finally introduced, in a parenthesis, the information that Mary had just taken her up to see the Reverend Mother.

Lady Carberry consumed rice pudding, and asked an intelligent question or two, with a forbearance that caused Sarah to congratulate herself on her tact. But there was no gaining an advantage over that lady. When the questions had been asked and answered, one sentence shattered Sarah's complacency.

"And why couldn't you tell me that at once — instead of all those goings about it?"

Dear, dear! thought Sarah, diplomacy was a disappointing science. She would go upstairs as soon as she could and just look over her letter to Jim again. Why was Mary such an interesting person?

Chapter VIII

(1)

The views upon the convent current in the village suffered but very little modification as time went on. Subconscious public opinion had deeply suspected that within a week or two, at any rate, some mask or other would be thrown off, and figures would emerge in order to set about some mysterious business of bewitchment or proselytism. It was not seriously credible that confinement and prayer were really the objects for which so much preparation had been made. And the fact that no mask had yet been thrown off made the nuns all the more dangerous.

There began then very soon, in the public houses of Manningham, that slow stream of comment and rotatory argument that continues in them, I believe, even to the present day. There were practically no data to argue upon; nobody but a tradesman's boy or two and a laundress's assistant ever approached the house, and these had nothing to report except the appearance of a curiously dressed woman with her head wrapped up, who spoke in a very un-English manner. The argument therefore must always be of an *a priori* nature.

Naturally the squire came in for a quantity of comment also. He had been certainly popular; a man does not play for the Gentlemen of England without becoming a kind of compelling demigod, scarcely human. And to this had been added Jack's own extreme geniality and approachableness. He had given a cricket ground to the village as soon as he had arrived in the place; and on certain glorious evenings he had himself bowled at the nets for a few minutes to the chieftains of the village team. But his last mood had bewildered all the world. It was not that he lost his popularity. Rather he was contemplated with a kind of pity, as a pleasant man suddenly struck insane. The burning of his bats, the rumor of his prayers, in fact his whole violent change of front, had tossed him back into the atmosphere of suggestive mystery in which, as a Catholic, he had first arrived.

A small event, however, took place at the very close of the shooting season that once more complicated the situation.

There was gathered at the lodge gate on the last day of January a group of men and boys, in leggings, armed with heavy sticks, at half-past ten o'clock; and it was understood that the Wetherly coverts were to be beaten for the last time. It was an almost perfect shooting day — turquoise sky, frost in the air, and a small breeze. Three or four retrievers pulled small boys about at the ends of chains; low conversation filled the air; and Mr. Truman in a velveteen jacket stood a little apart like Napoleon before a battle. It was known that six guns were required; three were to be provided by the house, three more were to come from a distance — personages known as "the Colonel," Mr. Francis, and "Parkinses." The Colonel had already whisked up the drive in his dog-cart, a vision of red face and cropped white hair, beside his man; Mr. Francis, even now, could be discerned walking up from the station carrying his gun; and simultaneously half-past ten struck from the church clock.

There followed the clash of a gate within the park; and three minutes later Jack and his four guests appeared — the Colonel, magnificent now in his loose knickerbockers of loud check, his gaiters, and his Norfolk jacket, and the three men staying in the house. Jack, it was evident, had no intention of shooting; he had not been out once this season, and now his stockinged legs and low shoes made it plain that today was to be no exception.

There was a short pause while "Parkinses" was still expected. Yet he should have come by the ten fifteen, and Mr. Francis reported no glimpse of him. Jack strode about, bare-headed, swinging his stick, and giving directions to Mr. Truman, while the beaters stood in groups, shifting slowly from one leg to the other, the dogs tugged, and the guests said a good many things over and over again to one another.

The tableau was broken by a telegraph boy. Jack took the orange envelope and tore it open.

"Parkins isn't coming," he said; "wired for — or something. Well, it can't be helped."

Mr. Truman saluted.

"Beg pardon, sir."

"Yes?"

"Can't do the Wetherly coverts without six guns, sir," he said. "We could do with eight."

Jack jerked his head impatiently.

"Well, who is there? You can't take a gun! You'll be wanted."

Mr. Truman made no remark. And the church clock struck the quarter.

The guests looked at one another, and at Jack. There had been almost the beginning of a faintly unpleasant scene in the smoking room the night before. The youngest of the men, who had been with Jack at school, had attempted to rally him genially on his Puritanism; but the extreme impatience of his air, coupled with a single remark as to "a man's own business," had caused an uncomfortable pause. (Algy Lennox had made one or two bitter little mental notes on the apparent failure of religion to make a man behave decently.)

So every one looked at every one else first and then at Jack, in dead silence. Jack was observed to bite his nails.

"Damn it!" he said suddenly. "Truman, send one of the boys up for my gun. I shall shoot vilely; but it can't be helped. Oh! And tell him to bring a cap. I've come out without one."

Rapid and almost feverish conversation broke out upon the instant, as the boy vanished at a run through the park gate.

"Let's be getting on, anyhow," observed Jack. "We've a good half-mile across the fields. Yes, we may as well spread out. There may be outlying birds."

(2)

Lunch was to be eaten in the outhouse of a farm at one o'clock, and Mary and Sarah were to be present.

At a little after twelve they came together up through the coverts that had already been shot, guided by the sound of firing, and emerged at last upon one of the broad rides — trunk-roads, so to say — that cut this patch of

woodland into three or four large copses. Straight in front
of them, with his back turned towards them, facing the
tall, leafless trees beyond, stood the Colonel, his legs
about a yard apart, waiting. Mary whistled gently to
make their presence known, lifted her eyebrows in inter-
rogation; and, reassured by his nod, sat down on a stump.

It was a delicious day; and the two had not said anything particularly vital on their walk uphill. The world up
here looked very charming — the wall of wood before
them rose from the green darkness of rhododendrons and
undergrowth into a perspective of filigree against the radiant sky; and it was not too cold for enjoyment. All was
at present silent; the beat was a long one, and the men,
Mary supposed, some half-mile away. Neither yet had the
game begun to appear.

There is a curious meditative, almost hypnotic mood
into which one falls at such times. The objective faculties
are fixed intently upon external expectation, and the subjective powers work in a mill-like kind of way, serene and
redundant. There was a background always to Mary's
thoughts now — dating from the previous summer, but
established more firmly than ever now by the happenings
of the last month. The nuns, the past, the future, the con-
vent-needs, Jack — these recurred like figures in a
zoetrope, gently and not unpleasantly revolving.

Yet there was a sense of discomfort, for all that.

She began to wonder faintly what exactly Jack was doing. He had said at breakfast that perhaps he would start
with the shooters, and since he had not come back to the
house, she imagined he was with them still. At any rate,
she would see him presently at lunch. . . .

A movement from Sarah brought her to facts again; and
she looked up to see the Colonel bending this way and
that in an effort to see through the complicated undergrowth in front. A brown body whisked out like a streak
away to the right; there was a formidable bang, a mutter,
and, far away, she heard the patter pass away and cease.

Then she sat up to attend: she loved such days as these.
They were objective and distracting. . . .

The approach of driven game through a wood is as incalculable and as mysterious as the advent of spring. Cer-

tain things always happen: there are always a few ideal
shots to be had — swift birds coming straight and high
like projectiles; a cunning group taking advantage of
every shred of cover; a certain proportion of rabbits that
appear and vanish again like fast-bouncing cricket-balls;
hares that emerge suddenly, sit up and look, and then do
something unexpected; certain inexplicable pauses, and
equal inexplicable torrents of flying targets — all these
phenomena take place in the average drive. The skill
bears upon the discerning of which are which, and the
meeting of each in its proper manner. Mary was well entertained today. . . .

She had the pleasure of seeing half a dozen quite excellent shots — again and again she saw the streak overhead, smooth and curved, heard the bang, saw again the
curve broken, and after an ecstatic pause heard the mellow thump on the dry leaves. She counted seven rabbits
killed quite perfectly as they whizzed across the ride, and
two hares. Further, she had the pleasure, no less keen,
though different, of observing four times a clucking
pheasant pass unscathed, triumphant and hysterical, re-
prieved for one more summer among the woods.

It was always delightful to watch this Colonel. He was
not good enough to be at all infallible; he was not bad
enough to be disappointing. And he looked so capable, so
business-like, and so steady. He smiled so frankly when
all went well; he was so obviously indignant with something other than himself when it did not.

Again the thought of Jack recurred. . . . Ah! What a pity
it was. . . .

A beater or two emerged presently, and the Colonel
turned round.

"Done pretty well, Mrs. Weston," he said, "for the last
day. Ah! Lady Sarah."

He took off his cap with an air.

It is always suggestive to watch the two sexes on such
an occasion as this. The situation is so obviously a rever-
sion to a primitive type. The men lord it always; the
women submit femininely. The women are there on suf-
ferance. They stand for the squaws who should presently
gather and cook the game by the campfires of the tribe.

They are politely snubbed, gently mocked, and they play their own parts perfectly. The men at the best are tolerant and kind. Chivalry vanishes, or is retained only by a series of violent efforts. And the men, again, are so complacent. There is a sense abroad of duty done and hardships endured.

The Colonel was magnificent. He descended to small talk with a magnanimous air, and Sarah played up to him beautifully; while Mary, who though she loved it all, had never been quite sure that the business comprised the whole duty of man, observed them philosophically. But her philosophy received presently a small jerk.

She heard Jack and Mr. Truman in earnest conversation approaching round the corner, and an instant later saw them appear. From Mr. Truman's left hand depended a dead cock pheasant (head keepers will seldom condescend to carry a rabbit), and over Jack's shoulder was an undeniable gun.

He broke off in the middle of a sentence as he caught his wife's eye.

"Why, Jack," she said, "whose gun —?"

He dropped his eyes.

"Parkins didn't turn up," he said in a slightly high voice. "I'm taking his place."

He paused for an infinitesimal instant.

"I'm so glad," she said. "Sarah and I will stand behind you at the next drive. May we?"

The next drive was even more favorable to spectators.

The line of guns was drawn up in a grass field outside that which was the very pick of the woods, and Mary and Sarah, standing a yard or two behind Jack, had a view of the entire line from end to end. Algy Lennox was to their immediate left, and the rest, down to the stout Colonel, dwindled far away to the right.

Mary was conscious of such a mixture of emotions, and all of them so slight that she was quite unable to formulate any conclusion. She tried to tell herself how sensible Jack was and how pleased she ought to be, yet simultaneously she was aware of a faint resentment that was wholly without justification. It took shape in a resolution to watch Jack's shooting in serene silence, and to praise him very enthusiastically indeed for any good shots that he might make. Also she determined to exchange no glances with Sarah at all. It was all very unreasonable, and she knew it.

But Jack's shooting was so singularly bad that there was little opportunity for enthusiasm. He stood like a rigid statue, with a kind of determination apparent in the curve of his back, and he missed everything except one rabbit, which, looking at him with a hesitating air, he shot straight in the face at a distance of fifteen yards.

The performance began with a pheasant, rising slowly and perpendicularly out of the undergrowth in front. Two barrels full of shot rent the air about him, and he disappeared, crowing, back again into the wood. A hare followed, crossing smooth ground at a good steady pace, and grass sprang twice into the air in his rear. Then came a bustle of pheasants one after another, exploding like fireworks. The rabbit came next and died. Some more pheasants followed and lived, and so forth.

There was a dismal little pause as two beaters appeared and a retriever.

Mary drew a breath.

"You got that rabbit all right," she said.

Jack paused before answering.

"Please don't stand quite so close again," he said. "It bothers me."

(3)

"May I come in?" said Mary at a quarter to twelve that night, tapping at the door of Jack's bedroom.

It had been rather a dreary evening. Two or three satisfactory people had come in to dine; the three bachelor guests were quite pleasant people; yet the thing had hung fire. Jack himself did not seem altogether at his ease.

She had had no opportunity of speaking to him alone till now, and even now she had not the least idea what she wanted to say. Everything surely was as satisfactory as it could be. Jack had shot again, not in the least because he wished it, but simply to fill up a vacant place. And why shouldn't he shoot, anyhow? Was not this kind of reasonableness exactly what she had urged upon him so often?

Yet she was uneasy; she felt there was something to be said, though she did not know what. She sat up in her dressing-gown in her own room, told her maid not to wait, and had listened urgently for the closing of Jack's door beyond her own and the vibration of his footsteps.

"Oh yes; come in," he said.

He was standing straddle-legs, with his back to the fire, in his smoking-coat, and did not move as she came in.

"What is it?" he said.

"Oh, nothing," said Mary comfortably. "I must sit down a minute. Your fire's better than mine. Did you have a good day?"

"Oh, it was all right," he said. "I forget the bag; it was pretty decent."

Mary arranged herself delicately in a chintz armchair and spread her feet before her. Then she took a sudden determination.

"I was awfully glad you shot," she said. "What was the matter with Mr. Parkins?"

He did not answer her question.

"Are you?" he said abruptly.

Mary looked at him with a deliberately assumed wonder.

"Why, of course," she said. "Haven't I asked you again and again?"

Jack grunted.

"But, Jack —" She stopped.

"Yes?"

She took the fence at a rush.

"I mean I'm awfully glad that you did it just this once. I don't mean —"

He waited, silent.

Again she took it at a rush. She had no intention of saying this kind of thing when she came in just now, but somehow the pleasant intimacy of this room, the firelight, Jack in his smoking-coat and the rest of it — this suddenly broke down at least one or two of her barriers. She leaned forward a little, looking into the fire.

"I mean I'm glad you did it just this once. It was an entirely right and reasonable thing to do. But, you know, I don't feel as I did a couple of months ago, or even as I did when you didn't go after the hounds."

"How do you mean?" came in a carefully deliberate voice.

She glanced up and down again.

"Well, I've changed rather," she said. "I mean — oh! I may as well say it right out. I mean that I think there is a good deal more in your point of view than I thought at first."

There was a dead silence. She felt she had taken some plunge of unknown significance.

She had seen nothing at all in Jack's face as she had looked up just now. He had put his bedroom candle on the mantelpiece, and he himself was in shadow. She looked up again, half-nervous, and saw only that he was looking at her. Then he moved a little.

"Tell me," he said. "How do you mean?"

Mary leaned back once more, clasping her hands behind the loose billows of hair that her maid had just arranged. Somehow this seemed to her a critical conversation; she did not know why. She supposed it was because she was going to make a confidence, and she was not quite sure how much she was going to say, nor, in fact, how much she had already said. So she determined to be easy and natural.

"Well," she said, "it's rather hard to put into words. I — I think I should say that — that I rather agree now with what you said about being more — oh!" she wailed suddenly, "this is horribly priggish. I can't keep it — but, being more, well, serious. I'm — I'm not quite sure that I think shooting and — and cricket — and — and this sort of life is quite ideal after all. Oh, Jack, please don't think me a prig. I can't put it like you. . . . Oh, what would Sarah say?"

She was taking refuge in mock-misery, and knew it. But she thought it the only way.

Jack turned abruptly to the mantelpiece, took off it a small china bowl clasped by a small china boy, and began to examine it with an intent, connoisseur-like air. For an instant she thought him a little irresponsive. Then she decided it must be through an anxiety not to say too much; it was through depth of feeling that he was silent.

"Oh, you're beginning to think that too," he said slowly. "Do you mean —"

"No, no," cried Mary, suddenly frightened. "I don't in the least want to do what you suggested at first. I mean about monks and nuns. That's all perfectly impossible. But I mean in other ways. I think you've been perfectly splen- did, and I want to help you, really. And I think your shooting today was the best of all. It shows you're — you're finding your balance again. It seems to me that things will be easier now — on both sides. I don't in the least want you to make these things a regular business again, as you used. But I want you to be able to do them when you ought; and to be a good magistrate, and land- lord, and all the rest; and — and — well, say your prayers and be properly pious. I — I think it's splendid," she ended abruptly.

"I see," said Jack shortly.

"You know it's that convent," she said, "partly" (relieved now that she-had got her confession over); "they've done me a lot of good —"

"But I want to know," said Jack, putting the china bowl carefully back again, "I want to know exactly what you wish. Do you mean that you think —"

"I mean I'm going to be converted too," said Mary. "There! That's it, in a nutshell. I've been thinking a lot. Oh, I know that Sarah'll howl; but I shan't tell her. It's not her business. She can find out if she likes; I don't care. And it seems to me that we can just go on living here as before, only — only be pious too. It seems to me that your ideas are perfectly splendid; the convent and everything. I can't imagine why we shouldn't, both of us, be really good Catholics, and yet go on here. (She was beginning to talk rather feverishly, and was aware of it.) I don't believe for an instant that we ought to give it all up and be some- thing else. And I wanted to tell you that. I don't in the least agree with the ideas you had at first, you know, and I never shall. I think that was real fanaticism, you know — all that about you and me going off to the convents, or living in a gamekeeper's cottage. You and I aren't made for that, are we? Oh, I'm sure you see that now. But I wanted to tell you that I do agree with the way you're doing it now — and — and that I won't be tiresome. Do you see, Jack?"

Again there was a moment's silence.

Mary felt her excitement pause for a moment, like a wave before it breaks. The impulse had come upon her so suddenly that it seemed like an inspiration But she was driven too by another motive which she refused to recognize.

The point was, how would Jack take it? She waited with an extraordinary expectancy for his answer. It seemed to her as if some kind of sentence was to be pronounced. Jack's face was still in shadow; and in that moment of time it appeared that tremendous issues were being decided, utterly disproportionate to the situation as she had stated it. Again, she knew, but refused to recognize what those issues were.

Then the tension broke; and when Mary went to her room five minutes later, she knew, with a sinking at her heart, that judgment had been deferred.

All Jack had done was to kneel suddenly forward and kiss her.

"Thank you, my dear," he had said — no more than that. Then he stood up, nodded goodnight, and turned away.

So Mary sat some half-hour more before her fire, motionless.

Chapter IX

(1)

Lady Carberry was not feeling very well. In a word, it was digestive. . . . But such troubles as these may mean a very great deal after a certain age and to a certain constitution; and little Dr. Basing recommended that her drive should be given up for the present and that she should remain in the house for a week or two.

So the little ceremonial ceased. The fat horses waxed slightly fatter; the aged lodge-keeper, whose duty it was to be standing by the gate bare-headed with a bent back at twenty minutes to three, snoozed uninterruptedly in his chair instead; the coachman remained half an hour longer in the steward's room after dinner; and when three days further had elapsed, Miss Fakenham was asked to come down.

It all fell pretty heavily upon Sarah, whose duty it became to hang about and do nothing in particular. She took second place, definitely and clearly, to her ladyship's maid, and was instructed to wait upon that lady for orders. Miss Fakenham's arrival, therefore, was something of a relief.

But it was a very dreary time: the slender stream of guests dried up; it was impossible to accept invitations; and Sarah was reduced to long and lonely rides — not too long, as her mother might want her — and to seeing what she could of Mary at odd times.

Of course Mary let out fairly soon by hints and implications what was in the air, and the dreariness increased even further for her friend. It seemed to her exceedingly hard that this most natural and easy-going friend should take a turn of this kind. They had something resembling a small tiff one day just before Easter. They seemed, said Sarah, to be drifting apart.

"I can't understand," said Sarah, "why you need make such a fuss. It seems to me that you were much nicer before."

Mary paused with her hand on the garden gate. She had walked up in the afternoon to inquire after Lady Carberry, and Sarah had walked down with her as far as the gate to the short cut across the park.

"I don't think that's the point," she said.

"It is for me," said Sarah. "Besides —"

"Well?"

"It seems to me it's the real point for everyone. Surely religion can't do anything better than make people friendly and natural and all the rest.

There's this world for certain; and as regards the other —"

"Yes," said Mary.

"Well, as regards the next world, no one knows anything for certain."

"Catholics do," said Mary, quick and sharp.

"So you say."

Sarah was certainly a little cross today. She had had a trying morning of it. The doctor had come as usual, and been rather gloomy: he had refused to give any kind of assurance as to when the old lady would be about again. And she herself had been sent for twice to be found fault with. Mary, then, seemed to her the last straw.

"You're a little fractious," said the girl, smiling.

Sarah made a small impatient sound.

"I hate all that sort of helpful cheerfulness," she said.

Mary let the gate swing to between them, and her face darkened ever so slightly.

"All right," she said. "Goodbye."

"Goodbye," said Sarah, with sudden dignity.

It was all very tiresome and troublesome, thought Sarah, as she went back to the house. She knew perfectly well she had behaved rather badly; but she preferred to say that Mary had. Then, two days later, came a sudden event that drove these things away.

She had been up to see her mother about twelve o'clock, and found her even more severe than usual. The beef-tea had not been properly prepared, and it was entirely Sarah's fault for not overlooking the servants more care-

fully. What, it was asked, would she herself do when she
had a house of her own, if she could not even keep
well-trained servants up to the mark? Would it not be better if Miss Fakenham took over the entire charge of the
house for the present? And so forth. The worst of all was
that it was entirely impossible to snap back. More, the old
lady lay in awful dignity, crowned with a black lace
shawl, her ruddy face pinched and fallen, with disagree-
able-looking pouches beneath the eyes. The whole room
too suggested a pathetic imitation of a presence-chamber:
the large four-posted mahogany bed, the satinwood toi-
lette table decked with silver objects, the faint smell of
furs, dresses, eau-de-cologne, the deep carpet, the
bath-rug, the little row of miniatures, the solemn chintz
furniture, all somehow combined to suggest a great personage fallen low, surrounded by possessions which, with
digestive troubles, she could not properly enjoy.

"You should be more thoughtful, my dear," observed her
mother when the daughter had been sufficiently crushed.
"When your poor father died I never left him night or
day."

"But, Mother, you're not so ill as all that!"

"We never know," said the old lady, who knew perfectly
well that she was going to recover, and had told Dr. Basing with some warmth that very morning that she would
not be treated like a helpless invalid. "We never know. I
only know that you should be more thoughtful. The
beef-tea was most tasteless this morning; I could scarcely
manage more than a spoonful or two. . . . So just remember, my dear, in future."

"I'm very sorry, Mother; but really, the beef tea —"

"Yes, my dear; I do not expect you to prepare it. That
would be too much to ask. But it's the general tone of the
house that shows itself in little things like that. If the
servants had been kept up to their work this would not
have happened. Now go and enjoy yourself, my dear. A
good brisk walk before lunch would do you good. Just give
me that prayerbook, and the miniature of your poor father, before you go. I like to have them beside me. . . . And
tell Linton to come to me immediately. And please, my
dear, see that the baize door is kept closed at the top of

the stairs. I think that is not too much to ask under the circumstances."

Sarah looked at her, torn between compassion and resentment. It was this kind of thing all day long.

Certainly she looked ill this morning; her ringless old hands jerked gently and peevishly on the silk rug that lay over her; and her face was lined in iron-looking folds. The scorned beef-tea stood in a small white fluted covered vessel on the pedestal by the bedside; and two toast crumbs, one on the very end of the old lady's nose, made her dignity the more pathetic.

Sarah made suitably filial remarks and went downstairs.

The luncheon table too increased her sense of dreariness. It was so exact in its appointments, each of which was dictated by irrevocable laws. The butler was so immutable, the food so exceedingly well cooked. And yet the chair of the mistress of all was pushed back against the wall, her place at the head of the table, so sacred was it, rested vacant, and the roast lamb lay instead before Sarah's own seat in the middle of the long side facing the windows. Neither was Miss Fakenham helpful: she sat subdued and gloomy opposite Sarah, answered all her remarks correctly and volunteered none of her own.

It was as the sweets were being actually placed upon the table that the blow fell. A bell was heard to ring; the butler nodded swiftly and silently to the footman, who vanished. The butler, when all was set, vanished also; and two minutes later reappeared, slightly breathless.

"Her ladyship is taken suddenly ill, my lady. Her ladyship's maid —"

Then the two rose and fled.

(2)

Mary first heard the news from Dr. Basing himself in the afternoon, and it fell on her with that sense of bewilderment which such news, regarding one whom one rather dislikes, always bears with it.

"Dead! You don't mean it!"

The doctor quieted his horse and leaned over the rail a little nearer. It was just outside the park gates.

"Indeed, yes," he said; "it was what I feared. The heart was weak. It was all over by five minutes after I got there."

Mary turned her pony's head on the instant and was off.

The house was in the same sort of breathless condition, suggesting without manifesting disorder, in which, as in a bad dream, she remembered her own house hardly more than seven months ago. It looked like a familiar face in a swoon. In the hall, down which she had so often seen Lady Carberry proceeding as on some high day, were small evidences, scarcely noticeable, yet taken together, significant of a real disorganization. A bright red and black cricketing cap, plainly the property of a footman, lay in the midst of the majolica plate that held the calling cards. (The butler secreted it deftly as he came to the door). An umbrella lay all across the floor, and a white fluted covered vessel stood on the seat of a polished wooden chair. Whether it was these things, or her own knowledge, or whether conceivably some actual shadow of emptiness cast from some plane of which we know nothing — at least there was desolation here, and a certain horror of darkness.

She went swiftly through into the morning room, a cave of firelight and dying daylight stealing through unshuttered windows, and there started up a figure hidden in a deep chair that threw itself, wild-eyed, into her arms. . . .

"And the worst of it all," moaned Sarah presently, "is that she didn't know me. And the last thing I really saw of her was when she was cross with me. Oh, my dear, does she understand now, do you think?"

Mary tightened her arms round her friend.

"My darling, of course it's all right. Don't think of it like that."

"Yes, yes; but what does she think of it all now? Tell me. You Catholics say you know."

Mary hesitated. Was purgatory assimilable by Sarah just now? And yet, if ever, purgatory were obviously necessary! . . . She hesitated.

"The Rector's been up here; he's been telling me about heaven and all that; but — but, Mary dear, I — I can't think of Mother. . . like that. Do you really think —?"

Her voice faltered and stopped.

Then Mary made an attempt. Truly she did her best; she insisted on happiness for all those who followed the light they had; she toned down certain points, which need not be discussed; she said that she quite agreed that heaven and palms and harps were a little difficult just at present, considered as an environment for Lady Carberry; she hinted gently.

"And what I'm going to do next, goodness knows," moaned Sarah.

Mary's trickle of consolation dried up on the instant. There was really no need for consolation.

An hour later she came out again. Oh yes, she had been upstairs and seen the satinwood dressing table, and the silver ornaments, and the mahogany bed, and that which lay on it, august and terrible. A nurse sat there by the bed. Sarah kneeled by her. Three candles were burning, and a little fire, before which hung a sheet or two, burned on the hearth. Miss Fakenham, Mary remembered afterwards, was somewhere in the room — a mourning shadow.

Sarah came down again with her, through the house so deathly still, clung to her again, and listened without hearing to the last words that Mary pumped up for her with intolerable effort.

Yet as the girl drove away again into the darkness, in spite of what she had seen and the sorrow of her friend, she was thinking of neither of these things, but of that interior conflict of her own which once more surged within her.

(3)

Jim was lying in bed in a room in his aunt's house in London when he heard the news by the first post.

It was a room so entirely characteristic of its inhabitant that it is really worth a description. First, it was papered and painted throughout in creamy white, with the exception of a light green frieze of the exact tint of apple leaves in sunlight, which color was repeated in the short silk window curtains, furniture coverings, and carpet. All the furniture was of mahogany, brought to a high pitch of polish (it was of some period or other, but I entirely forget which, if I ever knew); it had spindle legs and a particular kind of curve in its lines. The bed too was of mahogany, very delicate and exquisite, with a beautiful little inlay in the curved bed-head. There was not a great deal of furniture; the room had an empty aspect; but it was a very expensive emptiness.

Upon a discreet-looking upright couch at the foot of the bed lay Jim's clothes, ready for assumption. (His man had called him half an hour before, set out his bath-towel, dressing-gown, and placed a little early-morning tea-set of pink china beside his bed.) His clothes, even empty of Jim, were a caress to the eyes, so perfect were they; and by their side lay a pair of his famous clocked socks with suspenders attached.

But the bed itself and its occupant formed the climax, so white were the sheets, so delicate the silk bedspread turned back over the foot, so beautiful the pajamas, and so quiet the owner of all.

(I love Jim — as I have said before — at least I love mentally, to walk round him, and look at him, and paw him with reverential fingers. He is so perfectly finished, so completely true to type, so utterly contented.)

Further, I forgot to mention, on the table by his bed lay a small vellum-covered book of French poems, a silver cigarette case, and a matchbox that struck a light almost entirely unaided. And on the spindle-legged table beyond the couch rested four more books — no more — in a little stand. He was lying very quiet and thinking very hard; and, if the truth were known, I expect he was experiencing the supreme struggle of his life. He was wondering whether he would go to the funeral or not — no more. It would take place in three days, he was informed by his aunt's letter, that still lay open on the bed; and he was to send a wire immediately. So his bath cooled rapidly in the next room while he fought it out.

It was a struggle, because he chose to make it the symbol of a conflict in which he had long been engaged. The point was: was he to marry Sarah or not?

The alternatives lay before him, ranged down to their minutest details. Jim was essentially a bachelor; persons of his temperament always are; they are gloriously sufficient to themselves; their atmosphere is so individual and personal a thing that the risk of an alien intrusion is a danger seldom faced. Who could tell, for instance, whether Sarah's taste would rise to all that was represented by this white, apple-green, and mahogany? And if not. . . .

On the other hand, there was a great deal to be said for it. An individualistic and artistic bachelor is apt, when he reaches a certain age, to be treated even too much as an individual and too little as a social personage. He ceases to be able to shoot or play billiards, or even fish as well as he would like; and philosophical conversation cannot please forever. But the husband of Lady Sarah must always be taken into consideration. There would be two houses at once, and a third to follow on his aunt's death, besides quite a decent income. He need no longer stop in his Civil Service: he might even begin to add once more to his first editions. And, after all, Sarah was not a bad sort, all things considered, and might be capable of a good deal of improvement.

So Jim lay and considered it, with his sleek head black against the linen and his eyes closed.

Lady Carberry's death he did not even pretend to regret, except for the fact that it brought things to a point. He would no longer be able to play about down there. Sarah, undoubtedly, would drift off into other circles presently, and might — it was really quite conceivable, after all — she might find someone even more to her taste than Jim. It was now or never. . . .

A small, bulgy, china clock on the mantelpiece beat nine in the tones of a distant cathedral. Jim opened his eyes and touched the bell by his bedside.

"Oh, just turn on some more hot water," he said when the man came. "I shall be down in half an hour; and there'll be a wire to send as soon as I come down."

So the great decision was taken; and Jim considered it all over again under innumerable aspects as he ate a kidney and a half and drank some coffee before setting out for Whitehall. (The kidney was slightly dry, he noticed; he would speak about it. No, on the whole, he wouldn't; it was his own fault for being late; and the coffee was so superlatively excellent that it really made up for the other.)

Ten minutes later, again, he was in the hall, still thoughtful, slipping his arms into the coat respectfully held up by Charles his man.

"No, I'll take the umbrella," he said. "I think it might rain. No cab; I'll walk part of the way anyhow. The wire went all right?"

"Yessir."

Then he went out and turned briskly up the pavement to the left.

So the mysteries of Life and Death are wrought and interwoven.

(4)

I think, too, it is worthwhile to describe the funeral. No less than two columns of the county paper were occupied in its chronicle, recording the list of mourners, the special train from town, the mob of carriages and cars at the churchyard gate. Further, the churchyard itself figured at length, the exquisite symbolism of the sun that came out, the white surplice of the venerable Rector, the extraordinary beauty of the singing of the hymns "For all the saints" and "Now the laborer's task is over."

Lady Sarah's distinguished grief-stricken figure made its appearance four times in the two columns; and a word of tribute was paid to the broad-mindedness of Mr. and Mrs. Weston, and especially the delicate sympathy of the latter, who, for the first time since they took up their residence at Manningham, entered the parish church. It was remarked also that Mr. James Fakenham supported his aunt on this melancholy occasion, and drove back with the mourners to the house of sorrow.

To Mary the experience was one of almost unrelieved horror.

She arrived with Jack ten minutes before the service began, and, sitting in the church in the seat assigned to her, watched through the low, clear glass window that which the newspaper described as the "funeral *cortege*" (without the accent).

For the first time in her life she saw a plumed hearse actually in existence, and stared with almost superstitious terror on the twelve black erections, which with their long fringes resembled so many long-haired faceless heads nodding in mute sorrow. She saw too the great coffin, silver-plated, clamped and bound, slide out from its end on to the shoulders of six men in black frock-coats, and watched its progress up the path, with the Rector in front, reading aloud words which she could not hear, while his surplice blew open from the neck. Then came the mourners and the crowd.

Presently when the church was filled — I omitted to say that Chopin's funeral march was being played meanwhile by the village schoolmistress — the organ boomed out again into a hymn, studied closely by Mary, recounting the glories of God's saints and the song of Alleluia which is theirs.

She reached out a hand and took Sarah's, who stood next to her — herself speechless. Death, it seemed to her, was terrible enough without this kind of unreality; yet Sarah smiled at her, as if comforted through her heavy veil. Jim, Mary noticed, stood beyond Miss Fakenham next the aisle, with a respectfully bowed head.

So the affair went on. Once or twice she stared out again at the plumed heads that waited twenty yards away down the path, then again at the Rector reading, with that scholarly expression for which he was renowned in the district, an enormous portion of Scripture containing a few passages of amazing beauty and a good deal that was completely unintelligible to modern ears: "There is one glory of the stars . . . and another of the moon. . . . One kind of flesh . . . another kind of flesh"; and then, ever and again, at the monstrous shape before the chancel steps, loaded, piled, and heaped with white flowers as a symbol of innocence and simplicity.

And it was the body of Lady Carberry, she reflected, that rested there.

The second hymn at the graveside crowned her abhorrence. It began, certainly with sufficient beauty of expression, by announcing that "the laborer's task was o'er," that "the battle day was past," and that "the voyager lands at last upon the farther shore." It concluded, as in every verse, with a word upon the "servant" of God sleeping in Him.

Oh yes, the hymn was a beautiful one, bringing tears to the eyes. (Sarah broke down and sobbed halfway through.) It was sung reverently and softly; and the sun came out, as recorded by the *Gazette*, and shone from curtaining western clouds. And the Rector uttered the last words with an almost perfect intonation; and yet, and yet.

Well, in a sentence, what was there in common between all this tenderness and confidence and the life of the old woman whose body lay in the midst?

Mary struggled against the thought — it was horrible to think such things — yet, was it not an indisputable fact that the life that had ended had been one of utter and complete selfishness? She had been hard upon all who knew her; she had sinned by every sin of pride and complacency, and even the smaller kinds of tyranny, that it was possible to imagine; she had spoiled, so far as it was possible for her to spoil, the life of this poor girl beside her, who sobbed and sobbed at the thought that their last words had been words of reproach and fault-finding, though not even on her side — this poor girl, who, in the midst of her agony, had had time to wonder what was going to become of herself. Certainly the old woman had lived a conventionally good life; she had outraged no proprieties, had brought herself within the reach of no human or social law; yet if there were a divine law of love anywhere in the universe, her life had been but one defiance of it from beginning to end. She had no friends; she had only unreal shadows of herself. There was not one soul in the universe who in a week's time would really regret her, or one life that would be the poorer for her loss. This passionate crying of the girl, these discreet eye wipings of Miss Fakenham and two other middle-aged ladies — these were at the most purely symptoms of nervous emotionalism. In a month from now Sarah would be happier and freer and more effective than ever in her life before; and as for this grave concern on the faces of the Lord Lieutenant of the county, the magistrates, a dozen farmers — tenants, of course — Jim Fakenham, and the rest of the mob — this was worth exactly as much as, considered morally, as the black coats and gloves that they wore upon their bodies.

And it was this woman who was the laborer and soldier and traveler of God, who had won her reward; and it was from the lips of the soul that had inhabited that body that the eternal Alleluia was presumed to be pealing. Was there not to be one cry for mercy, one confession of failure and misery, one utterance of faith and hope in a compassion utterly undeserved and forfeited? . . .

"The grace of our Lord Jesus Christ, and the love of God, and the fellowship of the Holy Ghost be with us all evermore," said the Rector comfortably. And the choir sang Stainer's *Amen*.

Husband and wife drove in silence through the park gate. Mary had promised Sarah to come up a little later when the mourning guests had gone.

Then Jack turned to her in the brougham.

"My dear," he said, "don't look so overcome."

Mary said nothing.

"Well, she was a good old thing, I suppose," he said.

Mary assented with a nod.

"And I suppose Sarah'll go and live with an aunt or something," he went on. "She's well enough off, anyhow. There was Jim Fakenham there; did you see him?"

Mary sighed.

"Oh, Jack!" she said, "it really was awful, though. That hearse, those hymns . . . everything. That's what's called a bright funeral."

Jack made a small demurring sound. (He looked extraordinarily odd, thought Mary, in black gloves and trousers.)

"Yes," he said, "I suppose so. But I don't see why they shouldn't. They don't pray for the dead, you see, so I don't see why they shouldn't put the best construction —"

"Oh, Jack! you don't believe that for one instant."

Jack looked out of the window.

Even in their own delightful drawing room Jack's black suit cast a certain dreariness. They had tea instantly, but everything was a little sepulchral, for all that. Once again

Jack remarked upon Mary's manner; and this time she seemed to resent it a little.

"Oh, don't bother, my dear!" she said. "Sarah's on my mind, rather, too."

"Too?" questioned Jack.

"As well as Lady Carberry," said Mary deliberately.

She rose and went to the window, leaving her cup half-drunk. The sun had set a few minutes before beyond the western slopes, and the air was of that dying luminosity that resembles a hope that is going downhill — exquisite, tender, and melancholy. The clouds had cleared yet more before sunset, and there shone, high up, coming and going, seen as within folded-back curtains, a single star like a crumb of glass. Beneath the slopes lay, dull and menacing, dark ash-colored, darkening as she looked. A little wind shook the dwarf-ivy at the window and sank again. It seemed to Mary as if everything waited for some solution — some key-word to set all in order. Were things generally really so futile and meaningless as they appeared. Or was there, after all, an answer — a missing letter that would make sense out of nonsense? . . . And if so, was it what she suspected? . . .

Mary turned round abruptly.

"Where are you going?" asked Jack, lowering his cup.

"I'm going up to church for a bit," said Mary and went out.

Chapter X

(1)

It was Miss Groves, lady's maid to Mrs. Weston, who first noticed that the mistress's health was not all that it should be. She was a discreet personage of forty years of age, and had nursed Mary as a child; so not one word was breathed except to Mrs. Reinher, the housekeeper, who had fulfilled the same duties towards Jack. Yet what she had to say amounted to little enough. Mrs. Weston, it seemed, was usually now to be found lying awake in the mornings; she continually dismissed her at nights comparatively early, presumably with the intention of sitting up; she was beginning to be a little dark under the eyes; she fell into silences when her hair was being put up; she did not always drink her early cup of tea. It was not alarming; but the facts were noted.

Other persons also noticed small silence, brooding, and, if it must be confessed, slight irritability. It is a distressing fact that the most august griefs produce such symptoms.

At the convent too it was noticed, though not one word was uttered on the point, that the charming Mrs. Weston did not come to see the nuns any more. She was in the chapel, certainly, at Mass every morning; she was occasionally discerned there by the rustle of her dress at odd times during the day; but the parlor knew her no more. She was as generous as ever; bundles of spring vegetables appeared in embarrassing profusion; even a message or two was left that if anything were needed, news was to be sent down immediately: one of the farm light carts was required to call three times a week for instructions. But Mary did not appear.

Sarah's contribution to the mass of evidence is inconsiderable; for Sarah had gone to an aunt, as Jack had foretold, and the two together to Switzerland as June began. There was an impression too abroad, among Sarah's friends, that Mr. James Fakenham's holidays this year

were falling unusually early, and that he mentioned more
than once the delightful opportunities for recuperation
offered abroad at a time when hotels were comparatively
empty, in such places as the Tyrol or even Switzerland
itself.

It was on a delicious day about halfway through June
that Madeline, one of the nondescript girls in caps and
black dresses already mentioned who seem to frequent
convent kitchens, was looking out of one of the few windows on the kitchen side of the house that commanded
any view whatever of the outside world. The room was on
the first floor, and she could look out over the yew hedge
that rose immediately below her window straight down a
ride that led on level ground into the heart of the wood.
There were a few minutes more before she would be
wanted in the kitchen; so here she stood and stared, notic-
ing the cool green shadow under the tall trees that met
overhead, the flecks of sunlight and the dusty-looking atmosphere in which whirled ceaselessly myriads of tiny
summer afternoon insects. It was not an exceedingly wide
view, since the lower half of the window was filled with
frosted glass, and it was all that she could do, standing at
her full height, to raise her eyes over the central win-
dow-bar. She was therefore entirely invisible to anyone
approaching from without.

As she was on the very point of turning away, she noticed a white figure, with something scarlet moving about
it, coming extremely slowly up the ride she was watching.
A rabbit that a moment before had suddenly sat up with
cocked ears in the middle distance dropped and vanished;
and a minute later the girl could see who it was that was
coming.

To those who live in convents a comer from the outside
world is always slightly interesting; and the sight of Mrs.
Weston set in motion in the girl's mind a train of thought
not indeed exactly envious, but of a faintly tantalizing
nature. She herself proposed some day to enter the convent as a lay sister; it was the obvious thing to do. She
had been caught somehow in its train; she had been swept
off with it to England; there was nothing else she particularly wanted to do. But she was still aware of external

interests; and it struck her now as she looked vaguely out at the girl, not ten years older than herself, who came along so leisurely under her red sunshade, bare-headed, in her white dress, that it must be exceedingly pleasant to be the mistress of a large domain, to walk where the mood calls, at four o'clock in the afternoon, to have a quantity of servants, and to have no duties at all which cannot be deputed to somebody else.

The figure came along very slowly, straight towards where a gate in the hedge gave entrance to the path that, straight forward, led to the transept door, and curving to the right round to the lodge gate and the front of the convent. Madeline supposed that she was coming to pay a visit to the church, but watched as a child watches, purely, so to speak, for the academic interest of the thing, to see which path she would take.

The latch of the gate seemed a little difficult, and the sunshade, that up to now had hidden the woman's face, suddenly slipped back as she put her hands to it. Madeline still watched, and then, in a moment, was startled by the white pallor of which she caught sight. Was that look, she wondered, merely one of impatience with the latch?

The gate opened and closed; and Mary stood there for an instant hesitating. Her face looked out again, her eyes seemed to meet Madeline's own; and the girl started back, partly from a sense of being caught watching, partly from that look of misery that was now so unmistakable. When she peeped again she was only just in time to see Mary's dress vanishing round the corner in the direction of the lodge.

Madeline ran downstairs, through the cloister at a more discreet pace, and came towards the inner passage leading to the gate as the bell overhead jangled once.

"Can I see the Reverend Mother?" asked Mary, without a word or smile of greeting. Then without waiting for an answer, she turned aside into the parlor.

(2)

The Prioress, looking presently through the two gratings, and peering as well as she could at her visitor's face, noticed too that something was wrong.

It was a look of extraordinary weariness that she saw there. During the first sentence or two of ordinary greeting there arose upon the eyes and mouth the conventionally appropriate expression, but it faded again in a moment, leaving the eyes heavy and almost somber, the corners of the mouth turned down, and that same deadly tiredness she had seen upon her first entrance.

"You have come to see us again, then, Madam; and Monsieur your husband — ?"

"Jack's away for two or three days," said Mary dully. "He comes back tonight."

"And you are lonely? I am not surprised; when so charming a —"

Mary jerked slightly with an impatient movement, and the nun broke off.

Then there fell a silence.

(It is not very easy at first to exchange confidences through two gratings. It is a little like making love on a telephone. There is a sense of firing a gun and waiting for an indication that it has reached its mark. But it has, too, its advantages.)

The Prioress broke the silence, leaning a little nearer.

"So you have come to see the poor nuns again, Madam?"

"I have come to see you, Mother," came the dull voice again.

"You are in trouble, Madam?" came back after a pause.

Mary bowed her head.

"I am in bitter trouble," she said.

The Prioress shifted her position once more.

"Tell me, my child," she said softly.

"I — I don't think I can."

"Oh, my child, yes. It eases the soul. Tell me simply and quickly."

Mary looked up at the head bent towards her and caught, or thought she caught, the glimmer of kind eyes through the veil.

Then the floodgates opened. Mary talked rapidly, jerkily, emphatically, her voice rising as she spoke, and the Prioress listened, with scarcely a word of answer.

"I must tell you, but I am a coward, a deadly coward. I — I hesitated even at the gate just now. I never meant to come; but I can't bear it; I can't bear it; it's killing me. Well, it's a long story. It's gone on for nearly a year — since Jack's illness. I've told you about that. You remember?"

"I remember."

"Well, that was the beginning, at least practically. You remember, Jack was dying. The doctors were there and Sarah. I prayed. Oh yes; but it was no good; I knew it wasn't; it never is."

"Well, then Jack died. I saw him die before my eyes, and the doctors told me so. Then Sarah tried to take me away, and I wouldn't go. I screamed, I think. I wouldn't let myself believe it."

The Prioress leaned forward again, and her voice came clear and almost sharp.

"My child, be tranquil. You must tell me tranquilly."

Mary raised her terrified eyes and let them fall again slowly.

"I will, Mother," she said. "Thank you."

She drew a long breath to steady herself, unclasped her hands, and clasped them again. Then she went on, without the ring of hysteria in her voice. It was more as if she were repeating a lesson.

"Well, Sarah left the room after that, to see the doctors. I told her she must leave me for two minutes with Jack. I knew quite well what I wanted to do. It was quite deliberate; it was that that has made it all so bad. I told Father Banting that, again and again; but he wouldn't believe me. He said it was not a deliberate vow, and that I had no time for consideration."

"But, Mother, you know how one can be deliberate at a time like that, even in a second or two; and I had at least three or four minutes."

"What did you do, my child?"

"Well, I looked at Jack lying there, and I simply could not bear it. I didn't think Jack had died exactly in mortal sin. Oh, I don't know what I thought. He had received conditional absolution; but I knew his life hadn't been anything particular. But that wasn't the only thing: I wanted him alive again. It wasn't only that I wanted him with me, but I couldn't bear to think of him as dead. Oh, Mother, death is so ghastly."

"Tranquilly, my child."

Mary shivered a little and settled herself again. "Well, when Sarah had gone, I knelt down by Jack and looked at him. They had put a crucifix in his hands. . . . Then I — then I —"

"Yes, my child; be tranquil." . . .

Mary was silent a moment.

"It's hard to put it into words, Mother. I didn't use any words — at least, out loud; but I meant it, and expressed it, inside, you know, as deliberately as I possibly could. . . . It was this: I said to God, absolutely knowing and meaning what I said, that if Jack could only be alive again, I'd offer myself entirely to Him forever, that I wouldn't shrink from anything, that I'd do anything He wished — I meant, of course, in big things —"

"Did you have any idea of what you meant by that?"

Mary bowed her head.

"Yes, Mother," she said in a tiny voice.

"Tell me, my child." . . .

There was dead silence.

"Tell me, my child. . . . No, tranquilly." . . .

Mary, who once more had looked up with a quick movement, looked down again. She began mechanically, yet with an appearance of extreme care, to twist her rings slowly round and round.

"I knew nothing about the Religious Life, Mother — about the rules about a husband and wife, and so on. But the thought of the Religious Life came quite clearly into my mind. I didn't understand in the least how or where, or anything like that; but I included it in my mind, though I loathed the thought of it. And I included it; I meant I would do it, if I could, and if God asked it of me. Of course I thought it really impossible."

The Prioress leaned back slowly.

"Yes, my child; continue."

"Well, I did that — I did it twice; with my eyes tight shut and my hands on the bed. It was all perfectly deliberate; and I was quite quiet, and then —"

"Yes?"

Mary began to shake. The Prioress's hand rose with a kind of soothing, commanding gesture.

"Then I opened my eyes," said Mary very low indeed, "and I heard something; then I saw Jack opening his eyes; and the crucifix slipped out of his hands — his fingers. . . . Then he said something. . . . I screamed." . . .

"That is enough, my child. Be quite silent a moment."

Mary looked up again. Her lips, her eyelids, her whole head shook so violently that she could scarcely see. She steadied her chin on her hand, her elbow on the ledge, and she saw for a moment, plainly enough, the veiled, quiet old face opposite, with closed eyes. Then the eyes opened, and Mary dropped her own.

"Continue, my child — quite slowly."

Mary drew a long breath. The worst was over, and the rest comparatively simple.

"Well, ever since then I've been fighting against it all. I tried to make the doctors say that Jack wasn't really dead at all, and of course they said it, and that satisfied me in a sort of way — at least I made it satisfy me."

"I comprehend perfectly."

"Then the awful thing happened." (Mary's voice faltered slightly.) "Jack proposed the very thing itself — I never told you that, Mother — Then he said *the very thing* — that we should both enter Religion."

"Yes?"

"I said I wouldn't." (He had found out all about it from books and priests.) "I entirely refused. I said all the — the *sensible* things. You know. . . . I said them to myself, and to Jack, and to Sarah, over and over again. I persuaded myself; at least I half-persuaded —"

"But yes; I comprehend perfectly."

"Well, I wasn't happy; I was wretched. I — I caught at things — anything to salve my conscience. The convent was the first thing. (You know I was against that at first? Well, I was.) And then I caught at it; I made myself think it would do for the — for the sacrifice of myself. I did all I could for it; and all the while, right down, I knew it wouldn't do; though I don't think all the time I knew that I knew." (The Prioress nodded gently without interrupting.) "And then you came; and I thought that the extra

things might make the difference — the getting up earlier; Father Banting being about always — Oh, that was
before; but it doesn't matter. And then you came —"

"Yes, my child."

Mary gripped herself again with an effort.

"Then you came — and you showed me the dead body —
you know — the sister." (The Prioress raised her old eyes
steadily to the girl's an instant.) "Yes — well, that was
another blow; I don't know why, but it showed me it
wouldn't do — that I was shamming — playing fool. And
then I talked to Sister Teresa. It was horrible. . . . She
made me understand perfectly, in just a sentence or two.
It came down on me like — like a gas, or a hand; and I
fought it and got free. That was why I never dared to see
Sister Teresa again. I — I couldn't bear myself —

"Well, then I began to think about Jack —"

"Yes?"

"Well, that distracted me a little. I began to pretend to
myself that really and truly it was my duty to keep Jack
within bounds — that — that he would never make a
monk, that he was a fanatic — and that therefore it was
no good my being a nun. (Oh yes; I had it clear enough by
then!) And then Jack went out shooting one day, after he
hadn't for ages, and I made that an excuse. I said to myself that that was a sign, so I backed him up. I pretended
that I knew his vocation better than he did. I told him
that he must be just a good Catholic. I — I hindered him
as much as I could. I had already refused, in spite of everything, to release him; and I made it worse by trying to
cheat him. And all the while I knew perfectly well that he
ought to be a monk. No, he has said nothing; not a word.
He promised he wouldn't; but — but I'm ruining him, and
I'm cheating myself; at least I — I — almost succeeded in
cheating. I think I should have . . . but then — then Lady
Carberry died. Oh, it was one thing after another; one
thing after another . . . like — like blows of a hammer.
Not one of them alone would have done it. Some of them
were just little taps. Oh, there were hundreds more, I've
almost forgotten: little sentences in books — a bird flying
in a particular way — anything would do.

"Yes. . . . I know it sounds silly; but Lady Carberry's death woke me up again. I don't know why. . . . Somehow it made death frightfully real. . . . Yes: I know she was very old; but that didn't matter. She wasn't the sort of person that dies — there was a sort of eternity about her. . . . And the funeral — all about the saints and the laborers. . . . Oh, I can't explain, Mother — it's endless. But it woke me up again. . . .

"And then . . ."

There was a pause.

"Yes, Madam?"

"Well, then I set myself down to kill the thing. Sarah was away — I had plenty of time. I used to go and try to hypnotize myself — yes, before the Tabernacle — into believing it was all nonsense. . . . I even began to play with my faith — to wish I wasn't a Catholic. Oh, Mother —"

"Yes, my child?"

"And I can't bear it — I can't bear it."

"There's been no sudden event since then, my child, to make you —"

"No, Mother. No; no; it's just everything; and — and —"

There was a sudden break in the girl's voice, and in an instant she was down, her head on her hands, her hands on the ledge, sobbing as if her heart would break.

(3)

"Now listen to me carefully, my child," went on the Prioress five minutes later. "You are quiet now? You can attend to me? Eh well, I shall make you a little discourse.

"You have done that which is very common in the world. You have attempted to silence the voice of our Lord speaking in the heart. You have played with grace — ah, I know it very well. It is the temptation of all who know anything of the inner life. It is their only temptation after a while. And you have tried to give to our Lord other things — things which He did not ask of you, to serve in place of that which He did ask of you. And in effect you have been unhappy.

"I do not think you know anything yet of what the interior life truly means; no, nothing at all; not so much as a child like our Madeline here. And the very first thing that our Lord has asked of you, you have refused to give it to

Him! That is not such a piece of generosity as would show
that you have progressed very far! Eh? Is it not so? . . .

"Yet our Lord is so generous that He has asked that one
thing of you, though knowing that you would not give it
Him! And your generosity! Ah, a fine one, is it not? — to
offer our Lord this and this and this, which He does not
want, and to refuse Him that which He does!"

(The Prioress's voice softened suddenly.)

"You have given Him vinegar, my child, instead of the
wine He asked. . . .

*   *   *   *   *   *   *

"Eh well, listen to me. (No, my child, I did not wish to
make you cry. . . . Be tranquil then, and listen to me.)

"Eh well. We must ask ourselves why it is that our Lord
asked such a thing at all. . . . I will tell you. It was because He saw in you a power, a capacity, is it not so? . . . A
seed (no more than a seed, my child) . . . yet it was there,
and He saw it. Now our Lord does not trouble Himself. . . .
I should say that He does not trouble souls for whom He
has no intentions — such as can do nothing great for Him.
. . . He leaves them alone, I think. . . . He gives to them
such grace as they need, and He leaves them tranquil. It
is a good sign then that you have been unhappy. . . .

"What, then, does He wish from you now? It is certain.
A reparation of your fault. And that fault was as I have
said.

"Now listen carefully if you please, for this is a little difficult.

"Our Lord once said, 'The kingdom of heaven is within
you.' . . . There is, that is to say, in each soul an interior
castle, as our Holy Mother Saint Teresa tells us, and for
many that interior castle is at rest. Our Lord dwells there
in peace; He gives such graces as are necessary, but He
does not proclaim Himself.

"Now, with you it is not so. He has proclaimed Himself
in you; and you have answered Him, We will not have this
Man to reign over us.

"It was at Monsieur your husband's deathbed that you
offered yourself to Him, knowing what you offered; and

He answered you from the castle. Until then you had not known that He was there. And He begged you to give Him the key of that castle — to surrender yourself to His Will, and you would not. You have offered Him this and that in its place. There — I will say no more of that.

"But you have kept the innermost place of your heart to yourself. You would not give up all: you had no confidence in Him.

"Whether or no you had indeed a vocation to Religion I do not know; that is not our affair. Our affair is only that we should have no reserves from Him. It may well be that He will send you back to serve Him in the world. . . . No, my child, you do not believe that, I know well. Eh well, so much the better.

"Well, then, this is what you must do. There is no question of it at all. Monsieur your husband returns this evening, you tell me? You must go to him immediately; you must say to him that you are ready to do anything that he wishes in the matter. . . . No, be tranquil, my child; listen to me. You must say to him that you believe that you too have a vocation, or at least that you are willing to offer yourself. You need not tell him all the tale; you need but say as I have said.

"And when that is finished, with a full heart, then will be the time to speak of it further, to consider whether or no it is possible. But you will have repaired your fault then; you will have offered yourself fully. . . .

"Now go, my child. . . . No, not a word further. Come again tomorrow. . . .

"Ah, you are happy now! Is it not so?"

Chapter XI

(1)

There is no manner of life which so teaches control of the features as that of a butler: in comparison with it that of an actor, a religious novice, a diplomat, or a Jesuit sinks into nothingness. Persons are born or die, the house is in flames, yet a butler is impassive; it seems that his small square whiskers hold his features gripped as in an iron frame.

Mr. Parkinson was relaying the table for his master's dinner at half-past nine; the mistress had dined as usual at eight. And although he himself had been present and watched her carefully throughout, no expression of any unusual kind had crossed his face, nor the faintest novel tone found its way into his voice. Neither had he said one word to anyone on the fact that she had refused soup and fish, eaten largely of mutton, and had radiated such ecstatic and excellent content that he thought her beside herself altogether. She had talked to him a little, since nobody else was present, and had said a number of rather odd things. Finally she had told him to bring coffee into the smoking room, and had given careful directions as to the master's dinner. Mr. Parkinson was to wait upon him, was to say that the mistress was in the garden, but would be in again at ten. She had thrown herself with such passion into detail in itself unimportant that even to Mr. Parkinson it was evident that there was emotion about; and as to the character of that emotion her face spoke eloquently.

All he permitted himself to say in the steward s room during his hasty supper a little before nine was that the mistress seemed very pleased to have the master home again. He said this just before the telephone bell from the lodge gate announced the passing through of the motor.

The master looked very different as his coat was taken off in the hall, and his hat and stick put away.

He had been off to the other side of the county on some agricultural affair, staying with the Lennoxes, and had been absent four days. And this was the first time he had slept away from home since his illness last summer. Apparently the visit had not been a success.

He asked shortly after the mistress.

"Yes, sir, the mistress is very well. She asked me to say, sir, that she was out in the garden and would be in at ten o'clock. The mistress told me to take your coffee to the smoking room, sir."

Jack nodded and went to wash his hands. As he washed he glanced out through the open window into the solemn jeweled dusk and wondered where exactly Mary was.

This dinner was very different. Jack sat in silence throughout; he ate of everything; he drank three glasses of claret; he said not one word good or bad. He sat, between the courses, rather hunched up, twirling a glass in his hand and staring. It was a queer contrast.

When the dessert things were put on he leaned forward, took four strawberries, which he ate rapidly, obviously thinking of something else, and got up immediately.

"Coffee in the smoking room, eh?"

"Yes, sir, immediately."

"Is it ten o'clock yet?"

"Close upon it, sir. Shall I tell the mistress?"

"Er — no; don't bother."

Then he was off, crossed the hall, and vanished into the smoking room. Mr. Parkinson heard the door shut rather loudly.

(2)

Jack threw himself instantly into a chair, stretched out his legs and closed his eyes. Certainly he did not look very well; there was a sort of heaviness about his good-humored mouth and eyes that made him appear almost sullen.

So he remained, perfectly quiet, obviously not asleep nor even sleepy, for there was a certain tension about his features: once or twice his blue eyes opened, and the perfect intelligence and even fixity in them showed that he was very intent upon something. The coffee came in presently; and as soon as the door was closed again, he helped himself quickly to two cups one after the other, and drank them in hasty gulps. Then he lay back again.

As he lay there the anxiety on his face deepened again; once or twice his lips moved as if rehearsing some sentence; once or twice he changed his position with a jerk.

After two or three minutes he got up quite deliberately, took a pipe from the rack, blew through it once or twice, and examined it. Then he hunted about on a side table, pulled out at last a tobacco jar, and unscrewed the lid. There was a little tobacco there, left there by some guest — perhaps Algy Lennox himself — and he began, with an oddly nervous sort of air, to cram a little of this into his pipe. Yet when it was filled he hesitated, and so stood, the pipe in his hand, looking now at it, now at nothing: once he glanced quickly and guiltily at the door as if he heard some sound. Then he put out his hand to the matches, took one from the roughed-glass globe on the chimney piece, and hesitated again.

It was a perfectly ordinary scene, yet minute as filigree, and obviously significant of some sort of indecision that was very nearly tragic. It seemed that something of enormous import depended on to whether that pipe were lighted or no. It was obvious too that it was not its mere smoking that mattered; it was the occasion and the act: there was symbolism in the air. Then suddenly, as a footstep came close outside, he thrust the pipe quickly behind a framed photograph and sat down. You would have thought that he had not moved for half an hour, so perfect was his pose as the door opened.

Mary came in swiftly, closed the door behind her, and turned.

"Jack!" she said.

Her face was alight with excitement, radiant with happiness and a strange look of expectation. She was in white from head to foot, and there were flowers in her hair. She might be a bride on her wedding evening. Her face was pale, but her eyes shone like stars. Jack looked at her and sat up. Then he stood up.

"Here I am," he said.

She seemed to recover herself; she came forward and kissed him.

"And you've had a nice time?" she said.

"Oh yes; all right."

She sat down abruptly on the arm of the chair he had just left; he went and stood by the mantelpiece, wondering.

It was plain that something was in the air, he told himself; and for a moment or two he lost his own sense of misery. His own became merged in a greater emotion.

"What is it?" he said shortly.

She looked at him for an instant in silence. Then she too stood up, seeming to drive down by sheer will the passion that shook within her and escaped in silence from her eyes.

"It is this," she said. "Oh, I won't waste words. I've come to tell you that I consent."

"What? — I don't understand."

Her face broke into smiles and her eyes suddenly filled.

"Oh yes you do, old boy. You know. Don't look like that. It's perfectly true. I've come to tell you that you've been right and I've been wrong."

He clasped his hands suddenly behind him.

"I don't understand. Tell me," he said in a quick, dry voice.

"Come and sit down. Yes; I mean it. And I'll sit here. I don't want you to see my face. I'm — I'm too happy for anything. Yes; I insist."

He came forward stupidly, still but half-understanding all that she meant, and sat down. She once more arranged herself on the arm of the chair, supporting herself along the back. (As she began to talk, he was staring in front of him with relaxed hands; but presently he had shifted a little, and was shading his eyes; his face turned from her, motionless.)

"It is this," she said in a quick, low voice. "This is the sum of it. You remember what you asked of me after your illness — about the Religious Life? Well, I said I wouldn't. I was wrong. And I knew I was wrong. I've been fighting against it ever since; and I see now —

"Listen. You don't know what happened when you died. I haven't told a soul — except in confession — oh, and the Prioress this afternoon. Well, when the room was empty I

knelt down and offered myself to God — if only you could
live again. And you came back — you came back, Jack.
Oh, Jack! He accepted it, you see. You were perfectly
right. You did die; and God brought you back. And then I
— I refused my part of the bargain. The minute you said
it I knew that that was the thing — that I should be willing, at any rate — and I wasn't. I — I excused myself; I
jumped at what the doctors said. I wrote to Sir James. I've
got his letter upstairs saying that it was not death, but
only suspended animation. I tried to make Dr. Basing say
you were mad. I did everything. Oh, Jack! I've been so
mean. Suspended animation!

"It was because I was a coward. I couldn't bear to give
up all this. I didn't understand. But I do now. Oh, Jack, I
do now!

"And — and I want to ask your forgiveness. I've been a
beast to you. I've hindered instead of helping. I've kept
you back from your vocation.

"You haven't talked much lately about these things.
And I must make a confession about that. I thought it was
because you were — were giving in — going back again.
But I understand that now too. It was because I couldn't
share. I've watched you, Jack. I've seen you making your
meditation.

"Then the shooting the other day. That was all lies too. I
don't mean I don't think it all right; but I mean as to what
I said, about being a country gentleman being best. I
knew that was lies. Oh, Jack! What a liar I've been — a
liar and a cheat.

"Well, that's all over. (No, my dear, don't interrupt till
I've done.) I went to see the Prioress today. I couldn't bear
it any more. I told her everything; and oh, it was a relief!
And — and she said such things to me, but not half-bad
enough. I've finished it, once and for all. It's done now,
and I'm so happy I don't know what to do. Do you see,
Jack? I've come to tell you at once. I couldn't bear to see
you till I could tell you. Oh, Jack, kiss me — though I
suppose you oughtn't to — not any more."

She turned her tearful, flushed face towards him for the
first time, and saw how his head was turned from her,
shaded by his hand. She thought she understood so per-

fectly, and her reward in that instant compensated for everything. He was overwhelmed with happiness. He could not take it in.

She put her hand gently on his head.

"Poor old Jack!" she said; "but it's all over now. Kiss me, Jack."

Still he did not move.

She slipped off the arm of the chair and kneeled half in front of him, taking his other hand in hers.

"Forgive me, Jack," she said; "give me absolution."

Then she kissed his hand gently.

And at the touch of her lips he tore it free and turned such a face on her that she shrank back.

"Why, Jack!" she said.

"You don't mean it! You don't mean it!" he cried.

"I do — I do."

"You don't! I don't believe you. You're — you're — playing a trick."

"Jack, what's the matter?"

He sprang up.

"I don't believe a word of it. You've been spying. You've been finding out things. Look here!" He banged aside the photograph frame — it fell with a crash on to the fender; he tore out the pipe.

"Look here," he said. "Look at this. Do you understand now? I'm sick of it all. I've been a damned fool."

His hand shook, but he snatched up the match — a miserable little symbol that stood to him for so much — dashed it alight, and put it to his pipe. It was silly, theatrical, abominable, and trifling; yet his passion was so great as almost to ennoble it. She stared at him, white-faced, sunk back on her heels.

"There," he said. "Do you understand now?"

He pulled furiously at his pipe, sending out wreaths of smoke.

"You had better understand it at once," he said. "I'm sick of the whole damned thing. I've been playing the fool for months, footling along with things, and trying to be pious. It's all rot. Look here —"

He snatched at his coat pocket.

"There's a letter that came for me at the Lennoxes'. It's to play again in South Africa. I haven't answered it yet, but I'm going to. I'm going to say yes . . . . Pack of rubbish . . . . Just because I was ill." . . .

He tossed the letter towards her.

"Don't look like that, Mary. There! I'm sorry. I oughtn't to have said all that." (He stooped and picked up the letter, laying it on the mantelpiece.)

"But I've been a fool, and I'm furious with myself — a silly, posing fool. And all those asses at the Lennoxes' finished me. No, you're all right, old girl. You haven't done anything you shouldn't. It's I who've been the fool. And now I've gone and given the thing away by building that rotten convent. We must see what can be done. Perhaps we can get rid of them."

He paused again.

Mary rose to her feet in dead silence and stood there looking at him.

He turned away his face and affected to probe his pipe with a penknife that lay on a little tray.

"Mary, I'm sorry I was violent. I meant to tell you quietly. But what you said — There — I'm sorry. Are you going? All right; we'll talk later. That's best. Look here. I'm really sorry."

(3)

Half an hour later he was again sitting motionless in his chair.

He had had time to think and grow cool again, and the shame at his own violence had gently passed away. Of course he would apologize to her again presently. He must go in and see her before he went to bed.

So there had risen within him again that attitude of mind to which he had now been approximating for three or four months — that solid sensible mood which had always been his until the event of last summer.

He lit his pipe again, stretched out his feet, and began to review things.

First there was the shock of his apparent death and his recovery. It was remarkable, but, after all, such things had happened before. That odd sort of vision he had had of the doctor and Sarah walking on the grass; that yet

more odd impression — all part of the same thing, of
course — that he had become aware of a real world of
spirit, and all the rest. Well, that was just the delirium of
his illness, and had persevered in an unusual degree. It
was all really the "subjective" self (he was pleased with
the phrase; he had read a little article in a monthly review at the Lennoxes' on the point.)

Of course it was that; it was quite obvious. People who
died did not recover. Therefore he had not died.

The coincidence of Mary's prayer! He saw through that
in an instant, of course. Why, wherever had there been a
deathbed of a husband at which a wife did not pray like
that? And did the husband always recover? Very well,
then.

How long had the impression lasted? Well, vividly, only
for a few days. He remembered saying to Mary that he
must act at once, that he must not lose the impression.
That was pretty soon after. Then it must have been about
then that the thing was fading — exactly as one would
expect. With convalescence came sanity.

Why then had he gone on acting as if it was still real to
him?

He pulled on his pipe thoughtfully, trying to analyze his
own psychology. It was not very easy, but he began to see
presently. (Somehow his little scene with Mary had
cleared his mind wonderfully. He was able now to look
back and criticize himself. Up to that point, in spite of his
efforts, he had not been able to dissociate himself from his
past. It had been like a man trying to look at his own
back!)

What, then, was the reason? Yes, he saw. He had been
still afraid that the thing might be true; his will, so to
speak, had run on by impetus after the first emotional
impulse had ceased. Even the process of convent-building
had been sustained by this impetus. He had been acting
rather superstitiously, remembering the emotion he no
longer felt.

Certain little points began now to stand out clearly —
their significances, unknown at the time, were obvious
now.

There was the sucking at the empty pipe. That was on the evening after the nuns had arrived. That is to say, he had fixed his will up to that point, and relaxation immediately followed its consummation. How natural that was!

Then there was the arrival of the new horse, and the little scene as the hunt went past. That had been a fierce little struggle — really the first of all. Of course he had beaten down the desire. . . . But it only showed how morbid he was when he could take so seriously the difference between riding alone and riding after a pack of hounds.

Then there was the shooting incident. That had stood for a lot to him — far more than he had thought at the time. It had meant a very real break. . . . He smiled, in his sanity, as he recalled the sense of guilt with which he had killed his first bird that day — his discomfort at Mary's presence. (How abominably he had shot too!)

And now, here was the final smash — that is to say, his final reemergence into reasonable thought.

What had brought on this final smash, for which all those other incidents had been a series of preludes?

First there had been his days with the Lennoxes. It was the first time he had been away from home — away, that is to say, from the power of association — and it had been a curious revelation to him, or rather reminder, of what real human life was like. The Lennoxes were Catholics? Oh yes; Algy had been at school with him. Algy and his wife nearly always went to their Easter duties. They had built a house for the priest too. (That reminded him. Father Banting must really be got down to the village again somehow. It would never do as it was.) Yet the Lennoxes were quite ordinary people. You might stay with them for weeks, and not dream that they were Catholics at all! That was the proper way. Religion ought to be well kept in the background. Of course it was all true in a sort of way, but . . . .

Then there was the conversation at the Lennoxes'. Those "asses," as he had described them just now, had begun by ragging him rather, till they saw he didn't like it. Then they had stopped. It had stung rather. And then Algy had talked to him so sensibly just after the arrival of the letter.

Then the letter itself had done a good deal. (He smoothed it out on his knee and glanced at it again.) How sensible and manly it was — just businesslike. It was from good old Dick. Dick said something perfectly courteous about certain rumors he had heard as to Jack's having given up cricket, but refused to believe it. Jack couldn't be such a fool, said the letter. Then came the offer.

What rot all that had been! Why the devil shouldn't a Catholic play cricket? Why the Church allowed recreation even of kinds that others thought dangerous, such as horse racing. What a mad ass he had been! Why even Mary had laughed at him! And Father Banting, too he had been very plain about fanaticism, and had even urged him to go on with his sports.

But the final thing had been Mary just now.

Jack crossed one leg over the other, beat out his pipe into an ashtray, and resettled his position.

He hadn't answered that letter. Why not? Well, it had seemed more decent somehow to tell Mary first. Oh yes, he had intended to tell Mary, of course. That was why he had the letter in his pocket. But then before he could get a word out had come this beastly scene. He had behaved like a brute. (Yes, he must look in at Mary and really apologize. But of course Mary would understand. She was so sensible, at least she had been.)

Of course she didn't mean what she said just now. It was just a bit of morbidity, the result of seeing him day after day going on with his prayers and his ridiculous meditation and all the rest of it. (Oh, that meditation! What a burden it had been!)

Yes, that was it. It was all his own fault for behaving like a fool. He must tell her that, and it would be all right again.

Well, it was her suddenly saying that about being willing that had caused all the row. It had been so unexpected, and when he was already in a devil of a temper.

The letter fell from his knee, and he picked it up. Yes, he must answer it before he went to bed. That would settle it.

Tomorrow? Mass? No, he was too much done. Besides, it wasn't Sunday. Really, this nonsense about daily Mass was too much. No, he'd go on Sundays, of course. He must set an example. And perhaps on Thursdays. Well, he'd think about that. There was no hurry. Today was Monday.

That letter. Oh yes, he must answer it.

He got up, carrying the letter, and went across to the writing table, near the window. But even then he hesitated. He put the letter carefully down, and stood looking at it. Why what in the world was he hesitating about? Why the deuce shouldn't a Catholic play cricket in South Africa? He looked up meditatively to the window. Yes, that was right; the windows were wide open. What a heavenly night!

He leaned on the sill and stared out.

The enormous night lay there before him, mysterious and infinite. The world seemed very quiet. Below spread the park in the dim darkness, blotted here and there by clumps of trees. No lights sparkled in the village. It must be getting late. And above him lay that gulf of stars, immeasurable, remote, and watching — a vast span, cut overhead by the parapet, arching down opposite to the tops of the hills across the valley. There came to his nostrils the smell of the sweet earth and the dreaming flowers, to his ears the silence of English country at night, as familiar and living as the sleep of a child. It seemed friendly indeed, but full of secrets, and extraordinarily solemn. A kind of memory, like a far-off echo, came to him of his dreams a year ago when he had thought himself dying, of the lawns of the old house, the gavotte, his parents, the river and the water-plants, and the rest. There was enough in common between the emotion of those things and of the solemn moonlight. But he thought of them with an almost entire contempt. . . .

There he stood for a full minute, looking, smelling, listening, and hesitating.

Then with a jerk he turned away and sat down at the writing table.

Chapter XII

(1)

Once more there was a little excitement in the village, as at the arrival of the nuns, when it became known that Lady Sarah and her husband were to stay at the Hall for a fortnight. The event of the last few months were perfectly known, even to an elaboration of detail, in that strange manner in which secrets do get out.

First there had been the letting of Lady Carberry's house — or rather Sarah's — for a term of two years, and the going abroad of the mistress. Then, like a thunderbolt, the news of the marriage in October, scarcely six months after the old lady's death. Mr. Fakenham was only known as a well-dressed figure who occasionally walked through the village with his trout-rod; but it was known that he was an old friend, and had stayed with her ladyship in several consecutive years. On the whole the affair was approved of, particularly when it was considered that Lady Sarah's sole remaining aunt with whom she had gone abroad had also died in August, and that the girl had no other relations in the world. A husband was the best thing for her under the circumstances.

Once more, therefore, at the close of an afternoon in late November, there was gathered a little group at the lodge gate to see the brougham drive through; and it was thought that it would be a pleasant distraction for Mrs. Weston, all alone now, through the absence of her husband in South Africa.

Sarah herself was very content as she drove up to the house. She had had a delightful month, very quietly, with her husband in Wales — that husband in whom she still felt a very considerable pride. He was really a very clever man; he was entirely presentable, and now that he had resigned his position in the Home Office, he was free to come and go with her as she liked. He had not been very well; the routine of the office was very trying to his nerves; and the fact that now he had no earthly reason for

continuing with work that was distasteful to him had finished the affair finally. He had told her, in a burst of confidence, that there was any amount of occupation in the
world generally for a man of his tastes; and he had begun
once more his collection of first editions. It was a very
pleasant life that these two were to lead in future. They
had let the Manningham house for the present, but they
were already negotiating for another; they were to divide
their time between town and country; they were going to
enjoy themselves very much indeed in doing nothing in
particular.

"My dearest," said Sarah, and threw herself into Mary's
arms in the hall.

Sarah's first preoccupation, when the two were alone after tea in the morning room, was to say a word or two
about the difficulties of dressing suitably in her double
character of bride and mourner.

I forget how the matter had been solved by Madame
Valerie, but Mary assured her that it had been solved satisfactorily; and told her, in other words, that her appearance was heartless neither to the dead nor the living.

That was all right then; and Sarah began to attend to
her friend.

"And you, dearest — how are you? You're looking rather
pale."

Mary said she was very well indeed.

"And Mr. Jack? Has he reached Capetown? Aren't you
fearfully lonely?"

"I had a wire yesterday," said Mary. "He begins to play
next week."

There fell a little pause.

Sarah had written demanding explanations of the very
short sentence in which Mary had informed her of Jack's
change of plans, but had had no answer. She was determined to have one now; but did not quite know how to
begin. She threw back her boa a little further and leaned
forwards to the fire, stretching out her hands. The wedding ring was there.

"Tell me sometime, dearest, won't you, all about Mr.
Jack; I didn't quite understand —"

"There is really nothing to tell," said Mary quietly, "except what I told you. Jack changed his mind about cricket, and has gone out to South Africa to play."

"That's what you wanted him to do, isn't it?"

"Yes."

"And — and it's all right."

"Yes, it's all right," said Mary.

"Really and truly?"

Mary nodded.

Well, that was the end of that, for the present. Even Sarah saw that it was no good going on just then. But as they talked of all the things that they would talk about — of Jim, of the wedding, of Switzerland, and the rest — Sarah was observing with all her might. The impression she received could not be put into words; she could not even formulate it in thought, beyond telling herself that "something" had happened. Mary looked really perfectly well; she was charmingly dressed; she talked naturally and easily; she asked the proper questions; she made the proper answers; and yet something hung down like an obscuring veil, through which glimmered formless things whose nature could not be detected. There was a gravity about her, yet not a gravity different either in kind or degree from gravities that Sarah had observed before; there was an air of reticence, yet of a reticence that she had seen before, and that had broken suddenly and abruptly into whirling confidence. Only, this evening, this did not break.

At dinner it was the same. The three talked genially, pleasantly; Jim made the kind of remarks that he did make in congenial and admirative company; Mary appreciated them beautifully, as Sarah, glancing up quickly, observed with pleasure; and everything went very well indeed. Yet there was this kind of note sounding in the background; Mary presented only one superficies of herself, the rest was somewhere else.

The husband and wife talked it thoroughly well over that night — Sarah in bed, Jim smoking a cigarette on the hearthrug after half an hour alone in the smoking room.

"It's all a matter of temperament," said Jim.

"Yes, I know, but it isn't Mary's temperament. That's the point. Mary's not a bit like that really. Why, six months ago she'd have told me the whole thing in ten minutes. Something's happened, and I don't know what. I believe she's been alone here ever since her husband went."

"It's temperament for all that. You must make allowances for temperament. It's only a part that you haven't yet seen. But it's a part."

Sarah was not attending.

"Tell me again what Algy Lennox told you."

Jim sighed and flicked away his ash.

"Oh, nothing much. They were ragging Weston in the smoking room, and he lost his temper. Bad form that."

"Which?"

"Both. Why can't people mind their own business. Well, he lost his temper. And two days later Algy heard from him that he'd accepted this invitation."

"That's all?"

Jim nodded. Sarah sighed and drew the bedclothes close under her chin.

"But I don't understand why Mary isn't pleased. It's what she was always wanting him to do. Why, she burst into tears when she found him burning his bats."

Jim said nothing.

"And now — Jim dear, what do you think?"

"Perhaps she's turned religious too."

Sarah was silent a moment.

"No," she said, "not like that. You're wrong there. Mary's thoroughly sensible. Of course she's more religious than she was; but —"

"She goes to Mass every day," observed Jim; "she said so at dinner."

"Yes, I know; but that's not —"

Sarah stopped again.

She felt extraordinarily piqued by the situation, and rather resentful too. She was in a particularly expansive mood just now. Her mother's death had relieved her from a real moral incubus, her new-found liberty, her hotel life in the summer, her marriage — all those things had combined to make her so; and it was really annoying to meet with reticence from one whom she considered she knew through and through.

"Go and ask the nuns," said Jim suddenly, throwing the stump of his cigarette into the fire behind him. Sarah started.

"Jim, that's perfectly brilliant. I will. The mother's sure to know, and I'll get it out of her. Now, please don't dawdle any more. I want to go to sleep."

(2)

There was an excellent opportunity for this next morning. Mary told her, with quite the right amount of regret, that she had a hundred things to do, and wouldn't be free till eleven. So about a quarter-past ten, after a large breakfast, up went Sarah.

The little parlor appeared to her more repulsive than ever. Not content with *Sainte Thérèse*, someone had hung up yet another appalling effigy, of a shaven man in brown and white, clasping a book, beside the other picture. This time Mary was not there, and there was no need, therefore, for any kind of pose; she could study during the few minutes of waiting, honestly and sincerely, not the details only, but the entire effect of this little room. Yet its message was as illegible to her as hieroglyphics. It must mean something — she saw that; it must stand for some aspect of life, yet it was one she could not interpret. It could not be a sheer love of ugliness, not even simple carelessness, that was the ideal; for the boards were spotlessly clean, the table exactly in the middle, and even a bunch of flowers upon that. Well, she accepted the fact that it meant something she did not understand, and concluded by the same act of thought that it was not worth understanding: it was plainly medieval and foreign and second rate. Probably, too, all the nuns were rather middle-class.

When the curtain was back at last, and the proper things had been said, and mutual inquiries made, Sarah started for her goal with superb assurance. She knew perfectly well that she, with all her experience and tact, would get out of this guileless old creature all that she wanted without difficulty.

"Reverend Mother," she said, "I want to ask you about Madam Weston. Can you tell me what is the matter with her?"

"Eh? Is she ill?" asked the veiled enigma. "Madam was at Mass, I think —"

"Oh yes: I don't mean in that way. But about Mr. Weston and all that. Mary seems unhappy — well, not perhaps unhappy, but strange."

"I regret it infinitely," said the old lady. "Monsieur her husband is away; and the loneliness perhaps —"

"No, no, my Mother. I do not mean with regard to that. But Mr. Weston has changed his manner of life again; and it seems to me that Mary is not very happy about it. Six months ago —"

"But, Madam, explain yourself, if you please. Monsieur Weston is an excellent Catholic —"

"Oh yes, yes. I don't mean that," explained Sarah, a little irritated at the very slow comprehension of this old lady; "I meant with regard to other things. Monsieur Weston was so strict a few months ago; and now all is changed again. I don't understand Mary in the least. Six months ago she was urging him to be — be ordinary" (Sarah wondered for one wild instant whether "ordinaire" exactly expressed the thought) — "to be like other people, and now that he has commenced again she — she seems not pleased."

"Eh well," remarked the old lady, in a conclusive kind of voice.

This was not illuminating; and Sarah began all over again. It was annoying to have so small a vocabulary; it was annoying to have to discharge this slender weapon through two banks of grating; but it was simply maddening to find on the other side a stupidity even greater than she had supposed. It appeared as if no combination of French words could convey even a hint of the subtle question she attempted to put. She was aware, of course, that every woman who could deliberately (and even more, if acquiescently) confine herself "between four walls" must have been exceptionally dull, even before she had become a nun; but this dullness seemed to her remarkable. Once only did she suspect for a moment that the dullness was assumed; and that interpretation vanished a moment later as the old lady began to discourse on health in general, with a particular application to Mrs. Weston of so sensitive a constitution. Sarah put it all as patiently as she could, over and over again; and each time, before she could drive the point home, some smooth surface was interposed, and the conversation slid off at an angle. She gave it up at last, trembling a little with indignation.

"Eh well, Reverend Mother," she said (she was very much pleased with the naturalness of her *Eh bien*), "I see Mary has not confided in you."

"Eh," came back the murmur; "but to you, her friend, Madam, no doubt —"

"And, of course," went on Sarah rather hastily, entirely unable to resist a little dig, "living as you do in the convent, it is impossible for you to understand what goes on outside."

"Yes, yes, Madam; we are but poor nuns who know nothing. You will pray for us the more, is it not so?"

The answer was perfectly courteous, almost deprecating. Yet for a moment Sarah again wondered whether the mind behind were quite as flat as appeared. But no; it was impossible that this nun should know anything. The stupidity was too well marked. Besides, was it not to be expected? . . . and so on.

"Well, goodbye, Reverend Mother. We are to be here a fortnight —"

"And you will come again to see us, will you not?" said the tranquil voice, "and give us the news? Come as often as you please, Madam."

And Sarah went away with her suspicions lulled.

(3)

Her direct assault upon Mary — for, of course, she made one, and that no later than that very evening — was, at any rate, decisive for the time, though not in the way she intended.

The two were sitting together as they had sat last night. Jim, who had got thoroughly wet through in the afternoon, and had half-dressed on coming in, had wandered away to the smoking room in dress trousers and a Norfolk jacket; and an excellent opportunity displayed itself.

She began with a stratagem.

"I went up to see the Reverend Mother this morning," she said, "as I told you. We had a delightful conversation about you, my dear."

Mary lifted her eyes and let them fall again.

"Really, darling? How extraordinarily interesting it must have been. What did you say?"

"Oh, we talked about you?" said Sarah vaguely, trying to get a world of suggestiveness into her voice. "Mary dear, do you know you've become quite different since I saw you last?"

"How do you mean, my dear? Deterioration?"

Sarah looked up from the low stool which she had drawn quite close to the fire. But Mary's face was quite impassive, with a flicker of only the very faintest humor upon it. She was sewing gently at something or other on her lap.

"You're different," said Sarah emphatically. "Tell me. Have you had a row with Jack?"

Mary fumbled in her workbox, drew out a letter and tossed it to her friend.

"Read that," she said. "Yes, I mean it."

Sarah read it: it was a very friendly and cheerful note from Jack, quite in his old manner, dated from Madeira or Gibraltar or somewhere.

"I don't understand," said Sarah.

"Well, my dear," said Mary sedately, "you asked me whether we have had a row. I ask you, Does that note look like it?"

"You're trying to fence," said Sarah, struck by a brilliant inspiration; "you don't answer."

Mary laid down her work and looked straight at her friend. (It must be remembered that these two really did know one another quite well.)

"Do you mean you want to know whether Jack and I have had a breach, and that my air of mystery means that I am a broken-hearted and deserted wife?"

(It was a good sentence. It had been carefully prepared by Mary two days before.)

"Well, yes, more or less," said Sarah.

"Then I'll tell you, No. Jack and I are excellent friends. Quite excellent. Can I do anything more for you, my dear?"

"And you've had no rows?"

"Oh, my dearest, of course we've had rows. And so will you and Jim, before long. But we've always apologized and made it up, quite beautifully; as I hope you and Jim will."

"And there's no row on now?"

"Absolutely none. We're on as excellent terms as ever."

Sarah stared at the fire without speaking; she heard only the lap of the flames and the gentle rip of the thread through the silk beside her. Then she sighed loudly.

"Oh well, if you won't tell me, you won't."

The rip of the thread ceased.

"Sarah," came a stern voice, "will you kindly tell me exactly what's in your mind?"

"It's this," burst out Sarah indignantly. "There's something up. There's this thing of Jack's — I mean his suddenly changing round again and becoming just what you wanted him. And there are you, as grave as a cat, telling me nothing, and trying to pretend that there's nothing the matter. You didn't write anything to me. You won't tell me anything. All right, then don't. And there's that stupid old woman up there —"

"What old woman?"

"Why, the Reverend Mother, of course! I could have — could have slapped her face; only there were the bars between."

"Then you went up to find out all about me, did you?"

"Of course I did!"

"What! After your experience with Father Banting too — that old sheep, as you once called him?"

Sarah looked slightly offended.

"And she didn't understand what you wanted?" pursued Mary relentlessly.

"No; she was too stupid. I never met such a —"

Mary's face rippled all over with laughter.

"You really thought that?"

"Why, of course — what else could I think?"

"Do you know who the Reverend Mother once was?"

"Once was! Why, I suppose she was always a nun, wasn't she? At least —"

"Have you ever heard of Pauline, the writer?"

"I've read her books, of course," said Sarah sulkily.

"Well, she is Pauline. Or she was, forty years ago."

"Pauline! Do you mean —?"

"I mean what I say. Only you mustn't tell her you know, please. I only found it out by chance."

This was so bewildering that Sarah ran clean off the scent. But she was whipped into it again.

"Whether she knows or not, is not to the point," went on Mary severely. "Only perhaps you'll remember next time that we aren't all abject fools. I should have thought your time with Father Banting would have taught you that. Dear Sarah, I love you, you know; but really you're rather stupid about Catholic things. I know you only think it a matter of temperament and all that, but I assure you there's more in it than you think. We do know our job, you know." (Mary broke off.) "And do you really think that if she did know anything she'd let it out to you?"

"I — I thought, perhaps — " began Sarah feebly.

"Just so. Well, we can leave that. Now you come to me. Well, I'll tell you this much and no more. Something has happened; but nothing more is going to happen. It's all done with. (I think you're the most inquisitive person I've ever met in all my life, or I wouldn't tell you even this.) But it's all done with. Jack's going to play cricket in South Africa, and is going to play very well too, and make a great many runs. And then he's going to come back here and play all the summer. And then he'll shoot in the winter. And I shall go on doing what I've always done; and you and Jim will come and stay here every year. And we're all going to live happily forever afterwards. There; that's enough, my dear."

Mary patted the silk on her knee contentedly and observed Sarah with a large smile.

Sarah thought very hard indeed for about ten seconds. Then she threw herself back on the stool, clasping a knee.

"I see," she said, really trying to keep resentment out of her voice. "Now let's talk about something else."

Chapter XIII

(1)

It is curious how some houses, more than others' seem, in the absence of their owner, to be eloquent of that absence. Some houses are sufficient in themselves, complete and entire; it is they which are the substance and their inhabitants are but accidental. With others the contrary is true; and every detail and combination of their rooms cry out for and imply a vital presence.

Manningham Hall was of the second class, and even Sarah noticed it. The effect perhaps was a simple thing after all — the result of two or three caps in the hall, an empty pipe rack in the smoking room, a couple of chairs before the hall-fire, obviously the special property of the host. The rooms were human enough and individual enough to postulate on human individuality.

Now Sarah was not very clever, as will have been perceived; and it took her some time to be aware of this, and a longer time to express it; but she expressed it at last; and she thought it rather silly even as she said it.

She and Jim had been to church in the morning on their second Sunday, and the combined effect of certain hymns, and of the sight of her mother's grave — (she had taken a large wreath of chrysanthemums to lay upon it) — had produced an introspective kind of mood. She had also seen and shaken hands, after church, with the tenants of her own house across the valley — people of no importance; and emotionalism descended upon her. She walked up from church with Jim, rather silent, with her head on one side, and went on into the house alone when he said he would take a stroll and meet Mrs. Weston coming down from Mass. She went into the smoking room — she did not quite know why — and sat down before the fire.

It was a very pleasant room, with an aspect that has already been described — and, still rather sentimental, she let her eyes rove round it.

There was nothing peculiar about it; it was extraordinarily ordinary, entirely true to type, in its faint smoky smell, its extreme comfort, its deep chairs, its emblems and books of sport, and its empty pipe rack. Jim smoked cigarettes only, of course, and his silver case, with his small inscribed matchbox, lay forgotten on the mantelpiece. They seemed an intrusion.

Over the mantelpiece hung two framed photographs on either side of an oil painting of a horse in a stall. One photograph presented a cricketing group, with Jack, strangely childish-looking, dandling a bat in the center, and a coat-of-arms painted above; the other a lawn and a great shuttered house, backed by towering limes. She believed this second photograph to be a picture of Jack's old home. The lawn had a tea table and chairs set out on it, she noticed.

Between the fire and the door was an old cracked bat in a glass case, with an inscription on a tarnished silver plate let into the splice. Next to the fire was the pipe rack.

Then, as she looked, the personality of Jack descended upon her as a cloud, and she set herself once more to regard the problem connected with him. . . .

Yet she got no satisfaction from it. No data had been added beyond the single assurance of Mary that "something" had happened (and that she had known before). So she lay back in Jack's chair, and with the pipe rack before her eyes, and the two photographs over the mantelpiece, and the ancient bat that had escaped the fire, and the suggestion, rather than the smell, of smoke in her nose, considered him absorbedly.

A spatter of rain, and voices in the hall, and the sudden clatter of a dog's paws on polished boards, and a cheerful cry of "Get down, sir," from Mary, brought her out of the chair again and into the world of men. Yet the sensation did not leave her.

(2)

(The following section can be omitted without detriment to the story. In fact, I am not sure that the story is not much improved without it.)

Some other little things happened on that Sunday at Manningham that I think are just worth writing down.

They are of complete unimportance in themselves, and they may be completely unimportant even when correlated with facts. At any rate, let us have them.

It is within the bounds of possibility that a certain groom may be remembered, whose name was Jim. (I am sorry it is the same name as Mr. Fakenham's; but such was the fact.)

It was Jim's business to give a look in at the stables before going down to the village to church; then to lock them up, and place the key on a certain nail outside the harness room door.

So, at about twenty minutes to eleven, as the bells were in full blast, Jim came out from the back premises, in his black trousers and red waist coat with his white silk tie properly knotted and secured by a fox-head pin, and opened the stable door. There was some kind of a sharp movement as he entered from the further end, so he went past the other stalls up to that of the "new horse," Charlie, whom Mary had managed so admirably on a previous occasion. There was something the matter with Charlie: he was apparently uneasy, and it was some movement that he had made that had startled the boy.

He was in a loose box of his own, being an excellently behaved creature, and could roam about in it at his will. Now, however, he was in the further corner, backed up against his own manger, with his head high and his eye rolling, exactly as if a stranger were making too free with him.

Jim looked in over the top and made the proper remarks. Charlie whinnied, high and fretfully, tossed his head again suddenly back; and the boy could see that he was shaking from head to foot.

"Now then!" said Jim again sternly.

Charlie paid no attention beyond suddenly breaking from his position, darting forward to the corner nearest the door, yet away from Jim, and again standing and shaking.

This was very serious; and Mr. Perks, the coachman, must be informed forthwith. It looked like some kind of a fit.

Jim drew back the bolt and went in. (Charlie paid no attention to him whatever.) He looked round the box, beat
his foot once or twice, and said "Shoo." It was just conceivable that something had got in that had no business
there — a strange cat, a particularly large rat, even a
snake. Jim's imagination rose to that point. Nothing
whatever happened.

Then (I have this from Jim's own lips) he was aware
that some sort of movement took place close beside him,
so localized that he glanced quickly behind him, expecting
to see Mr. Parks himself. There was no one there. Then he
had a sort of feeling that there was someone near the door
of the stable, and he craned up on tiptoe to see. Again
there was no one. Jim called himself a fool, and looked at
Charlie once more. The horse still looked uneasy, but the
appearance of tension was gone, and he allowed himself to
be slapped and poked without resenting it. His skin was a
little moist, but the shaking was all over; and Jim presently went out and thought no more of it.

The second odd little thing that fell out at Manningham
that day happened to one of the gardeners. It had come on
to rain suddenly the afternoon before, and Ferguson, the
second gardener, had left one or two little things on one of
the upper lawns, intending to do something in one of the
greenhouses till the rain was over, and then to return and
fetch them.

Well, the rain continued, and he forgot. He went
straight home to his cottage from the glass house, and left
the things lying about.

At about ten minutes to eleven on the Sunday morning,
as Ferguson set out on his Sunday rounds from his cottage above the house (he was a convinced Presbyterian,
and would almost as soon have heard the Popish Mass as
attended the ministrations of the Establishment), he suddenly remembered his omissions. This would never do.
Things must not be about on the Sabbath. He had intended to go to look round the home farm over the other
side, but he thought he might as well extend his round
and gather up the things. Everyone else would be safe in
church.

He came out from the walled kitchen garden straight on
to the upper lawns, between the convent and the house,
and was advancing to the wheelbarrow, which was only
too plainly visible, when quite distinctly he heard someone call him from the direction of the house. He looked,
and there was no one. He advanced again, and again,
clearly and plainly, he heard his name called.

Ferguson was a Lowlander, and he had therefore none
of the charming superstitions to be found further north.
He had not the faintest suspicion but that one of the men
wanted him, perhaps to take a message somewhere. It
would not be quite proper to shout back, so he wheeled
about and turned down the path towards the house, half-
expecting to see a head thrust out through the window of
some back premise. There was no one there. Neither was
there anyone on the gravel sweep. Neither was there anyone about the stables, to which he went on immediately.
(Jim had disappeared five minutes before.) Ferguson was
so puzzled that he penetrated even into the kitchen department, but there was no one there but a scullery-maid,
singing a hymn as their custom is, line by line, very
slowly and emotionally while she scoured copper pans.
No, the men were all gone ten minutes ago, she said.

So Ferguson went on to the home farm, once more entirely forgetting the wheelbarrow.

The third odd little thing that happened was so very little that I am really ashamed to mention it. It was this,
and no more.

Miss Groves, lady's maid, had a slight cold this morning, and thought she wouldn't go to church. As soon as
eleven o'clock struck and the bells stopped she had occasion to go to the morning room for something or other. So
she came out of the door below the stairs to cross the hall,
and began to cross it. Halfway she stopped and looked up,
because she was suddenly aware that someone was leaning with his arms on the rail and looking down on her
from the gallery that ran along the upper part of the hall.
She did not see this person, she informed people later,
except out of the corner of her eye; and when she turned
and looked there was no one there.

Now these things were absolutely the only unusual events that happened at all on this Sunday morning, and they are all so small and so easily explicable that I scarcely know why I have described them.

For example, horses do sometimes behave in an odd manner. Almost anything will make them do it. An unusual sound associated in their minds with something exciting is quite enough. And grooms and people of that kind are notoriously unsatisfactory witnesses even as to their own sensations.

Next, gardeners do forget things, and then remember them, and then forget them again. And gardeners, as well as other people, do sometimes think that they hear their names called when there is nobody to call them.

Lastly, nothing is commoner than for ladies' maids to see things out of the corners of their eyes and imagine themselves to be observed when they are not.

Finally, servants' hall evidence is very nearly the worst evidence in existence under all circumstances, and servant's hall evidence collected after the event is simply trumpery.

However, the things were reported to have happened, and they were all written down in a notebook by a thin man with gold eyeglasses and an academic air not more than a fortnight later, who came down from London on purpose on behalf of some publication or other, and they all appeared in the ensuing number, disguised by initials and studious misdirections.

I give them, therefore, for what they are worth.

(3)

Sarah put her sensation into words that evening. It had been an unwholesome kind of day — windy in the morning and too warm for November, windy and rainy in the afternoon. And the day had closed in early with a heavy sky, racing northeastwards all in one piece, flushing angrily in the west, with the winter sunset ending suddenly in a gash of yellow over the hills and then swiftly falling darkness. The two women had been out in the woods walking over a mile of fallen leaves up the long rides, in and out, telling of secondary matters, each thinking the other a little superficial, and had come back over the hill towards the house as the early dusk was falling. It was very much Sunday and very much November. Tea was a delightful thought.

It had been planned that Mary should be back in time for Benediction at the convent at four o'clock, and that Sarah should or should not come with her, as she felt inclined. Mary, Sarah considered, was one of those charming people who leave their guests, with full sympathy, to the mood of the moment.

At the chapel door she had hesitated; then she had followed Mary in.

But the twenty minutes' service had only deepened the emotional dream in which she seemed to move today. She had let her eyes stray from the pointed candle-flames, bright and comforting, to the pointed windows, austere and chilly, looking, too, now at the heavy figure of the priest, his profile, ruddy and white, his deep-faded cope, and at the tiny server who moved with such deliberate childish dignity; listening again, in a dull kind of impatience, to the voices of the village people in the transept behind her, staring up at the high wooden roof, lost in gloom. It all seemed a very queer and unnatural way of worshiping God.

A thousand thoughts drifted by her; yet again and again she came back to Jack. Of what was happening there before her eyes, or was believed to be happening, she thought little or nothing, except vaguely of the amazing credulity of the worshipers. It was, in some fashion, the personality of Jack of which she thought — suggested to her, no doubt, by these evidences of his absence which had come before her today in this receptive mood of hers. She wondered what, really, in his heart of hearts, he thought of all this; did he really believe it? Then she remembered, with a curious little glow of satisfaction, that at any rate he had taken to smoking and cricketing again. He seemed, at that reflection, to be very much in sympathy with herself. . . . All this the quietly absorbing, suggestive spectacle continued to develop within. Outward appearances formed a vivid background to her thought.

How astonishingly difficult it is to put this kind of moodiness into words. Though I know Lady Sarah Fakenham extremely well, and have talked to her once or twice about this very day of her life as well as of the rest, yet I can understand little of what she felt. All that she was able to convey to me was that sense of deepening heaviness, mostly sentimental, not at all unpleasant, that came upon her in the smoking room in the morning after church, and increased upon her all the rest of the day, and running through it was a thought of Jack.

The day was practically gone when she came out again, following Mary, and down through the gardens to where the great house lifted its twisted chimneys beneath. Overhead still raced the sky, heavy as a blanket; dead leaves whirled and spun beside them, torn from the heart of the woods, and an incessant sound was in the air, the long hush of the wind through the stripped branches. From the window of the morning room, as they came over the last ridge, shone out the firelight. It was pleasant to think of tea waiting there, and the long evening. (Jim, she reflected, would probably be asleep still before the smoking room fire.)

The two hardly said anything as they went; but Mary pointed out, as they took the short cut past the kitchen garden, that one of the gardeners had forgotten a wheelbarrow loaded with flower-pots and a garden instrument or two. That must be seen to, she said. It must have been left there, unnoticed since the day before.

The glass door, too, into the hall had blown open as if someone had passed quickly through, forgetting to close it after him. But they went through, closed it, and passed on to the morning room.

(4)

It was just after the dressing gong had sounded that Sarah uttered her psychological state. She had stood up mechanically at the sound of the gong, though she had no intention of going for twenty minutes yet, and Mary had laid down some book or other that she had been reading aloud.

The room had been to Sarah that evening all that it had promised to be, as she had seen its window shining out on to the darkening gardens, and her animal emotionalism (for I do not even now believe it to have been psychical) had lain as in a warm bath for relaxation. They had had the lamp taken away, and in the firelight they had talked gently of ten thousand little things, with silences between. Jim had looked in on them once to make an inquiry as to where a certain book was to be found (he was on the track of first editions again, as in the days of his youth). Then they had lighted the candles and Mary had read aloud, I forget why or what, and Sarah had sat on her stool by the fire and listened and looked — now at the fire, now at her own ringed hands on her knees now at Mary's face, bent and attentive, half in candlelight, half in shadow.

Then the dressing gong; and Sarah stood up, stretching.

"Thanks, dearest; that's lovely."

Mary closed the book, and sat, her finger still in the place, meditating.

"Oh, I feel so funny," said Sarah suddenly.

Mary smiled up at her, obviously thinking of something else.

"Do you, dearest? I'm sorry."

"So very Sundayish," said Sarah. "I've felt it ever since this morning. Do you know that feeling one gets sometimes, that everything's sort of — sort of slowing down to a stop? Or else it has stopped, like a train between stations, and one's rather sleepy, and just blinks out at everything, and wonders who the man is going along the road, and whether he'll get there in time, and what his wife's name is."

Mary smiled again, showing her even, white teeth. Sarah did say this kind of thing sometimes, quite unexpectedly. It was, so to speak, Jim translated through her feminine medium.

"But the train always goes on," said Sarah. "At least, it always has with me."

Mary stopped smiling abruptly. And for an instant Sarah found herself wondering whether by any chance Mary's train had not gone on with her. There was that "something" that had happened. Then she remembered about Jack.

"I've been thinking about Jack all day long," she said. "I can't think why. I — why do you look like that?"

Mary dropped her eyes.

"Like what?"

She said it so naturally that Sarah concluded herself wrong. It was no doubt the effect of firelight.

"Ever since I went into the smoking room I've been thinking about him. There was his pipe rack there and the photograph of the cricket-group. What is that photograph, by the way?"

"Oh, it's a Stonyhurst group," said Mary.

"And the photograph of that house?"

"That's his old home, where he lived as a boy."

"And then this afternoon too. How extraordinary empty this house seems without him. Yes, I know that's not polite — quite a — a hostess in yourself, of course. Now there are some houses that aren't a bit like that. Jim's aunt's is one. It doesn't matter in the slightest if she's there or not, you know. The furniture goes on just the same."

Mary smiled again without speaking. She was not contributing much to the conversation; but it made no difference to Sarah.

"But here, somehow, it's all Jack. You aren't in it at all, my dear. At least it is so today."

"I know what you mean," said Mary evenly.

"And there he is, out in Africa, probably in a blazing sun, making hundreds of runs. How very odd and untrue that does seem. What's the difference of time between here and South Africa?"

"I haven't the slightest idea," said Mary.

"Dear me! What an extraordinary wife you are! Now if it was Jim making runs in a hot sun in South Africa, I should sit here, so to speak, with my watch on my knee. I wonder where Jim is? How quiet the house is! He's probably asleep again."

"It's time to go and dress," said Mary, without moving.

"So it is," said Sarah, and sat down again.

The house certainly was very quiet. The faint vibrations of ten minutes ago, as man and maid passed to and fro overhead, opening wardrobes, and setting down hot water, were all over. The table too had received its finishing touches in the next room, and the household was quiet.

Even the wind outside too seemed to have conversation;
but it dropped; and except for one instant in the silence as
the two sat, when there lifted a kind of big draft outside,
spattering the fountain over the pavement in the little
flagged court, the world seemed trying to rest.

It was quite interesting, thought Sarah, still in her sentimental mood, to sit here and listen to the quiet. Once
again, as she listened, a window opened somewhere, perhaps in the basement, and a voice said an inaudible word
or two, and there was silence again.

"It's as hard to go up and dress," remarked Sarah, "as it
is to go to bed. Why is life such a series of efforts?"

"Well, we must make one of them," said Mary reso-
lutely, getting up and blowing out the candles.

As they came into the hall, whence rose the staircase, in
Jacobean dignity, to the warm gloom of the picture-hung
corridors above, a great log crashed forward on to the
hearth. Sarah paused at the first turn of the staircase to
see Mary attempting to grasp it in the tongs and restore
it.

"Oh, you're doing it wrong!" she said, and came down
again in a hurry, as the smoke was eddying out, a thin,
pungent cloud, into the hall. But as she put out her hands
to seize the tongs Mary stood up suddenly.

"What's that?"

There was a violent vibration of the inner glass door of
the hall as the outer one opened, and the sound of footsteps on the stone. The next instant Parkinson came
through, with his hat on, in an ulster opened at the front,
showing his white shirt. He recoiled as he saw his mistress, and stood there, still covered, staring as if in terror.

But Mary said nothing. She stood there silent, still holding the steel tongs, waiting for who should follow.

Then the priest came through — a grotesque figure, his
skirts gathered in his hands, an old cloak thrown over his
shoulders, and a tall silk hat on his head. He held something in his hand that glimmered white in the light of the
hall-lamp overhead. The big outer door banged heavily
behind him in the wind, and the reverberation rang
through the house like thunder.

He came straight through, lifting his hat as he did so, and setting it on the table as he passed.

"Mrs. Weston — " he said.

No sound came from Mary.

"Mrs. Weston, may I — may I speak to you privately an instant?"

His kindly old face was all drawn with some emotion, and the rain through which he had come shone on his shoulders.

"A — a telegram," he said; "Parkinson received it ten minutes ago. It is from — from —"

Sarah cried out something.

"Yes; from Africa," he said. "It — it — bad news. He is ill — Mr. Weston is ill. Mrs. Weston, may I speak to you privately? Yes — yes — he died today."

Epilogue

There are a few things in this world more pleasant than a proper breakfast room in full summer at about half-past nine o'clock — harmonizing, as it does, the simplicity of air and sun and lawn and flowers — all moderately ethereal joys — with the grossest carnal suggestion of kidneys and amber marmalade and steaming silver coffee pots. Such a harmony as this makes it possible sometimes for the most *blasé* to be tolerant.

Sarah thought so, at least, as she came down and regarded the scene, pushed her head out of the window and her nose into the very heart of a crimson rose, and turned once more to the table. Three or four letters lay there by her plate; she opened one, glanced through it quickly, and sat down.

Ten minutes later Jim appeared. He was a little tired, he explained; there was a rebus bookplate that had kept him puzzling till after midnight: he was convinced he had solved it at last.

Sarah nodded, then passed over the note she had first opened.

"At two o'clock," she said. "We must not be there after that."

Jim yawned delicately.

"Is my presence really necessary?" he asked.

"Of course it is," said Sarah energetically. "I couldn't bear it alone."

Jim went to the sideboard with pursed lips as if he were whistling. Sarah stared meditatively at his brilliant socks.

"Poor dear!" she said suddenly.

"Yes, I am rather —" began Jim.

"To think of it coming to this," she went on without the smallest attention. "And I warned her. Oh, how I warned her not to be morbid!"

Jim selected a kidney.

"Catholic — and temperament," he observed. "Two in-
scrutable mysteries."

"I suppose we must say something nice to Mrs. Aberford. Oh, Jim!"

"Who's Mrs. Aberford?"

"Oh, an old aunt. She's dug out from Scotland somewhere — 'to give her away,' as they say."

"Give her away! What the blazes —"

"Oh, I don't know. It's one of the things they do. And
don't make the obvious joke."

Jim looked a little hurt.

It was a gloomy breakfast after all, in spite of the amber
marmalade and the sunshine and the roses and the kidneys. Jim made an attempt or two at conversation, but it
was a failure. Sarah sat, picking a scrap or two of food,
staring before her, and Jim gave it up.

He could not understand, he told himself, why she was
so concerned. Surely she had known, two years before,
that it would come to this. Mary had written to that effect
within a month of Jack's death, remarking that she was
going abroad first to get things into focus, but hinting
plainly enough what the result of it all would be. Then
there had followed another pause, then another; and then
three months before they themselves had taken possession again of their own house the last stage had been entered upon, and Mary had entered the convent as a postulant. Absolutely the last detail had been fulfilled by the
arrival of a little red-lined paper announcing that His
Lordship the Bishop of Pentapolis would give the habit to
one postulant at 3 p.m. on the Feast of Something or
Other, at Manningham Convent, that vespers would be
sung at 2 p. m., and the sermon preached by the Rev. Father Badminton, S. J. There had been no abruptness; the
thing had developed as surely as an engagement develops
into marriage. Why then sit over kidneys in the morning
sunshine dumbfoundered, on what was, so to speak, the
wedding day? There the thing was — perfectly hopeless
and morbid, of course — but if people liked that sort of
thing it was obviously the sort of thing that such people
would like. Live and let live! Meanwhile, there were first
editions and bookplates, and real strenuous life for the

wholesomely minded. So he was not greatly occupied with the thing. He reflected only that he would have to lunch at a quarter to one.

And while Jim pondered downstairs, Sarah went up to look at the baby.

It had arrived six months before, and was enthroned, with a nurse, in what had been Sarah's own nursery and schoolroom years ago. Somehow or other it seemed to her symbolical today; and she stood with her back to the fireplace, regarding it in silence as it went up and down looking over its nurse's shoulder. It appeared to her almost infinitely pathetic that Mary had had no child; it would have solved so much. A baby was surely the outward sign of what life ought to be; it stood for reality and facing facts and all the rest of it; it gave a sense of permanence and continuance and all the rest of it. Whereas Mary's dreams — how desolate and fruitless!

She did not exactly formulate these ideas, but they passed imaginatively before her, one by one, and she thought herself very feeling. She perceived the contrast between this homely nursery with its white furniture, its gay carpet, the little brass-railed cot, and so forth, and a nun's cell as she knew it to be. The one stood to her for sanity and wholesomeness, the other for a despair of life. Obviously one's chief duty to the world was to live in it as permanently as possible, and a child — as Zola and Mr. H. G. Wells have mystically represented it — is a real fulfillment of that duty. And that child in its turn would pass on the torch of life, and so on — yes, and so on.

She felt a little melancholy as she looked, yet utterly certain that she was right. Of course Eternity and all that was all right for the individual, but there was also the duty of forgetting self in one's children. Whereas poor Mary ended with herself: there was no more to be said.

She took the baby for a minute or two into her own arms and held it there. The warm touch and movement were reassuring. Then she gave it back to the nurse and whisked out of the room.

(2)

The sweep of gravel outside the chapel was crowded with vehicles as the Fakenhams drove up in their beauti-

ful motor at about ten minutes before two. The heat was
considerable here, and Jim, who had lunched grudgingly
though quite heartily at a quarter before one, paid very
little attention to Sarah's remarks, as they waited for a
carriage resembling a pantomime comic cab that occupied
the steps. Yes, he assented, obviously that was the back of
a Roman Catholic ecclesiastic getting out of it. There were
all kinds of other people there, some known, some unknown; and all bore themselves with an odd air as they
nodded and exchanged remarks. The occasion might
equally well have been, judging by their demeanor, a
cheerful funeral or a very melancholy wedding; such a one
at which the bridegroom, for instance, might be deaf or
paralyzed.

Their turn came at last, and in they went, stumbling
along in the sudden darkness, led by a smiling young
woman in a black silk cap shaped rather like the head-
dress of Red Riding Hood.

Then Sarah began to look about her in earnest.

Little by little the glare of sunlight in her eyes passed,
and this is what she saw. Immediately in front of her, beyond the single row of heads that occupied the front
places in this public transept, rose up the light iron
screen; but the door in it was set open, and two or three
odd figures, looking rather like modest French peasants,
passed in and out continually, obscuring that which lay
behind. She could just make out heads, but no more. To
the left stood the altar on its two or three steps; and six
candles burned behind upon the gradine. A carpet
stretched from its foot down to where the moving group
revolved. Then suddenly the group partly dissolved; and
Sarah — with a sudden catch of her breath — saw Mary
in three-quarter profile, kneeling at a *prie dieu* facing the
altar. Beyond her, slightly behind, showed Mrs. Aberford's
severe Scottish countenance framed in a purple bonnet.

Mary's appearance was a complete surprise, and a
shock, as horrible as if she had been dead; for she was
dressed as a bride from head to foot, in an exquisitely
made costume, white silk, lace veil, orange blossoms — all
complete — with her hair elaborately coiled and puffed
upon her head. A painted candlestick, some four feet in

height, stood beside her, and the light from the candle fell
full upon her face. She was kneeling upright, with open
eyes, looking serenely before her.

The sight was horrible to Sarah — arresting and shocking; for she had last seen her in black for her husband. It
looked so heartless, she thought; and, above all, that radiant face, as young as if a young girl. And the reason
shocked her again as she considered it — ah, to think that
this was Mary! Her eyes filled with tears that ebbed
again.

The door beside the transept suddenly opened and two
priests came out with a boy or two. She looked at their
faces as they took their places, and hated them. That cal-
lous brute in a cope with his wooden demeanor — he was
the successor of that tiresome old Father Banting, wasn't
he? — dead three months now. What was it all to him, but
one   more   hysterical   woman,   under   a   piteous
heart-breaking mistake, embracing an unnatural life that
he himself dared not live? No, no; there were pipes and
alcohol and a decent bed and good food for him — and for
Mary, well, for Mary, what Sarah now knew by heart.
What was that which he was saying in his brazen voice?

"Deus in adjutorium. . . ."

Some gabble or other.

Then, for an instant, her thought was struck dumb, for
in answer, away from the right, over that shuttered
screen, came the weirdest sound she had ever heard; it
was like wind, it was like the cry of migrating night-birds
on the northern fens — it was like the voices of the dead.
Yet there were syllables, in it, syllables that must surely
mean something, on but two notes, the tonic and the leading notes — no more. So it wailed and ceased, unearthly,
terrifying, horrible; and again in answer without a tremor
the brazen voice from the seat opposite.

What in the world did it all signify? What did it stand
for?

There was a subsidence into seats almost immediately,
and Sarah, beginning to think once more connectedly, yet
still to that intolerable accompaniment — two notes and
no more, unsupported by organ or harmony — glanced
again at the other priest, whose face she could see bent

over his book. She hated him too. He was commonplace, she decided, unimaginative, imperceptive, with his reddish hair and big nose on which perched a pair of gold-rimmed spectacles. He slightly resembled a chestnut horse, she thought. Then again she looked at Mary, immovable and upright on her knees, looking before her.

For how long the affair went on Sarah did not know. It might have been twenty minutes, she considered afterwards; but the appalling monotony of the voices soon overcame their absorbing horror, and she listened with scarcely even interest after a while to the change of voice that began each psalm on a higher note. Only once she started a little, as one of these single voices began containing in itself, it seemed, the very essence of the grave — thin, high, vibrating, and windy, as a ghost might sing. The censing of the altar later gave her a moment or two of interest, and she paused in that endless treading of the mill of thought and memory and prospect, to watch the wooden-faced priest going about his business to the chink of chains, and to sniff sharply that strange, haunting, sepulchral odor that floated in an invisible film down into the transept. Jim coughed softly and patiently beside her, as a kind of tolerant protest, she thought. She was glad he had so much philosophy to sustain him.

When the sermon began she sat back with curiosity to hear what would be said. She had decided that the matter of it would probably be defiant, and certainly rhetorical. A ceremony like this sorely needed a very river of emotion to flow over its horror. There would be talk about Brides of the Lamb, and convent ecstasies, and midnight vigils, and the thrill of the Bridegroom's kiss.

Yet there were none of these things. The affair was commonplace and even dull. The preacher, standing on the altar-step just above Mary, after a sign of the cross and the placing on his head what Sarah just knew to be a "biretta," began his deliberate little discourse and flowed on tranquilly to the end. She could scarcely remember afterwards what it was about. She just remembered that the text was something about "Ye are dead, and your life . . ." She forgot the rest.

It began with something about "congratulating our sister "on the step she was undertaking today. There followed a little description of the Garden of Eden — a thing
of whose very existence Sarah was exceedingly doubtful
— and a contrast with it of the world at the present time.
The beauty was still here, said the priest, but there
"lurked here what had been lacking there " — sin. He
went on a little about this — with illustrations and exam-
ples, and remarked that it was for this reason that certain
"elect souls, called specially of God," left the world, not
indeed to run away from evil, but to deal with it the more
effectively.

(That, Sarah reminded herself, was sheer nonsense. It
was even untrue. For all the world knew perfectly well
that the Religious Life, at least this kind, was simple
cowardice and selfishness, however much it might be disguised, and that the whole object of nuns was to try to
escape from worldly troubles. Sarah sighed as she considered the fact that her mare was lame, that her dentist
had been very discouraging last week, and that there was
that tiresome Colonel and his more than tiresome wife
coming to stay that very evening. . . . . Well, troubles must
be borne bravely. Meanwhile, poor dear Mary! To think
that she thought she could escape from troubles within
convent walls! What a delusion! — since human nature is
the same everywhere, and bears its own troubles with it.)

She was so much occupied with interior refutation that
she missed a good bit of the discourse. When she was able
to attend again the priest was, almost timidly, she
thought, claiming that at least this Religious Life ought to
show to the world that there was such a thing as faith. He
commended to the consideration of any Protestants that
might be present the reflection that somehow or other it
was a fact that there was an exceedingly large number of
persons in the world, of whom this "sister" of ours is one,
who deliberately, after full consideration, preferred to live
this life to any other. It was at least remarkable that in
the face of those who at the present day maintained almost openly that the senses alone offered solid pleasure,
there was another kind of joy sufficiently convincing to
make girls and women who had all to lose from the

worldly point of view by their renunciation, give up once
and for all everything that for the worldling made life
worth living, and embrace a life in which bodily comfort
was reduced to a minimum.

It was an involved sentence, and Sarah despised it with
all her might. Besides, the matter of it was ridiculous. It
was all just self-hypnotism, as Jim had told her at the
beginning.

As she finished these strictures the sermon ended, and
the two priests with their attendants went out in silence.

There followed a rather uncomfortable little pause. People began to rustle and whisper. Sarah heard a sharp sentence or two from somewhere behind.

"They say she's heartbroken, poor thing."

"Yes. I shall be at home tomorrow, dear, any time after
four."

Sarah jerked her shoulders impatiently and looked at
Mary again.

Still the moments went on. Then suddenly she made a
discovery: that in the shuttered screen on the right that
cut off the nuns' choir from the sanctuary a grating was
open, and she could see even from her seat, for it was
hardly three steps away, straight into the choir proper.
But it was difficult to see anything satisfactorily. There
was woodwork, yes, of unpainted deal, and yes — that
was a human figure beyond that desk, motionless. Then a
shutter slid again into its place without a sound. Sarah
determined, if there was an opportunity later, to shift her
seat a little in order to see better.

Then, abruptly, half a dozen figures emerged from the
sacristy door, one of them a burly man with dark complex-
ion and heavy eyebrows, in some kind of purple and black,
with a glint of gold chain and cross. That would be the
bishop, she thought.

She watched the vesting of him carefully, with scorn in
her heart. All this elaboration about nothing. Why could
not the man put on his clothes in private? The clothes too
seemed endless in number, and when all was done at last
and he stood up with his immense pointed miter on his
head and jeweled staff in his hand, she called him "Medicine man" to herself.

The medicine man, however, it seemed had business outside, for an instant later the group swept towards the transept and disappeared, passing within a yard of herself. A kind of flurry broke out in the benches, restrained by the attendants, and with an emotion that clutched at her throat Sarah suddenly saw Mary within a yard of her, passing swiftly on behind the clergy, dead white, yet smiling, with eyes like stars. Two little girls dressed in white carried her heavy brocaded train. Then the procession was gone, and Sarah cast herself into the scurry that followed, battling nobly with her elbows to see the end.

It was strange to come out again into the hot sunlight and to see the trees over the encircling wall. Sarah contented herself with thinking once more of the artificiality left behind, and of God's own sky and world natural about her. It was an immense consolation to her to reflect on this thought and to perceive, mentally, her own superior spirituality. Poor dear Mary! But what had happened to the procession?

Presently she found out.

A kind of semicircle had been formed about the porch-entrance to the convent, consisting of the congregation who had made the most speed; and into the pack Sarah presently forced herself, obtaining what was, on the whole, a very respectable position. And almost immediately she understood what was happening.

Within, the porch opened out a little, and in the space stood the bishop and his clergy, facing, slightly on one side, the door into the enclosure. This was at the instant shut, and immediately in front of it stood Mary, with her aunt on one side and the two little girls on the other. Then the door opened; and Sarah drew a breath.

Between the heads immediately in front of her, across the gravel, through the porch, beyond the groups within, she had her first clear sight — and indeed almost her last — of contemplatives with their veils thrown back.

She remembered afterwards the following points: —

They stood in a wide semicircle — she imagined about a dozen of them; she caught a general effect of brown and white and curious swathed headdresses. The Prioress stood in front. Behind them showed the dull white of the cloister and the glint of sunlit green beyond.

Of their faces she had afterwards a confused recollection, for the sight lasted scarcely a minute. But she summed it all up in whispers to a friend over tea in the phrase "unhealthy and morbid."

There was an odd irrelevance between eyes and mouth — they did not seem quite to belong; for the mouths were grave and natural, and the eyes deadly tired. In fact, they were not quite like the faces of living people. They resembled rather masks.

It was difficult for Sarah to define her emotions even to herself; for curiosity was so dominant that analysis was nearly impossible. On the whole, however, perhaps indignation, blind and unreasoning, was the next forcible sensation. She expressed it later by saying that at that moment the whole thing appeared to her even more abominable than she had dreamed. It was a kind of outrage upon the sky and sun and summer air.

Ah, the door was closing; and there stood Mary within, beside the Prioress, smiling. Sarah was distressed that their eyes did not meet. As the door closed she saw her friend's eyes begin to follow its movement with a strange expectancy.

There was a breaking up of the crowd; a murmur of voices; and again the bishop and his clergy swept back in the sunshine.

(3)

Of what followed in the chapel when Sarah, after a gallant struggle, found herself in the desired seat, she would have had a far more accurate knowledge if one of her neighbors behind had not maintained a steady whispered comment to someone else on all that took place. The bishop, who by now was stationed by the grating into the nuns' choir on the right, had his biography shortly retailed and his personal appearance disapproved of. Sarah turned a fierce cheek backwards now and then without avail.

It was exceedingly difficult to attend therefore to all that happened.

First, however, she noticed that the square window-like grating was swung back, and that it was possible to have a tolerable view into the place where Mary would for the future pass a large number of each set of twenty-four hours, that we call a day. It was not inviting: it was stone floored; it was walled for some four feet up by a partition of deal, beyond which, she supposed, the nuns sat in their stalls.

Then she noticed with a shock that they were actually sitting there, motionless as statues, shaped indeed like human beings, yet unrecognizable, since once more their veils hung down. And she had hardly seen this when without a sound Mary's own face, still crowned and wreathed, appeared at the square opening. A candle, she observed, burned like a star beside the face and shone upon the smooth texture of the cheek.

Then the bishop was speaking. There were questions asked. Sarah could just catch their purport, in spite of the shuffling and whispering about her.

What was it that she desired? Mary's grave voice, steady, clear, and deliberate, gave the answer: "The blessing of God. The Habit of the Order; and the companionship of her sisters."

("Or it was something like that," said Sarah later over her buttered toast.)

And was it of her own free will that she was there?

Indeed, yes.

Then certain folded objects were handed through by the bishop — a kind of bundle. (What theatrical nonsense it all was, said Sarah to herself! Why in the world make such a fuss about a little cheap stuff?)

And there were prayers in Latin being said now — an unintelligible mumble. Oh! what in God's name had all this to do with God's sky and birds and trees? The bundle was being blessed. Blessed indeed!

Then again the face vanished, and again one of those awkward pauses ensued.

Sarah, sitting back in her seat, began to reflect how much better she could have done it all. It was these pauses that were so abrupt and stupid. For herself, she would have arranged it quite beautifully. There should have been gentle hymns, cooed out of sight — nice peaceful things like Sunday evening — or at the least a little quiet organ playing. And incense too. A boy in scarlet, with a melancholy sweet face and golden hair brushed out like a halo. Ah! These Catholics didn't really understand the beauty of religion. Of course the whole thing was deplorable; but if it must be done, why not do it exquisitely? The affair was so abrupt — like gashes. It was so terribly workaday and business-like — like the delivery of a prisoner to a jail — no real sentiment or tenderness at all; and the attempts at it lamentable. The wedding dress, for instance; that was simply bad taste. It was as bad as Father Banting's pink angel.

She was brought back in a jump.

"How much longer?" asked Jim's gloomy whisper in her ear.

"I don't know. I —"

Ah! There was the face once more. Yet was it, indeed her face? There showed at the opening the head of a woman veiled in white, with down-turned eyes and closed lips. The lashes lay dead on the white cheek, and the very lips looked pale. The crown of hair was gone; instead the shroud-like veil. The wedding dress was gone, and the glow of blossoms, and the splendor of lace and silk; instead rough brown stuff shaved at the neck, and the edge of a heavy white mantle over it. So, motionless, in the square opening rested this woman's head and shoulders; and Sarah, craning this way and that, saw that she knelt upon a carpet on which lay a sprinkle of a few white flowers.

It was for a moment only. Then the figure vanished; and Sarah, edging out from her seat, careless of etiquette, was able to see beyond the bishop, from whom once more mumbled out some jargon or other, a long shape covered with a mantle that lay flat upon its face upon the carpet.

It was almost the crowning horror of all — the very pitch of all this theatrical unreality that veiled another reality so overpowering that Sarah was aware of its existence only in the formless pressure of fear that it exerted upon herself and her own fierce resentment.

Mary! Mary! By act after act of will and memory she tried to compel herself to know that this shape was Mary — Mary Weston who had ridden with her, laughed with her, smoked with her. There she was — the same person whom she herself had known, in whose company she had been in this very transept, lying flat upon a carpet with heavy men in fantastic dresses standing over her — there, behind bars more impregnable than of a prison, since they were raised and held in place by the prisoners themselves.

It was impossible for the imagination to take hold of the fact. It simply could not be Mary. The imagination must be right; the intellect wrong. Mary must be elsewhere — the thing was an illusion. It would be all right presently. The affair would be all over; the chapel gone like a dream. It was on another plane. Surely Mary herself would meet her afterwards, and laugh, and give her tea. . . .

The emotional movement passed; and she looked again intelligently. Yes, that was Mary, rising now, with another figure beside her, as the group of ecclesiastics moved away.

But her veil too was down. Was it possible that she had seen Mary's face for the last time?

Where were those two going? Ah! There was another figure come out from somewhere behind the deal boarding. Yes.

"Look, Jim; they're kissing — with their veils down."

Jim sighed tolerantly.

Then the grating closed.

Jim broke the silence in the motor five minutes later.

"Temperament, my dear girl, that's all. You must make allowances for temperament."

The End